# TRANSFORMATIONS

## BOOK ONE OF THE TRANSFIGURATION PENTALOGY

## JOHN DEJORDY

*Dedicated to Aaron "Greang" Retteen, whose insistence, pushing and friendship*

*transformed a few notes into what this book is today.*

The Transfiguration pentalogy:

**Transformations**

**Transitions**

**Traditions**

**Trainings**

**Transferences**

# Author's Foreword

2002. The war on terror had begun in response to 9/11, the Mars Odyssey found signs of water ice deposits, the movies *The Lord of the Rings: the Two Towers* and *Harry Potter and the Chamber of Secrets* were big in the theaters, and a little known website by the name of the National Novel Writing Month encouraged writers to write a complete 50,000+ word novel in just 30 days. I was its 2996th member.

In November of that year, I had come up with a little idea of a story. Five friends, embarked on a journey and I wrote:

*As I sit here in the cubby of a cave that has been become my home over the ages, I often wonder about Fate…Through one little push from Fate, a series of events, each a chain upon a chain delivered me to my present situation.*

And thus, I too embarked on a fantastic journey. The ideas were swift and I typed like a mad man, and by the end of the month, I had succeeded. With that bit of confidence, I neatly stored the file away, and moved on. I made notes, came up with new twists along the way, but never focused solely on the story that was my first *true* novel.

I've gone back each year and attempted a new novel, sometimes successful, and sometimes, not so. In-between then and now, I released a novella *Picayune* that will soon be an ongoing saga. But I always desired to return to my first story. In the novel's current form, I wrote about fate too:

*One little push from Fate triggered a series of events, like links in a chain, bringing me to my present situation.*

It is funny to think of everything that has happened since I started this and I wonder about fate. Would I have gone through it then, knowing what today would bring?

In a heartbeat.

It is my sincere wish that you enjoy my story.

# CHAPTER ONE

The Fury of the Wind blew debris into the cave's entrance. J.D.'s sanctuary sat at the summit of Mt. Mistmoor, the tallest mountain in the land. Listening to the storm, he closed his eyes and prayed the raging wind would drown out the sound of his heavy breathing. He knew his enemies searched for him, alert to the slightest whisper, and he hoped his den of magical protection would keep them at bay. If the wind carried his breath to them, they would find him.

His heartbeat pounded in his ears, the pulsing fueled by the sorrow of recent events. He fought the urge to cry, but a single tear escaped and trailed down his cheek. He opened his eyes and struggled to calm his breathing.

Exhausted from running for many months, he rose with a groan. His knees buckled, and he reached out to the wall for support. Straining to straighten his aching back, he shuffled to the entrance and peered out. He could barely see the gray silhouettes of the landscape far below. He punched the jagged rock, freeing a small shower of rubble and gritted his teeth. The unhealed scars from his last battle hurt more than his throbbing hand.

Large hailstones pummeled the entrance, and he took a few steps back. The raw dampness of the storm seeped into his bones.

He closed his eyes and concentrated. An additional onslaught of ice pelted his face, and he had to shy away. The ice quickly built up, building a thick wall that completely blocked the entrance, except for a small opening at the top. Feeling feeble, he pivoted back inside. Torches near the entrance burst to life, allowing him to survey the place he called home.

The dining table and four chairs to the left of the entrance wore a thin layer of dust. He leaned against one of the chairs for support, and the dust was instantly whisked away. A hutch next to the table remained closed, but the glass doors were clear enough to see the display of dishes and utensils within. John hovered near it, wondering if eating would calm his nerves. After opening one of the doors, he pulled out a tea cup and placed it on the flat surface of the bottom of the hutch. "Chameleon tea, please." The cup wiggled a little as it filled with the hot liquid. John took a few sips, before putting the cup down and searching the fairly clean cave.

In a darker section of the cave was a simple divan with a green spread. At the foot rested a small, round cushion covered by a tiny red blanket. J.D. clutched the makeshift bed to his chest and slumped down on the edge of the divan. Tears streamed down his face as he cried silently.

When he finally regained his composure, he returned the pillow and blanket to their original positions. He rose and shuffled deeper into the cave. Another recess held a large birch trunk and a gray cedar chest. The open trunk revealed heaps of colorful clothing.

He pulled out a shirt at random and smiled. The red, yellow, and green silk shirt reminded him of the times his friends dressed in colorful clothes to rebel against the black and whites everyone wore. The happy image faded, replaced by the shadow of raw memories, and he tossed the shirt aside. He ignored the chest and stared at a full-length mirror mounted on the wall.

He sighed and wiped some of the grime away from the dusty mirror. Leaning in, he barely recognized his reflection. It disturbed him to see the wisps of gray streaking his brown hair. Even in the dim light, he could spot the wrinkles that prematurely creased his youthful face. He huffed in disgust and smeared the image with his bloody hand. He snatched the silk shirt and used it as a bandage.

J.D.'s eyes drifted over the cave's other furnishings: a wooden desk and chair. Mildew covered the rosewood, obscuring most of the intricately carved deer and pheasants. He limped over and traced the chipped carvings with his fingers. The mildew left green and black spots of decaying wood wherever he touched. The sliminess added to the mess on his hand.

On the desk were three of his treasures. He picked up a silver figurine of a cat ready to pounce. Layers of tarnish obscured its former brightness, and he rubbed it with his thumb, trying to restore its luster. His efforts were futile, however; no amount of rubbing could erase the stain of time.

His hand shook as he returned the cat to its spot and picked up a small music box. The once-vibrant colors were dull and barely recognizable. He carefully opened his prize, hoping to hear its calming melody. The gears had yielded to years and weather, and he heard a warped version of the tune before the music stopped.

Snarling, he slammed down the box, cracking it. He smacked a dusty ball of ice between the cat and music box. It flickered a few times before glowing brightly enough to cast familiar shadows around the room. The ball's magic consumed the dust.

J.D. yanked the drawers of the desk open one after another, grunting as each empty one added to his anger. When he felt himself about to give in to rage, the bottom drawer on the right revealed the stack of parchment he sought. He grasped as many sheets as he could and slammed them down on the surface of the desk.

He slumped into his chair, and the wood creaked under his weight. His fists and body shook violently until he managed to get his rage under control. Bowing his head briefly in reverence for his friends, he sighed. A twinge of pain under the makeshift bandage drew his attention. He unwound the shirt, wiped as much of the blood and grime as he could, and tossed the rag haphazardly aside. He snatched a small jar from a side pouch on his belt and unscrewed the lid. There was barely enough of the gel, but he swiped his fingers, covering them with the last traces, and worked it over his injuries until the gel had eliminated all traces of damage. After glancing at the wall of ice, he plucked his quill, dipped it in an ink vial, and started penning his tragedy.

# PART I

**Salem, Massachusetts**
**Earth**
**1692 A.D.**

# CHAPTER TWO

*For Robert: May the fire in your heart be eventually squelched*

*As I sit in the cave that, over time, has become my home, I wonder about Fate. Funny, how it manages to dominate a person's life, even when that life has lasted as long as mine. It seems like only yesterday I was anticipating experiencing the joys and pains of adult life. One little push from Fate triggered a series of events, like links in a chain, bringing me to my present situation.*

*I was a person who carefully planned things. I never considered Fate, never believed in it. As I write this memoir, fable, or whatever you want to call it, I remember the line from Shakespeare's* As You Like It*: "All the world's a stage, and the men and women merely players." I wonder how Fate will portray us in its play. Had my friends and I read the script of our lives, I think each of us would have chosen a different author.*

I remember the day our lives changed as if it was yesterday. The date, according to the Gregorian calendar, was Wednesday, September 3rd, 1692. The sun's rays shone through the cracks in the shutters of my loft's window, waking me to a new day. The wonderful aroma of frying ham and eggs reached my nose. I jumped from my bed, dressed, and climbed down the ladder.

As I entered the kitchen, the aromas of my mother's cooking, combined with fresh fruit and tea, made me salivate. "Morning, Mother. Where's Father?"

Mother moved a strand of hair from my eye with a smile. "Oh, you know him. He's in his workshop carving a new table for the Millers. Could you watch the eggs while I go get him?"

"Of course." I went to the hearth as she left to get him. I flipped the eggs a few times before placing them on three plates. I had my mother to thank for teaching me how to cook. She never believed someone's sex should determine their role in life, so I learned how to do things that were considered women's work. Because of my mother's passion, we lived on the outskirts of town where she could live free from whispers about her *abnormal* lifestyle. After removing the ham from the fire, I set all the food on the table and sat down to wait for my parents.

My father strode in and slapped me on the back. "Decided to sleep in today?"

"No one rises earlier than you, Father. How is the new order coming?"

My father put up his hand. "No talking about work at the table." He waited for my mother to sit before saying the prayer. Although the meal might have seemed simple, it delighted me to taste how a few spices enhanced everything.

When our plates were empty, I began to ask my father if he needed help, but was interrupted by a knock on the door.

I answered the door while my parents cleared the table. "Hello, Diane. How are you today?"

Smiling, she curtsied. "I am well, thank you. Do you have time for a stroll?"

I glared at her drab gray and white dress and frowned. Her dark hair and emerald-green eyes were shown to better advantage in bright colors. "No," I replied. "I still have to do some chores and help my father in the shop."

My father came over to me and placed his hand on my shoulder. "I think I can handle the work alone today, son. If a woman comes calling, John, it is not polite to keep her waiting."

I nodded. "Thanks, Father."

I stepped outside and took a deep breath. Standing stiffly upright, I offered Diane my arm. "Shall we visit Robert's house before going into Salem?"

Diane laughed and slapped my arm. "Stop being so formal, silly."

I chuckled and relaxed. "Fine. Would you like to see my father's latest project before we go?"

"Certainly! I love your father's work."

We strolled to the shop, and I opened the door for her. In the center of the floor was a round table crafted from dark rosewood. Ornate carvings on the table's surface depicted waves crashing into one another. Along the edges were images of shells, starfish, and various fish. The round spindle legs were shaped like Ionic Greek columns. The table was a monument to Poseidon.

Diane ran her hand over the tabletop. "Your father does impressive work. You can't see the tool marks on his carvings."

"I've always been amazed at his craftsmanship." I sighed. "I will never be as good as him, but forget about that for now. We should go get the others."

Diane sauntered outside, and I ran after her. Together, we hiked to our friend Robert's house.

Diane took my arm again. "So, now that it's been more than a month after your nineteenth birthday, have you decided what you are going to do?"

"I could ask you the same. You will reach that age in a little less than a month."

She giggled and held my arm tighter. "Yes, but isn't it up to the man to decide?"

I wanted to answer, but decided it would be best to remain silent.

Robert's home was situated on a cliff with a steep private path leading down to the commercial docks. It reminded me of stories about a tyrant ruler towering over his peasants. The enormous gray house, with its many cornices and parapets, resembled a castle. On one side, near the path, was a tall lighthouse, but a high, well-kept hedge surrounding the land on all the other sides prevented anyone from seeing what lay on the other side of the hedge.

We approached the barbican entrance and saw that the guard had positioned himself beside the street. A man with a red face and tense neck muscles yelled at the guard.

The man poked the guard in the chest with his finger. "Listen, Woodrow, I demand to see Master Twinholm! How dare he charge such outrageous prices for tea and liquor!"

Woodrow pushed the man further down the sloped street. "You are lucky he still sells to you!"

We casually strolled to the main entrance, where Robert jumped out the door and bounded over to us. "Woodrow let you in?"

Diane met his eyes and went to take his arm. "He was busy, so we let ourselves in."

Robert yanked his arm free. "Are you insane? Woodrow will be furious."

"So?" I asked, annoyed at his reaction to Diane. His size intimidated most people, but even he normally succumbed to Diane's charm.

Robert huffed at me before looking down at Diane. The tension in his face relaxed. He offered her his arm. "Come. We should find Charles and Jean-Luc before trouble finds them."

I was the first through the gate, and as I left the estate, Woodrow sneered at me. "How did you get in, John?" he said, as Robert and Diane passed through the opening.

Before Diane or I could answer, Robert stormed over to him. "I would think the answer would be obvious. They entered when you left your post."

The guard lowered his head. "Yes, Master Twinholm. It will not happen again."

"See to it, or I will have to inform Father that you neglected your duty."

When Robert faced the forest with his back to the entrance, the guard sneered again, but didn't reply.

We crossed the road to a small, almost obscured path, overgrown with fall foliage, leading into the forest. As we travelled deeper, I marveled at the luminous reds, oranges, and yellows of the transforming leaves. Even though the forest was dense, and sometimes dark enough to block our view, bright sunlight penetrated the darkness, allowing us to find our way through a full season's worth of growth.

Diane wove around an oak tree. "So, Robert... John and I were discussing future plans."

Robert stopped and faced us. "Future plans? Do you mean today?"

"No, as in life."

"Well, I plan on working with my father until I can take over. And I always assumed you'd all work with me. Even though J.D. is annoying, he is smarter than any of my father's men. Heck, I even figured Cat would fit in somehow."

"Speaking of Cat," I began, "what are we planning to do in December for his eighteenth birthday?"

After a short time, we came to a slight hill with Charles's rickety shack on top. Ever since his mother passed away, his father played the part of a recluse, and our friend shared that type of lifestyle. We spotted a hunting knife at the base of a tree with its blade buried in the soil.

We found Charles dangling upside-down with a rope around his ankles. He was covered in mud, leaves, and twigs.

Robert circled the trunk of the tree. "Let's see, how do we get you down?" As he came out on the other side of Charles, he smirked. "Charles Avery Tomlinson the third, I presume."

We could all hear Charles getting ready to spit at him, but when Diane coughed, he swallowed it. "Just get me down, you pompous a—"

"Cat!" Diane called. "No need for that. What have you gotten yourself into this time?"

Cat put his hands up to his face and brushed away some of the debris. He seemed on the verge of tears when he fell. His quick reflexes allowed him to tuck his head and land on his back. He leapt to his feet and spun to face us. "I was setting game traps, and I forgot about this one."

Robert laughed loud and deep. "Typical. Well, at least it wasn't a spear-pit you forgot about, eh?"

Cat curled his fingers into a fist and didn't respond. After retrieving his knife, he inspected a line where a few quail, a turkey, and two rabbits were strung. He untied the line and flung the lot across his back. His unnaturally white teeth shone through the dirt. "I need to go to the butcher to see if I can get something for this."

Diane strolled to Cat and brushed him off. "We still need to get Jean-Luc."

"No, you don't." We jumped at the deep, monotone voice.

I spun around. "Jean-Luc!" He was taller than me, but shorter than Robert and broader in the shoulders than any of us. He folded his arms across his chest, showing off his massive forearms. Unlike most people, he always wore colorful garb, and today was no exception. "Well, we should hurry to the market, then."

Robert nodded at Jean-Luc. "That sounds like a plan. I have business to conduct, as well." He gallantly offered Diane his arm. "May I escort you?"

Diane grinned and slapped his chest. "I think I can maneuver better without hanging on your arm. Besides, I'm faster in the forest than you." With that, she bolted, surprising all of us with her speed, especially in a long dress.

I chased her past countless trees, up and down hills, and across a small brook. By the time I caught up with her, she had reached the road on the outskirts of town, and fixed her appearance so no one would know she'd been running. "How do you manage to run like that?" I panted, gulping air.

The rest of our friends caught up with us, and we walked together into town. Diane glanced around, patting her hair to ensure nothing had fallen out of her demure bun. "A lady can't divulge all her secrets."

The miller's wife and daughter heard Diane's comment, glanced at us, gasped, and disappeared into the mill.

Cat stretched his neck, trying to see over Robert. "What was that about?"

Robert scoffed and pulled away from us. "Why should I care? Let's get to the business of the day."

We hustled into the center of town, avoiding people when possible. The folk we did come across whispered and pointed at us. Recently, this reaction had increased until it happened every day, but we mostly ignored it. When we arrived at the butcher's house, Robert flung the door open, and we shuffled inside.

The butcher hung a shank from the ceiling and paused, glancing over to us as he inhaled deeply. "What is that stink?"

Cat bounced over to the counter like a gleeful child. "I have meat for you to purchase, Stephen."

Stephen spat in Cat's face, stepped back from his counter, and folded his arms across his chest. "I will not have anything to do with the likes of you anymore. Get out of my shop, the lot of you!"

"The likes of me?"

"I heard the rumors. I do not deal with folk from the Spanish Netherlands any longer. So you," he pointed to Jean-Luc, "and your circus freak, can get out."

Robert pushed Cat out of the way, reached over the counter, snatched the butcher by the collar, and jerked him forward. As he glared down into the man's eyes, Robert pressed his face so close that his nose squished the butcher's nose sideways. "Do you know who I am? Do you know who my family is, little man? I could have you licking the soles of my boots if I wanted. How dare you treat my friend that way?"

The man shook, and his voice cracked. "I-I-I don't have to deal with anyone I don't want to!"

Robert tightened his grasp on Stephen's shirt laces and lifted him off the ground. "You will pay Cat's father the full price for the game. Do I make myself clear?"

Diane stepped forward and placed her hand on Robert's shoulder. "Robert, please let him down."

Robert scowled at Diane, but after staring into her eyes for a moment, the tension in his face eased. He nodded at her before sneering at the butcher. He gently tossed the man back, still using enough force that it took the butcher a few steps to catch himself.

Cat looked at us as we left and then set his prizes on the counter.

The butcher leered at Cat, before glancing at the game. "I will deal with your father."

Cat nodded and slinked outside to join us.

I spun around to confront Robert. "What were you thinking? We all get supplies from him."

"Relax. I have dealt with him before. He might sound like a mongrel, but he seldom actually bites."

"What if you are not around?"

"We are *always* together, so what is the problem? Now, come, I need to visit the pub."

While we travelled through our little hamlet, I noticed people avoiding us whenever we approached. I refused to believe that anything was out of the ordinary. We had seen this behavior before, but something about today seemed different to me. I chose to ignore it. The sun was descending when we reached the inn's entrance. Robert nearly bowled over three girls who were leaving. He slammed his hand on the door frame to stop himself.

The youngest of the three, Elizabeth Parris, jumped to the side of the door and screamed. "It's them!"

Robert stared down at the trio of girls. "What are you babbling about?"

The eldest girl, Abigail Williams, glanced over at Diane, ignoring Robert. "Look at what the cat dragged into town, girls. Say Diane, what evils are you spreading today?"

Diane gazed at the girls, perplexed. "For Heaven's sake, what are you talking about?"

Elizabeth clutched her stomach when Diane mentioned 'Heaven,' and all three ran off. *Fleeing to church again*, I thought.

Robert huffed and took a few steps inside the inn. "Stupid girls."

I quickly stepped in front of Robert, blocking his movement. "Robert, they could cause trouble for us."

"They accuse people so they aren't accused themselves."

"And you don't think they will blame us?"

Jean-Luc joined me in the inn. "No sense worrying about it now. What's done is done."

Robert pushed past us and confronted the barkeep, who glanced away after listening to us and returned to prying the lid off some wooden crates with a crowbar. "I see you have my family's deliveries, Isaac."

Isaac spun around with the tool in his hand. "Right on cue. They said you'd be here shortly. How interesting."

Robert ignored the comment. "So, you will pay for your supplies now."

The man tossed the crow on top of an unopened crate. "I don't believe you will have to worry about payment. You will have your own troubles to deal with soon enough."

Robert snarled and stepped closer to Isaac. "And just what does that mean?"

"You will find out tomorrow. And as for you, J.D., perhaps you should talk to your father before then, no?" He returned to his work, staring into the crate and ignoring us.

Robert remained there, dumbfounded, until Diane gently tugged him away.

Peering into the corner of the dimly lit inn, I noticed my father standing with his back to us, addressing a few farmers. One of the farmers was also named John Dent, one of three others in town, which is why I used J.D. I pushed closer so I could hear him.

My father held up a few fingers while he spoke. "Three essentials feed a man. Physical, which is comprised of food, exercise, and work. Mental, which is anything that we learn or feel. And spiritual, filling oneself with the word of God."

John, a stocky farmer rose from his chair and waved his hand dismissively at my father. "So, you are saying that, if you don't believe in God, you cannot be a complete man?"

My father nodded. "Yes. And here is why…"

I grinned, knowing what he would say, but before he could truly begin his monologue, I coughed to get his attention. "Father, we need to talk."

16

The happy expression on my father's face disappeared as his eyes rested on us. "Finally, you are here. Go to my home. All of you."

Robert arched an eyebrow. "Why?"

My father furrowed his brow, more serious than I had ever seen him. "I said, 'go to my home.' Now!" He bowed to the men he had been addressing. "I must take my leave. Good day to you all."

Twilight was deepening when we left the inn. Outside, we broke into a jog to my family's house as the last of the day's light disappeared.

While we caught our breaths, my father braced himself in the frame of the door, his hand tracing the carvings he had done many years prior. He took a deep breath. "You must all leave."

I stepped to my father. "What?"

He spun around with tears in his eyes—something that I had rarely seen. "Those foul girls have accused you five of being a coven."

Robert scoffed. "I knew we should have whipped them when we had the chance."

"And that would have made them accuse us even quicker," Diane chastised Robert.

Cat paced side-to-side. "Why not arrest us then?"

My father faced him. "You know magistrates. They like their warrants all nice and neat. Hawthorne was investigating another charge on the other side of town. The girls didn't see me, so they have no clue that you know. I will give J.D. a map showing the best route to Reading. Once there, meet with Peter Smith, and give him a letter I will prepare. He will be able help, but you cannot return. Folks here will always believe those accusations and would take the law into their own hands."

I tried to compose my thoughts before unleashing them in a torrent. "It is a terrifying day when we must leave to protect our loved ones from the insanity of a bloodthirsty mob. Although I do not know what will happen to these girls, I hope they receive some punishment, either in this life or the next." I addressed my friends, "Go get ready. We will leave in the morning."

Robert glowered, "Why not leave now?"

Before I could answer, Cat replied, "Leaving by horseback at the dead of night is not the wisest of choices. Getting lost in the woods would be worse than being chased."

Jean-Luc approached me. "You have never led us astray. I know I speak for the others when I say, we will continue to follow your judgment."

The shock and disappointment stayed on my friends' faces as Robert, Cat, and Jean-Luc disappeared into the night.

I took Diane's hand into mine. "Would you like me to escort you home?"

Diane slightly nudged my side as she passed me. "Normally, I would accept, but in this case, I think it would better if we avoided being seen together." She stared into my eyes, seeing my concern, and she placed her hands on my chest the way she always did when she was serious about something. "I will be fine. Get ready for tomorrow." She pulled out an embroidered handkerchief, gently placing it in my hand. "You will always be my gentleman." I watched her saunter into the night.

After she disappeared, I inhaled the sweet aroma of the cloth before carefully folding it and tucking it in my belt. I was about to grin, until I saw the sorrow in my father's eyes. He followed me into the barn without saying a word. I ran my fingers through my horse's chocolate-colored mane then picked up his brush. When Cinnamon saw it in my hand, the stallion whinnied and nodded in anticipation.

My father spoke, breaking the silence. "Son, I wish there was more I could do for you."

I replaced the brush on its shelf. "Father, you have done more for me than you could possibly imagine. I am worried about you two, though."

"I can handle the magistrates and any problems with accusations about your mother and me. But there have been whispers about you and your friends for a while. Ever since Robert…"

My mother came in, carrying a pack. When I saw her forlorn face, I averted my gaze to avoid crying.

She rubbed her hand over mine. "It is some dried provisions, the blanket you always loved, a hand-ax, a few water skins, and all the bills of credit your father and I have saved."

I glanced up with tears in my eyes. "I can't take this."

"Take it John. Take it and live life with that spirit that I know you have." She leaned in and kissed my forehead, then took my father's hand and left.

I remained motionless for several long minutes, not doing anything before I stored the pack, finished grooming Cinnamon, and then retired for the night.

# CHAPTER THREE

As dawn broke, I peered out the open window. My restless night's sleep had me on edge. The gloom of the clouds hanging low in the sky blocked out the sun. A blustery wind howled, rattling the whole house, making me shiver even though I was still warm in bed. It was the type of day when I knew the sun wasn't going to show its face.

Hoping not to disturb my parents, I snuck down the ladder, only to find both of them in the kitchen. I chuckled at my mother. "I never could get anything past you, could I?"

My mother hugged me tight. "Be safe, and watch after the others. Your group's strength comes from the strong bonds you have."

"I will, Mother. I promise."

I extended my hand to my father. My father yanked me forward, and wrapped his burly arm around me. "Do our family proud, Son." He pulled away and handed me the map and letter.

I nodded, unable to answer past the lump in my throat. I ran out of the house to avoid bursting into tears and to the barn where I quickly gathered my provisions, and readied my horse. I set out for my first and closest friend, Diane.

The trip to Diane's house was short. We both lived on the outskirts of town, and my mind was so full of thoughts that I didn't really pay attention to anything or anyone. As I rode past the bend in the road that led to her family's residence, I could clearly see the white, two-story home. As I approached, I could smell the sweet aroma of the family's wine business.

In front of the house, on one side, was a large barn and on the opposite were rows and rows of vines. Even at this early hour, I could see her father, Pierre, working in one of the rows with a large wicker basket full of red grapes.

"Bonjour, J.D.," he greeted me with his large, ever-present smile. He was the type who could wring a laugh from the most cynical of men. Seeing him work in the fields always caused me stop and think. Here was a man who could easily afford help; yet he did the work of inspecting and removing the grapes himself. Perhaps he needed to do something, or perhaps he was a bit of a perfectionist. Seeing me, he went to an elongated lean-to, opened a covered vat, and dropped the grapes inside. I was about to speak, when he motioned for me to follow him into the barn.

I stared at the sky for a moment while the cold wind blew down my back. Without comment, I urged my horse forward through the open doors.

I crinkled my nose in anticipation of the wonderful sweet smell of fermenting grapes changing to a rank, mucky odor of manure, but was surprised when I couldn't smell any change. The inside of the barn was remarkably clean.

"John," he called to me in his thick French accent. It took me a moment to realize what he was asking since his accent and speed were always a challenge for me. "I need you to... guard my daughter."

"Of course I will!"

"Non!" He briskly jogged to my horse and seized the reins. With a harsh, raspy voice he commanded, "Promise me that she will not be harmed. Promise you will be her chevalier."

I nodded without hesitation. "Of course. You know how I feel about your daughter."

He shrugged his shoulders and nodded.

I tried to figure out if he'd understood me. "So where is Di—"

Diane entered the barn on her horse. She wore a hunter-green riding outfit, which shocked me. She wasn't side-saddle, and I had never realized that she actually rode horses, having never seen her on one before. Just thinking about how long I had known her brought back the memories of her on our first day of school. The images of Diane at the age of five drew a smirk to my face. My heart pounded in my throat, causing me to shiver.

It must have shown more than I realized because Pierre asked, "Tu froid?"

I wondered for a moment, trying to understand before I realized he was asking if I was cold. I shook my head. Diane motioned for us to follow. We followed her out the open door, and I couldn't help admiring her auburn hair in a bun, with some curls around her face. By the time we'd exited the barn, she had dismounted and was checking the straps on her filly, a white Andalusian.

Glancing over at me, she grinned. Her warm expression compelled me to return the gesture. Much like her father, she had the uncanny ability to project emotions onto others. When she smiled, people couldn't help joining her.

I rode over to her with a silly grin on my face. "Are you ready, Diane?"

"Give me a moment, John," she replied then took her father's hands in her own and kissed him on both cheeks.

"Que ton périple soit sûr mon ange," he said in a shaky voice. Tears welled in his eyes.

She hugged him tightly, spun to her horse, then stopped as if having second thoughts. Bowing her head for a moment, she mounted and rode over to me. "We should go." She matched her father's tone of voice.

"What did your father say?"

"He called me his angel and wished me safe travels."

We rode in the direction of the docks in silence. As we passed into the heavily populated section of town, the few people who were up at this hour seemed to avoid eye contact with us. They either pretended they didn't notice us and hastened their steps, or closed the shutters.

When we arrived at Robert's estate, the guard from the previous day stepped out. Tilting his head back to look down his nose at us, he huffed. "Master Robert will be with you in a moment. You may wait here."

Diane and I huffed at each other before she replied. "And if we don't want to wait here?"

Woodrow blocked the path of Diane's horse. His eyes narrowed and his upper lip curled. "Then you may wait over there, but you shall not enter the master's manor today."

Diane was about to reply when Robert rode up from behind the fence on a jet black stallion. The horse was huge, causing Robert to tower over us in the saddle. He had many things tied to his saddle, and carried a haversack. His Tyrian purple cloak with fancy gold trim flapped in the wind that blew with renewed force.

"We need to go now," Robert commanded. "Jean-Luc and Charles are already waiting for us." He spurred his horse to full gallop.

Diane and I followed him. Our horses easily kept pace with the behemoth. The wind whipped more and more debris into our faces with every stride, almost knocking us from our saddles. The air smelled stormy, and we rode past the main hub of Salem. The streets were deserted.

We rode to the edge of town and joined our other two friends. Jean-Luc's horse was about the same size and color as mine, but Charles's horse was the smallest and hadn't been brushed in years. Matted, unkempt hair covered the gray mare's shaggy body.

I shook my head at Cat. "You couldn't take time to brush your horse?"

Cat tilted his head to one side. "Why, what is wrong with Chaos?"

I shook my head at him. "Never mind. My father gave me the map to Reading. There are a few key spots where we have to take the correct fork in the road, but for the most part, it is straight on this road." I pointed west. "We should arrive there before nightfall if we go at a normal pace."

Cat peered down the road. "Why not ride harder and get there before lunch?"

"I don't want it to appear we are fleeing."

"But we are, aren't we?"

"Yes, but I don't want it to *appear* that way."

"Oh! I understand. Right. So onward!" He began to ride in front of us.

Robert reacted next, and the rest of us kept pace with him. "He will be a handful. So, J.D., what is the plan once we get to Reading?"

I thought about it before I answered. "We are going to meet with the man my father mentioned. He will help us with the…"

Cat wiggled in the saddle as he tried to ride in between us. "What if he won't help us?"

I sighed. "My father would not have sent us to see him. Besides, it is better than staying here where we'd be chained to the gallows, people would be brought to say anything they want about us, and the decision is determined on the spot without any chance to defend ourselves."

Robert waved Cat to the back. "And after he helps clear our name, what then?"

Diane spoke before I could answer. "I'd like to explore. To be the one that discovers the new things about this land. To do something that will be written about. But mostly, I want to live my life with my friends."

We rode up the inclined path and viewed all of Salem one last time. One by one, we crested the hill and stopped in a moment of shared apprehension. When we were about to round a corner that would forever take us away from our homes, Luke, a tracker by trade, greeted us. Dressed in leathers and carrying his bow, he emerged from some brush. His concealment had been so complete that we would have ridden past and never spotted him.

"Well met," Luke told us. "You would do well to hasten your pace. They are coming for you." He gestured behind us, at the path we had traveled. In the distance, dust clouds approached rapidly. "They are coming: the magistrates John Hawthorne and Jonathan Corwin. Those foul girls have blamed you for their curses. They went to your homes and discovered you missing and your families didn't even know you were gone. They are convinced you had prior knowledge, thus confirming to them what you are. Scouting parties have been sent to find your trail."

"And what of our families?" Four of us asked simultaneously. Only Charles remained silent.

"They are safe. I know the magistrates are only arresting those people accused by the afflicted, and, well, you are the only ones accused. If you run far and fast enough, perhaps they will tire."

I gawked at him in disbelief. "Why would someone like you want to protect us? You are one of those who usually gossiped about us."

"Gossip is one thing, but I do not believe in detaining people simply because girls say their mad actions are controlled by evil forces. I will not be the one who, by my actions, causes the deaths of others." With his warning delivered, Luke slipped back into the brush and disappeared.

Not waiting around to test the truth of his words, we bolted off, pushing our horses to their fullest strides. Diana's horse easily outpaced all of ours, so she became our lead rider, followed closely by Jean-Luc, then Robert and I, with Charles bring up the rear. As I occasionally glanced back at him, I thought it out of place. Charles should have outpaced us since his horse was the least burdened with supplies. I hoped he didn't want to confront our accusers.

We chased the cloudy sun for the rest of the day, following the path leading into the woods west of Salem Village. Strangely, we never came across any of the forks or markers mentioned on Father's map. We attempted several times to leave the trail, but the thick brush and trees confounded us. Each time we rested, our pursuers got closer.

Over the course of the day, they pursued us through the dense forest. Every time we stopped to catch our breaths and glanced behind us, we saw the encroaching dust clouds. The day seemed to pass in a blur. The magistrates and other witch hunters never relented.

Sunset approached, and we were desperate. We gasped and grunted. Our steeds were exhausted, worn by a day's worth of flight. We searched for any avenue of escape for the night— anything to give us a reprieve. We stopped on the road where the path bent sharply to the south. Frantically, we discussed alternatives, since running no longer seemed like an option.

Diane spoke first. "Did we make a wrong turn?"

Cat shouted at her. "What wrong turn? There were no turns! There were no people. Perhaps the woods are haunted!"

Jean-Luc rode up beside us. "We need to fight," he said calmly, like it was a normal conversation.

Diane gasped for air. She grabbed her canteen and took a drink. "I need to catch my breath. I can't fight anyone. What are you talking about?"

"We could kill them and hide their bodies." Cat took out his serrated hunting knife.

"Are you mad?" I exclaimed, riding over to him. "That is not going to happen."

"I agree," Robert said. "But we need another plan, and fast."

Cat jumped down and frantically looked around. "Maybe I can find some herbs to give the horses a boost of energy. Look! There is a trail in here." He entered what appeared to be a small, obscured path. It was not much, but any rest from the day's activity was welcome.

I jumped off my horse. "Everyone dismount. This is going to be tight." The path was barely high and wide enough for our mounts. We guided our horses into the forest. Cat led, his woodman's eyes seeking out the trail.

"How can you see any path? To me, it is more of the thick, impassable forest we've passed all day."

Cat chuckled as he continued through the abundance of wild bushes and low branches. "It is here, trust me. It is as plain as the path we were riding on." Even with Cat's keen eyesight, though, he continually misjudged the clearance and had to find alternate routes, especially with the size of Robert's horse. "Looks like an opening ahead," he said with excitement. Glancing back, I knew I would not be able to find the road again myself.

Cat pulled Chaos into the clearing then rushed back to help the rest of us.

Jean-Luc took Cat's and my horses, and we headed back to the main road.

Cat broke off some branches, handing one to me. "Sweep the path down there a bit. I will cover it here."

I did as I was told, while Cat obscured where we had disappeared into the trees. When I returned, Cat pushed me into the trail and bent back the brush and trees that had been trampled down. Joining the others, we all finally released our tension. We collapsed, exhausted.

Once we'd managed to catch our breath, we explored the grove that had become our refuge. It actually was larger than it had seemed at first. Oval in shape and nearly seventy-five feet wide, it appeared to be a long-abandoned homestead. The sides of the trees near the open space appeared as if they had been sheared off and were slow to re-grow, while the branches facing outward were wild and untouched.

We got to our feet and stumbled around the perimeter searching for other possible paths. I went with Diane one way while Cat, Robert, and Jean-Luc went the other.

When we met up on the opposite side of the entrance, Cat spoke. "There are no other exits. We found the only feasible way in. There is a stream on the border beyond the tree line opposite the entrance where the horses can drink."

We went to the horses and pulled off their tack and saddles and placed them on a dry patch of earth. We rubbed our mounts down quickly, letting them graze afterward.

"What's that?" Diane pointed to something I'd missed when we entered.

In front of the trees an oddly-placed, large obsidian slab jutted from the earth. It was slightly taller than me, broader than Jean-Luc, and very thick. The top of the stone was rounded in a half circle, and the sides were very straight. The stone appeared to be a black doorway into the massive, pure white birches that guarded the circle.

As I approached the stone slab, some trick of the dwindling light caused the engraved markings adorning the block to seem to change. "Did you see that?" I blinked my eyes a few times and tilted my head back and forth to ascertain I was not hallucinating as I watched the marks slide together at different angles.

Diane took my hand. "See what?"

"The markings seemed to move."

Robert laughed and slapped me on the back. "Good one— migrating engravings. What's next, ghost tales?"

With the rest of my companions, we studied the marker. The runes engraved on it didn't resemble anything I could piece together as words, although they were similar to Celtic. "Does anyone recognize what these marks could mean?"

Cat peered at it from a distance, as if not wishing to get any closer. After a long pause, he whispered, "It's not any type of Wampanoag or native writing that I recognize."

With hesitation, I reached out and touched the obsidian tablet. It was surprisingly icy to the touch. I jumped back, causing everyone else to jump. When I landed, my foot hit something buried under the grassy field.

I motioned to Robert and Diane. "Watch my back. Cat and Jean-Luc, watch the entrance." Kneeling on the sod, I attempted to push aside the dirt and grass. Whatever was hidden under the sod and earth, would, I hoped, help unravel the mystery.

Within minutes, I uncovered a strange, metallic door. Rectangular, it was monstrous, easily dwarfing even Robert's massive size. The sun had set, and moonlight shone on the metal, which appeared to be dull silver. Reflected light served to illuminate enough so we could see. On the door was a circular pull ring. Without thinking, I pulled, but I could not budge it.

"Jean-Luc," I called in a hushed whisper, "Get over here and help me."

Leaving his post, he ran to join me while Robert took his spot. "Need help, J.D.?" He put his hands next to mine on the ring. Together, we struggled with the door, unable to lift it at all.

"Robert!" I yelled, and then cursed myself for the loudness of my voice.

With a smug expression on his face, he motioned for us to drop the ring. "Let me show you two why I get things done."

We glanced at each other and smirked evilly, dropping the ring. Robert clenched the circle in both hands and pulled with all his might. His muscles tensed, but he had no greater results than the two of us.

I looked him in the eye. With a forceful, but hushed voice I said, "Together."

With the three of us grunting and straining, we managed to lift the door. Air rushed out with a hiss, and we heaved the metal door on its side. We cringed as we saw the slab fall, fearing the noise of the thick iron would alert our pursuers to our location. We were relieved when it landed on the soft earth without a sound.

We were assaulted by wafts of stale air and moist earth from the opening. Unlike the front, the back side of the open silvery door was black like a starless, moonless night. Not even the light of the moon could penetrate the shadow of the underside. The new opening revealed a staircase leading down into deep, impenetrable darkness.

Going to my horse, I withdrew a flask of lamp oil and one of my older shirts from my saddlebags. I hesitated to destroy the garment, but I needed some cloth for what I was planning, and it didn't feel right asking my friends to give up something if I was unwilling to do the same. Tearing the shirt into strips, I tightly tied them to two different branches. I thoroughly drenched the oil over them, and soaked part of the ground in my haste. With the new torches in hand, I headed for the staircase. Cat took out his tinder and sparked a fire on one, then used it to light the other. He handed one torch to me and took the other.

We were about to walk down the stairs together. Cat yelled, "Look!"

My heart raced, and the sweat from my hands nearly made me drop the torch. I faced Cat. "Now that you've scared us half to death, what are you talking about?"

"The markings! I can read them now!"

I spun and felt my eyes widen as I read the words etched in the stone.

*Don't be afraid*

After seeing the reactions of my friends, I looked at the opening of the clearing then back to the darkness. I tried to rationalize the message and hoped no one saw me tremble. "Let's see what this is all about." I nervously descended into the darkness, with my friends close behind me.

# CHAPTER FOUR

The curving walls of the staircase were cool to the touch. They were constructed of some type of rectangular metal bricks about one hand square. They were stacked tightly, with no space at all between them. I practically had to touch my nose to the wall to see the thin lines showing the bricks' edges. The torch light danced on the bluish-gray surface like a firefly invasion.

The narrow metal staircase stretched before us. It descended sharply into the gloom beyond the light of our torches. Along the way, we bumped into one another more than a dozen times.

"Stop pushing!" I struggled not to slip on the narrow steps.

"Just let me pass then," Robert huffed. "There has to be a bottom."

"Just take it easy, Robert." I held his forearm to stop him. "I would rather get there in one piece than tumble into the unknown." I could hear our collective breathing in the confined space, even over the chatter.

"What's that?" Cat jumped. "I heard something!"

The eerie sound of breathing came from around us rather than from us. We gave up on caution and hastened quickly to find the bottom of the stairs. My eyes darted nervously around. The stairs were immaculate with no trace of dust, no cobwebs, and no small insects, nothing that would normally be found in a subterranean passage that had been undisturbed for a long time. For some reason, the thought comforted me.

"It's our echo. Don't let your mind play tricks on you." I tried to sound as comforting as possible.

The air grew staler as we descended. We held our breaths to avoid the vile stench. Eventually, I could smell fresh air ahead competing with stale air behind.

"Look!" Diane approached the outline of a door resembling the monolith above.

Although it seemed to be metal, the door did not reflect the torchlight. To the right of the door, midway down the wall where a latch would be, a small, square metal panel hung. It was a bit larger than my hand with my fingers fanned out. This metal seemed as if it was created from the same material of the walls and stairs.

"What are you going to do?" Robert tugged my shirt as I inched closer to the door.

Ignoring him, I apprehensively let my palms touch the metal, anticipating the cold this time. It was warm to the touch. Carefully, I glided my hands over the surface, trying to trace the outline of the door, but did not find any seams. As my hand slid to the level of the small panel, the gentle pressure pushed the metal into the wall. At my touch, the door vanished into the ceiling.

Diane's scream of surprise resounded. We all focused on her, trying to calm our hearts. I swear I heard my friends' heartbeats echoing off the walls. When our astonishment subsided, we stepped cautiously inside, trying to discern anything that might explain why someone would bury stairs and whatever was beyond under the earth.

We entered a fairly large chamber. It was about the size of Diane's father's barn, almost twice as wide as it was deep. In the center of each of the walls was a large door inscribed with the same type of strange writings as the marker above, but with slight variations. The walls were made of the same type of material as the walls in the stairwell, but instead of being composed of bricks, these were smooth. To the right of each door was a small panel similar to the one beside the door to this chamber. Although we were deep underground, the chamber brightened. This light allowed us to dimly see basic details of the chamber, beyond what the torchlight revealed.

Robert confidently strode in, approaching the door on the opposite side from where we had entered. "Wait here. I will find out if anything is about."

We took in the weird ambiance. When Robert was halfway across, everything brightened as though lit by a score of lanterns, but there was no obvious source of light. I nearly choked. Robert jumped back to us in an instant, but the room remained bright.

"What the hell did you do?" shouted Jean-Luc.

Robert grinned and faced Jean-Luc. "Calm yourself, Jeanie."

Jean-Luc clenched his hands and squared off against Robert. "What did you call me?" His voice cracked with anger.

Robert raised his hands to his own chest. "Calm yourself, Jean-Luc. You know I did nothing. Perhaps the stories of witchcraft are true!" Robert half-grinned at us, and I was not sure if he laughed at our response, or at what he thought were his own cleverness.

I listened and tried to reason. "Are you being yourself, or are you trying to stir emotions?"

Before he could answer me, Diane confronted him. "How can you even say that in jest, Robert? Have you forgotten that we have been chased all day for that very reason? Are you so dense that you jump to the same conclusions as those who would have us killed?" She stared up into his eyes. "Now more than ever, we need to stand by each other and figure out where we are and what it means." She tilted her head to one side.

Robert succumbed to her charm, nodding. "I am sorry," he said in an unconvincing voice. "Does anyone have any ideas about what we should do?"

"Yes," I stated, recalling my previous thoughts. "We should explore these chambers. Perhaps we can discover what secrets they hold. But we should have a plan. I believe we should pick a direction and constantly go that way until we can no longer proceed. If we are somewhere large, we definitely do not want to get lost. I suggest we start at the left door and go from there. If this is anything like the catacombs of Paris, we can explore the entire thing by always taking lefts when a choice presents itself, unless it takes us back to the same spot. In that case, we'd take the very next right then follow the pattern again."

With surprise in her voice Diane asked, "How do you know about the catacombs of Paris? Have you been there?"

"I almost feel as though I've been there. My parents pressed me to study many cultures, from the Egyptians to the Norse and Celts and even the Aztec savages of central Mexico. I learned about layouts of various temples, pyramids, and catacombs."

Diane went to the door on the left, but Jean-Luc stopped her. "Let me go ahead, in case there are more hidden surprises, similar to the light Robert happened to trip upon."

Robert grunted and opened his mouth, but bit his lip instead of saying anything. We approached the door together and poked at the small panel to the right of the door. Jean-Luc mimicked my previous actions by placing his hand on the panel, but nothing happened.

"Gently push in," I offered.

Jean-Luc nodded and pressed the metallic panel. The door shot into the roof with a loud clanging that echoed in the barren chamber. I assumed the door would disappear into the ceiling, but

I jumped at the sheer speed at which it occurred. The chamber ahead of us changed from an eerie black to the same lustrous glow as the room we were in.

Jean-Luc leaned in far enough in to peer around. "All clear."

We crowded cautiously in, not knowing what to expect. Once Cat, who was the last of us, entered, the door came down with the same speed with which it had receded into the ceiling, shutting us in. In a panic, Cat tried to punch the door, but his fist hit only air as the door rose back up into the ceiling. He stepped back and waited as the door came down again. He repeated the action twice, letting his arm stay in the opening on the last try.

With the door open, he seemed puzzled. "Why doesn't this side have one of those metal squares?"

I peered around for possible exits. "None of them on this side have them. How weird. Cat, back away from the door, and we'll figure it out later."

Cat went to the door on our right while Robert stepped closer to the door on the left. The rectangular room was almost as empty as the one we had left.

Pointing, Diane asked, "What are those?"

Ahead of us were five thick, metal dowels sticking out from the wall at Diane's height. They were about an arm's length apart and four inches around. Under each was a small metal table.

I went over to the wall and pushed on one of the pegs. I shook in horror, as the dowel pulled my hand, and I stuck to the metal. I attempted to jerk free, but I couldn't budge it. "What in blazes?"

My friends spun in my direction. Diane gasped. "What's wrong?"

I held up my other hand to stop them from moving and pulled harder on the other one. I sighed with relief when the metal dowel relinquished its grasp on my hand on the third attempt. "I wasn't expecting the thing to be sticky." I touched my torch to the strange metal. Like before, the torch stuck to the metal as if by some magical means, although I would not have dared to say that witchcraft kept it still.

"It's possessed!" Cat cried and raced to the exit, causing the door to, once again, retract into the ceiling.

Diane clutched my arm and whispered in my ear, apparently afraid that someone unseen might hear her. "I do not like this, J.D."

"Everything will be fine," I answered aloud so everyone could hear. "Things are working differently here." I tried to sound reassuring, even though I was terrified out of my mind.

"Well, if we are following your plan, we go this way, so come on." Cat tried to pass Robert.

"Hold on, Cat. Should we not explore fully?"

"Fully? What else could there possibly be to explore?" He swept his arm around. "What do you mean? There is nothing else here, let's continue on." He hustled to the new door.

We were relieved to discover it opened without any action from us. The room beyond went from blackness to full brightness.

Cat coughed and covered his nose. "Oh my God, what is that horrible stench?"

A foul odor of decay that seemed to burn the hairs of my nose assaulted me, and I covered my mouth with my hand to prevent vomiting. Cat and I shuffled into the corridor to see a large pile of dust on the floor being sucked into small, circular holes in the ceiling. The rush of air blasting past us and into the ceiling was enough to extinguish our torches and leave us choking. By the time we had all entered the hall, the holes had closed, and the air smelled fresh.

"One, two, three." Cat counted the doors in the hall, nodding his head to each one as he did so. "Including the one we entered, there are nine doors total."

"Why do the two doors, the one we entered, and the one down there along the same wall, have no panel, while all the rest do?" Jean-Luc asked.

"Perhaps halls don't have them and rooms do?" I suggested.

"Where should we go from here, J.D.?" Cat asked. "Should we go to that far door, look in these on the way… or what?"

"Let's see," I responded. "If this leads anywhere, then we will backtrack. Let's take the door on our right."

The others nodded in agreement. We waited in front of the door, trying to prepare for anything that might occur. Jean-Luc took the lead, followed by Robert. Diane was in the middle, and I followed her. Cat took the rear and watched our backs.

"Get ready," Jean-Luc announced. After moving his head back and forth a few times, he informed us, "Looks like someone's bedroom."

I tried to see around him, but his size took up the entire door frame. "Either enter or get out of the way."

"Sorry about that," he said as he entered the room, and the rest of us followed behind.

The bedroom was fairly large for one individual, easily able to accommodate all of us with room to spare. In the far corner, a canopy bed with four carved, wooden posts nearly reached the ceiling. The large bed could easily hold three or more people and was covered in a green and brown spread. Across from the door, I saw a wooden desk crafted from the finest rosewood I'd ever seen.

The desk was massive, created from a single piece of wood. The sides were etched with scrollwork of leafy vines, each one displaying a different pattern of veins. The leg opening was flanked by three drawers on each side. In front of the desk was an equally impressive wooden chair. Outdoor scenes continued seamlessly from the desk, to the back of the chair, and back to the desk again depicting playful wildlife. Each animal was shown in the finest detail. From the delicate patterns on the fawns' backs to the wiry, disheveled fur of the wolves, I swore I could see muscles tensing as if they were ready to jump off the surface. Each leaf on every tree seemed different. Staring at the carving filled me with the feeling that I stood in a real forest watching a real scene. Even though my father was a perfectionist in his carvings, I tried to see the marks to determine the tools used on the wood, as I had examined my father's work, but the beautiful masterpiece was the Michelangelo's David of wood carvings, surpassing my father's work so much that I could not tell.

On top of the desk, a glass case contained an ornate hilt of a sword in a scabbard. To the left of the entrance was an equally stunning rosewood bureau, carved in the same manner as the other furnishings.

The bed was a welcome sight to my sore body, but the single bed produced a quandary over who should use it.

"What should we do about the sleeping arrangements?" Robert broke the silence.

"I'm not sleeping in here!" Cat yelled.

"Why not?"

"Are you daft? Why would we stay here?"

"Why would we not?" I countered. "It is dry. The bed looks comfortable, and we are hidden from view. There is really only one concern."

Cat folded his arms. "Oh? And what may that be, eh?"

"Obviously, we have to come to some sort of arrangement. The bed won't fit us all, nor can we share the bed with Diane."

"Pish!" Diane said with disdain. "We've camped out before."

"This isn't camping, and we weren't together."

Robert suggested, "Perhaps the other doors around this location might contain beds."

I blinked and stared at Robert. I would not have expected him to come up with such a good idea, or perhaps it was obvious, and I was too tired to have thought of it. I nodded in agreement.

Cat went to the first door on the right. He discovered a smaller chamber, with a bed and a small two-drawer stand. This bed's covering was bright red. Wasting no time, Cat lifted the bedding and mattress and dragged it back, placing it in front of the desk.

As he got the bed into the right spot, I went to the next door. Entering, I squinted at the brightness. The walls, ceiling, floor, and everything in the room were the whitest white. I dragged the mattress and bedding into the hall, letting my eyes gradually adjust. I lugged it into the first bedroom and examined what I had. The bed and blanket were white and immaculate. I put the bed next to the one Cat had brought.

The effects of the day were finally catching up to us. I stated, "I am going to get some supplies before retiring for the night."

"Who is going with you?" Robert folded his arms over his chest.

"I will go with you, J.D." Jean-Luc headed to the door.

Cat jumped up. "I will go also."

"Go fast," Robert ordered. Pointing, he added, "Cat, you act as guard. I will stay with Diane."

Diane rolled her eyes. "Yes, I will be certain to keep Robert safe."

Robert scowled, but didn't reply. He sat on the edge of the desk and folded his arms over his chest.

"So, what do you think we've found?" Jean-Luc asked me as we climbed cautiously up the stairs.

"I do not know, but I am sure I will find some answers. There has to be a logical explanation for everything we've seen."

As we reached the top, we poked our heads up and took a glimpse around. The moon had disappeared over the top of the grove and ominous clouds had rolled in, casting dark shadows over the trees and field.

"Come on," Cat whispered to us, jumping the last few stairs onto the moist dirt. Moving the torch around in a quick arc, he located the horses huddled together at the far end of the field.

I'd taken my first step to the animals when I felt a hand on my forearm, "We should check to see if the magistrates have stopped for the night," Cat told me in a whisper.

I leaned into Jean-Luc. "Go to the horses."

Cat crawled through the brush until he disappeared, while I watched his actions. A cold wind caused me to shiver.

When Cat reappeared, I asked, "Well?"

"All is clear." He brushed off the excess dirt and bits of shrubbery from his clothes. "In this dark, I can't tell what they did, but it appears someone rode past the entrance."

Jean-Luc had finished with his and Diane's supplies when Cat and I got to ours. We took a single meal's worth of food, a few empty sacks in case we found anything, and examined Robert's elaborate saddlebags. I shook my head at the exquisite food the servants had prepared for him. I opened a leather container and took a whiff. "Can you believe this—perfectly aged brandy?"

"And why are you surprised?" Jean-Luc countered, throwing the bags over his shoulders.

Taking the dried meats, Cat nodded. "Ready here."

We returned to the staircase, descending as carefully as we had the first time.

"How was everything?" Diane asked, as we entered.

"We had no troubles. We checked to see if the magistrates had found the entrance, then we got your stuff." Cat presented the bag to Diane.

I handed a satchel to Robert. "And here is your…meal. It must be nice to have someone to prepare your food."

Robert swiped his belongings from my hands. "It is. You wouldn't have me doing it, now would you?"

Before I could answer, Cat spoke with a mouthful of jerky. "So, what do you think we will find? Why would anyone build something like this in the middle of nowhere, hidden from view?"

"I don't have a theory yet," I replied. "We have to find out more before I can come up with something."

"Really?" Robert faked the sound of shock.

"Oh trust me, Robert," I said, catching the tone in his voice. "When I do, you will be the first to know."

Robert laughed, coughing up some of his drink.

Diane confirmed with Robert. "While you were gone, we decided that you, Jean-Luc, and Cat will sleep in the big bed. J.D. will get the bed that Cat brought in, and I will use the white bedding."

With this settled we went to our beds.

"Stop pushing," Cat complained, sandwiched between Jean-Luc and Robert.

"Stop complaining," Robert replied. "You could always go sleep alone somewhere else."

"You'd like that too much," Cat shot back.

"Do I have to separate you two?" Diane's tone was motherly.

"No ma'am," they answered sheepishly.

A long silence snapped when all of us broke into fits of giggles, making us even more tired.

"So, how do you get it to be dark, I wonder?" I covered my head to block out the brightness.

As if on cue, the light slowly dimmed, fading to blackness, and we drifted off to sleep.

# CHAPTER FIVE: DIANE'S INTERLUDE

Diane stirred first, awakened by a gentle breeze caressing her face. She sat up, and the light gradually increased. She got out of bed and left. The draft sent shivers down her spine, as it seemed to follow her down the hall with its many doors. She decided to explore the immediate vicinity. Knowing already where the first two doors led, she chose the next one.

Her fingers felt the cold metal panel, and goose bumps rose on her arms. She pushed, and beamed when the door quietly opened to reveal a dark passage. She waited for what seemed like several minutes for the light to brighten, but nothing occurred.

She was about to shrink back to her friends, unwilling to venture alone into the darkness, when she smelled a scent of roses. She leaned her head into the room, closed her eyes, inhaled deeply, and enjoyed the wonderful aroma.

"It can't be," she murmured. The scent washed away her apprehension, and she entered in search of the source of the scent.

With the only light coming from the hallway she left, Diane could only see the gray outlines of flowers. On the floor, tables, and hanging from the ceiling in holders, the potted plants crowded virtually every space. The deeper she shuffled her feet into the room, the more intense the aroma of roses became. She could almost taste it.

She stared, transfixed, for what seemed several minutes by a pedestal upon on which a rose rested. Unlike any of the other flowers, she could see its colors amid the grays surrounding it. The scarlet, burgundy, ruby, crimson, and red petals of this flower created an illusion of perfection as though the layers had been painted. Each petal was perfectly shaped in such a way that it accentuated the color of the tier beneath it. Even with the staggering number of flowers, Diane knew somehow she could pick out its scent.

The flower began to gleam with an inner radiance. Diane examined it closely and decided she must possess it. She reached out to grasp the rose, carefully trying not to touch any hidden thorns. As she was about to wrap her fingers around the delicate bloom, the slight breeze returned. The cool air blew over her hand and across the flower, drawing the color completely from it. The flower withered and crumbled to dust.

Diane jumped back, bumping into something large. Something not only large, but living breathed down her neck and chuckled with a deep voice. With her only exit blocked, she ran deeper into the darkness. After several minutes of running, she stopped to catch her breath, and mustered the courage to glance around and see if she was still being chased. The individual standing behind her was answer enough. Diane stepped back a few steps. The darkness betrayed her; she fell off an unseen precipice. As she screamed in horror, the blackness engulfed her.

# CHAPTER SIX: JEAN-LUC'S INTERLUDE

Jean-Luc yawned and stretched, pushing against Robert and Cat to give himself more space. Not finding a comfortable position, he sat up in bed and glanced around. He noticed Diane's absence and decided to stretch his legs while searching for her. He sprang out of bed and crept soundlessly to the exit.

He was unsure which direction to go. *Maybe she went to check the horses?* He spun left and nearly broke his nose when he slammed directly into a metal portal that didn't open. He grunted in pain and rubbed his nose. He tried exiting the corridor again, this time more cautiously, but still nothing happened. Pressing up against it, he tried to force the door, but it would not yield.

"This isn't good." Jean-Luc cautiously approached the opposite end of the corridor. When he reached the middle of the hall, the light flickered several times, and everything went black.

Jean-Luc stopped, allowing his eyes to adjust to the darkness. A familiar scent tickled his nose. "Diane?"

A muted cry caught his ear, and he immediately shuffled to discover the source of the sound. His destination was a closed door. The panel to open it did not work. He tried with all his might to lift the door, but its stubbornness was greater than his strength. Stumbling in the shadows, he located what he thought was the room his friends were sleeping in and tried to open the door. The sight of the door opening was a welcome relief. Running inside, he shouted, "Wake up! Diane is in trouble."

Squinting in the pale darkness, he saw that it was one of the rooms that his friends had raided earlier. Feeling a bit foolish, he went to leave, but the door refused to budge.

He heard a strange, soft female voice. "Contaminants discovered. Activating cleansing agent."

Jean-Luc, bewildered by the strange words coming from the walls, did not immediately notice the strange mist filling the space around him. "What in blazes is going on here!" He pushed the door with all his might and managed to lift it high enough that a tiny crack sucked out some of the cloudy, light vapor. The strange vapor irritated his skin, and he felt a bit woozy. He fell backward, hitting his head on the top of someone's boot. Before he blacked out, he heard a sinister laugh.

# CHAPTER SEVEN: CAT'S TALE

Cat shifted in bed. *How did I get talked into sleeping in this strange place, with mysterious, devilish devices about?* He tossed and turned until the urge to relieve himself got the best of him. He decided to check the horses and take care of his problem at the same time.

On his way into the hall, Cat noticed the barren walls for the first time. There were no decorations, no changes in color. There was nothing to distract the eye. He found the entrance room and shivered as he approached the exit door. When he opened it, snow blew into his face. The snow sparked a memory.

He closed his eyes and saw the snowball fight, for which he had spent an entire night preparing. Cat had crafted snowball after snowball and hid them in various nooks in the forest. When the fight began in the morning, he hit all his friends as he dodged their attacks. Wave after wave, he landed his snowballs, yet collectively his companions always missed. He threw another volley at Robert, watched his friend duck, and the snowball hit one of the horses his friends had taken.

"The horses!" he shouted, his daydream broken when he realized their horses had been fully exposed to the harsh elements all night.

Cat ran up the stairs a few at a time, only to slip and crack his left knee on a metal step. "Je—!" He stopped and bit his lip. *Lucky the snow cushioned some of the blow, or I might have done some serious damage.* He got back to his feet and dashed outside. Brushing himself off, he glanced at his bleeding knee.

*Stupid,* he cursed to himself, but the serenity of the snow on the trees and field calmed his nerves. He discovered the horses huddled together at the opposite end of the field. He hobbled over to Chaos and ran his fingers through his mare's course coat. "And John thought I was stupid for not grooming you."

A large, black bird swooped down, its claws extended. He easily dodged the attack, diving for cover in fallen brush. Peeking out, he did not see the predator. He got up and continued his search in the upper tree limbs to see if he could catch a glimpse of it, but the snow stung his eyes, and it was difficult to see anything, even something as big as the bird.

Moments went by, and still nothing announced itself, so he decided to gather supplies and return to the others. Checking his saddlebags, he discovered them empty. He went to Diane's bags, and all of her belongings were gone as well. One by one, he checked all the supplies, and discovered all his friends' belongings were missing. Cat spun, scanning the field to see if the items had somehow fallen out. Something out of the corner of his eye caught his attention, and he stopped.

At the entrance to the field, the brush had been cut down, leaving a gaping hole. He saw one of the magistrates with the large bird perched on his shoulder. The huge crow towered over the man. The bird flexed its talons, and it appeared as if it could have torn its master's shoulder to shreds if it had so desired. It peered at Cat. The blood-red eyes sent a chill down his already cold back.

"So it is you who practices witchcraft?" Cat stared at his foe, gritted his teeth, and snarled.

Magistrate Corwin towered tall and straight. "I believe that is a task best suited for you and your friends."

Under his breath, Cat murmured, "If I were to kill you now, only that bird and I would know where your body was buried." He glanced down and unhitched his cutlass, which he had taken before leaving the bedroom. He sneered maliciously, returning his gaze to his foe. The evil expression dissolved when he realized the bird was missing. That did not make a difference to him. All that mattered was releasing his rage.

Running to the magistrate, Cat closed the distance in the blink of an eye. He licked his lips and smirked when he noticed the fear etching the magistrate's face. He brought the cutlass back, taking time to savor the moment.

He cringed at a stinging sensation on the back of his neck and halted the death blow. He touched his neck and felt warm fluid. With his hand shaking, he stared at the crimson of his own blood. The world spun, and he held his breath to prevent himself from vomiting. A shriek from above caught his attention before he stumbled, losing his grip on the weapon. He fell to all fours and watched helplessly as the magistrate, with glee in his eyes, picked up the cutlass. Blinking a few times to fight the pull of unconsciousness, the last thing he saw was the swing of the blade before blackness engulfed him.

# CHAPTER EIGHT: ROBERT'S INTERLUDE

Robert was the next to rouse, feeling the absence of Cat, Jean-Luc, and Diane. Kicking the bed coverings to the floor, he saw only J.D. still asleep in his bed. Stretching his large frame on the bed, Robert scratched his side. Noticing his dry mouth, he decided that he'd rustle up something to drink and search for the rest of his friends. "They are probably discovering things for themselves—claiming things for their very own." The lighting increased, and he headed for the door. "Hope you can sleep with that cursed light, J.D." Robert chuckled.

Once outside, however, he was unsure how to proceed. He spoke aloud. "Should I get a drink first, or should I check. . .?" After a bit of a struggle, taking one step down the corridor then one step to the door leading to the exit, he decided it would be best to find the others first.

He went to the dowels and discovered articles of clothing and other things that had not been there when he had previously been in the room. The unusually-colored shirt and pants did not belong to his friends. He hastened over to the first dowel to examine the first item as if someone else was going to claim it before he could.

On the top dowel was a metal hoop, small enough that it would sit on his head like a hatband. It had a strange off-white radiance, giving the appearance of a halo.

Next to that hung clothes crafted of a material that felt like a fine but unfamiliar metal mesh. Robert ran his fingers over the matching green shirt and pants. They were joined together by a latch and a metal button-like device that fit inside one another. By pulling on them on the two sides, it was easy to tug them apart, and pushing them together formed a strong seal. On the table next to these clothes were thick, black leather boots.

"They are my size. How can that be?" Curiosity got the better of him, and he took the clothes and slipped back into the hall.

Going straight ahead, he attempted to open the door, but it would not budge. Shrugging it off, he went to the next door, which opened effortlessly. Stepping partially inside, he pulled the metal bed frame into the door passage. With the door blocked, he stepped inside the white room. The combined light from both hall and room was very bright. He stripped down to his undergarments and put on the green pants first. As he'd suspected, they fit perfectly. He did a few deep bends. No matter how he twisted, no matter how he bent, the clothes never pulled on his massive frame, but instead flowed with his movements.

He remembered playing at Diane's house as a child. He had tried on her father's silk shirt and been amazed at how it felt, but this was better.

Next, he put on the long-sleeved shirt. When he pushed his arm through the right sleeve, a black glove fell to the floor. Although he thought it strange that he had not felt it before, he figured it was another of the mysteries. He pushed his left arm through its sleeve, and another glove came out. This time he caught it before it hit the floor. Sitting on the bed frame, he pulled the boots onto his large feet. Like the shirt and pants, the boots were a perfect fit. He paced back and forth. Although brand new, they weren't rigid, as new leather boots would be. These felt better than his old suede slippers, which he'd worn for years.

Robert fastened the metal buttons. He tested the outfit, stretching his legs and swinging his arms horizontally. He was astounded at how good the clothes felt on his body. The material clung to him and felt light as air. He tried on the gloves, which fit but felt unusual. He went over and picked up his discarded clothes. He could feel them through the gloves, but he could still feel the gloves as well. The entire outfit felt different. Still, he felt it was a nice collection of clothes. He picked up the halo and was going to discard it, since it did not go with the rest of the clothes. "Why would someone doff the top part of the hat and leave the brim?"

Just as he was about to toss it, he thought, *Why not?* He set it on his head and ran his fingers over the hoop, from front to back. When he reached the back of the halo, his fingers traced over etching on the metal. The slight touch caused a pull on his stomach, with enough force that he staggered. He managed to steady himself on the end of the bed frame.

Looking down, he could see that clothes had changed slightly. Where the shirt and pants met, there were no seams; the outfit was now a single piece. The gloves and boots seemed to bleed into the one-piece clothing; the black gradually fading into the green. The entire outfit was like a second skin.

He reached up to try to detach the halo, but was stopped by something surrounding his head. The unseen force extended down his neck and into the clothing. He tried to calm himself, but panic was winning the fight. He stopped to think, but felt a strong pain and contraction around his waist where the shirt and pants originally met. Steadying himself on the bed again, he felt another force like someone kicking him in the stomach. It knocked him back to the wall. With his hand still resting on the frame, he yanked the bed back in with him. The door slammed shut, and the light went out.

Robert blinked a few times to adjust to the lack of light and was shocked that he could see. The suit tightened, enveloping him and cutting off his breath. He tried the exit, hoping his friends could help, but the door refused to work. Gasping for breath, he fell down as a funny smell surrounded him, as if bad, stale air replaced the good. He fought to remain awake, but he felt ill from breathing in the dizzying fumes. Everything became a fuzzy gray. As he was about to black out, he saw one of the umbra images advancing on him.

# CHAPTER NINE: MY INTERLUDE

After trying different positions to get comfortable, I awoke to a strong chill in the air. Looking around the bedroom, I noticed I was alone. "Diane?" I was surprised to see my breath in the cold air.

I sat up on the mattress and the room lightened. "Hello?" I called again, wondering what had happened to everyone.

I got up and left, rubbing the sleep from my eyes. I did not see anyone in the hall, so I went to check the horses, thinking that maybe my friends had done the same.

As I passed the dowels, I shivered. I noticed footprints leading into the hall I'd come from, but the moment I entered, a breeze kicked up and the tracks vanished, leaving a pristine surface.

The chill of the air bit my body. I tiptoed to the exit door with my arms wrapped around me. The door opened, but very slowly. About half a minute passed before it completely disappeared into the ceiling.

The scene stopped me. The entire floor was covered in a layer of snow. The door leading out of this underground enclosure was open. From the ceiling, a light snow fell, adding to the powdery stuff already on the floor. A strange gamy smell was in the air, perhaps deer or moose. Taking a few steps, I felt the crunch of fresh snow beneath my feet. Cautiously I crossed over to the stairs.

I saw a large doe squatting on the stairs. A sudden gust of wind caught the stream of pee. It marked me directly on the center of my shirt. The stench was powerful, almost revolting. Cursing under my breath, I said, "Now I need to get to my horse more than ever for a fresh shirt." I waited until the beast had finished and bolted up the stairs before I climbed the slick steps. About two-thirds of the way up, I noticed something crimson in the snow. It appeared to be blood. The snow was falling heavily, and any tracks—even those of the deer—had disappeared.

I sought the beast, but did not see it. The stench faded as I traversed the distance to the horses, or perhaps I was becoming accustomed to it. As I approached Cinnamon, the stallion bolted away from me. I tried a second time, and he bolted again. Grumbling, I pulled off my shirt. Bending down, I scooped up some of the fluffy new-fallen snow and rubbed it on my chest, letting the heat from my body melt it. It was a feeble effort to get rid of the sickening scent, but I hoped it was enough to at least allow me to approach Cinnamon without him sprinting away.

I advanced to my horse again with my hands in front of me. I gently called his name. I managed to convince my trusted steed to let me near him, but this time I noticed the horror in my companion's eyes as he stared past me. I turned and saw a peculiarly-dressed man. His clothes were immaculate and very ceremonial, much nicer than any clothes I had worn for Sunday church. The clothing was black as coal, making it very easy to spot him in the blinding whiteness. Over his head, he wore a black leather cowl that hid his face. In his right hand, he held a large scythe. Its long, curved blade was serrated on the bottom. In his left hand, he held a single red rose, its color so deep that not even the raging snowstorm could dull it. I stared at the man for what seemed like an eternity before he spoke.

"You will be making choices soon," his voice whispered in the wind. "Your choices will determine which avenues will be presented." He stretched his arms outward, as if to separate the items he carried.

"Who are you?" I demanded.

"Who I am is not important." His voice rasped in the raging storm. "You and your friends will have something to discuss very soon." With his warning issued, he swung the large weapon at my body with incredible speed and fluidity. His movement caught me off guard, but I did not jump, seeing that the distance between us was too great for him to hit his mark.

I was about to say something when I felt warmness wash over my body. Looking down, I could see the gash the blade had opened across my chest. My blood flowed down my torso, warming me against the coldness of the storm. Surprisingly, I did not feel pain; the keen edge of the blade must have cut very finely. I rose, unable to do anything except watch the snow melt as it hit my red torso. I stayed motionless wondering exactly who confronted me. *I need to see his face,* I thought and attempted to will myself forward. My body betrayed me, and I collapsed and eventually ended up on my stomach. I crawled, determined to see who the stranger was, leaving a bloody trail in the fallen snow.

The last thing that I remembered was the laughter. It gave me chills in the bones worse than those from any snowstorm. It started low, but was picked up on the wind and echoed off the dense trees until it throbbed in my head. I closed my eyes and waited.

# CHAPTER TEN

I heard a collective gasp as the five of us sat up at the same time. The illumination brightened and we could see we were all safe.

I tried to calm my ragged breathing and my trembling body. Once I caught my breath, I glanced around to see my friends in much the same condition.

Cat and Jean-Luc spoke simultaneously. "I've had the craziest dream."

We stared at each other, waiting for someone to continue.

I got to my feet and inched closer to the door, but spun around before reaching it. "Seems like we all might have had a dream. We should discuss them."

Still unnerved, one by one, we related our dreams and sat in silence until Cat said, "How is it possible that each of us dreamt about the others leaving?"

"Easy," I offered. "Have you ever had a dream where you were falling and you woke up with your legs kicking, or that you were in church listening to the bell, and then were awakened by the very same thing? Perhaps we each heard each other's restlessness, and our minds put that into our dreams. You know how when people have nightmares, they toss and turn? This chamber is small for the five of us, so it is very possible that we heard each other moving. I also suggest that with the scare we have had, combined with the nature of how we try to understand the unknown, things played on our minds."

"Yeah, sure, J.D., anything you say," Robert scoffed. "I am in favor of leaving. Is anyone with me?"

"Well," I began, "the magistrates are probably packing up camp as we speak. They are not likely to give up on us, so it is probably best to stay concealed here. The horses should still be fine. To that end, why not search around a bit more and see if we can find that suit of yours?" I desperately tried to suppress my chuckle to no avail. It quickly faded away as Robert came toward me, stopped only by Diane.

"Oh, Robert, just relax." She rubbed his shoulders.

He glared sternly at me before quipping, "Very well. At least I didn't get peed on."

We erupted in laughter and piled into the hallway. Everything was as we'd left it.

I focused on our task and walked down the hall. "Well, we searched these two, which leaves the other four. They are probably all for sleeping, but we should check. Is everyone in agreement?" I faced my friends. When Robert and Jean-Luc nodded, I went to the third door.

I noticed that Diane moved to the back of the line as I pressed the panel. As suspected, I discovered another sleeping chamber. In the corner was a bed covered with a pink spread embroidered with patterns of white and yellow roses. I detected a sweet perfume. I closed my eyes and envisioned fields of flowers. I looked back over my shoulder and saw Robert directly behind me, blocking my view of the others. I darted my eyes back and forth from him back to the bedspread. His expression of disbelief mirrored my own.

"What's in there?" Diane stepped closer to us.

"It's another sleeping room, Diane." Robert stepped in front of her, giving me enough time to compose myself before Diane saw my face. As I left, the door quietly shut.

I didn't hide my discomfort well. She asked, "What's wrong?"

"I am still a bit edgy from all that's happened." All of us showed some signs of wear, but I tried to hide my discomfiture about what I had seen and smelled.

Advancing to the next door, I saw Robert standing with his back to the door we had left. When Diane approached, he told her, "Diane, please continue on."

"Here we go." When the door opened, I stepped back, a bit surprised at not finding another sleeping chamber.

"What is it?" Jean-Luc stretched to see over my shoulder.

I tried to push him aside, but I couldn't budge him. "Please, Jean-Luc, let me investigate."

Jean-Luc stepped to his right. "As you wish."

Once past the threshold, the aroma of a pine forest washed over me. The space was double the size of where we had slept. The floor and walls were comprised of small, yellow glass squares, about the size of a standard horseshoe.

Imprinted on each square was a continuous green leafy vine pattern which twisted in different directions, making it impossible to tell where it started or ended.

I attempted to pluck a leaf from one of the branches. "It's so real."

On the left wall I noticed a wooden cabinet, about waist high and hewn from a single tree trunk. The pine had been carved with flowers and connected by the same vine that was on the glass. The two seemed melded together in pattern. On the top surface of the cabinet rested a bowl of the same material as the floor. In the bottom of the bowl was a hole surrounded by shiny metal.

"This resembles a wash basin, but there is a hole in the bottom." I glanced at Robert. "Why would they do that?"

Robert chuckled. "What? The great J.D. cannot figure something out? You're the brains, you determine what it is."

"Don't I always?" I examined the rest of the room. Atop the basin was a highly polished piece of metal extending over the center. Suddenly, the glass tiles above the cabinet became as reflective as a lake.

"What in the blazes?" I backed up into a pair of boxes carved in the same manner as the cabinet.

"What's wrong?" Diane yelled from the hall.

"Something surprised me, nothing more."

Deeper in, a strangely shaped object projected from the floor. Made from the same strange, yellow material as the wall, it had a circular bowl in front with a rectangular-shaped box which partially disappeared into the wall attached to the base. Inside the circular part was a good amount of what appeared to be water. When I bent down, water flowed down into the hole and disappeared and then refilled.

Directly opposite this was a square box set into the corner. The corners of the box were a shiny metal, but the walls were cloudy glass. The open door allowed me to see a circular shaft of metal coming out of the wall at about seven feet above the floor. It ended in a larger oval, metal object that was flat at the end. On the flat surface were small circular holes. This flat surface exactly matched the shape in the center of the floor.

After a quick glance around, I returned to the cabinet with the mirror behind it. I saw that everyone had entered, but were waiting patiently for me to finish examining the objects.

Cat strained his neck to see over Jean-Luc's shoulder. "A-a-any clues as to what this room is?"

I touched my hand to the metal over the basin. "Patience, my friend, and…"

I yelled and jumped back as I felt water hit my hand.

Robert grabbed my sleeve and yanked me behind him. "What happened?"

"Something came out of the metal."

"And?"

"Hold on, Robert. Let me try again." I approached the cabinet with caution and put my hand under the metal tube again. Cool water flowed like before, and the running water felt relaxing. I rubbed my hands together, and a little hole opened at the base of the metal piece and a second liquid was added to the water, causing my rubbing to produce a foamy result. Soap. I stopped rubbing and let the water rinse my hands. After I withdrew my hands from the basin, I shook off as much of the excess water as I could, thinking.

I glanced at the cabinets behind me. On a hunch, I opened the one on the left to discover large, soft towels. I used one to dry my hands.

When I finished, I peeked into the second cabinet, lifting the top. Inside was an empty metal box. As I went to lower the lid, I noticed that there was writing on the underside of the lid. In bold lettering the words "dirty clothes and laundry" had been imprinted on the metal. I closed the lid again and looked back at the strange thing in the back. *Is that a privy?* After my final examination, I came back, throwing the towel on top of the surface next to the water basin.

"This appears to be some type of place to wash. You can get fresh water from the basin for your hands. It's a privy in back and that..." I indicated the box. "...must be to wash your whole body. Who ever built this, must have liked to be clean. I suggest we use this. I cannot see any harm. Who wants to be first?"

We glanced at one another until Robert stepped forward. "I'll go first." Nodding in agreement, we all left Robert alone.

Cat sighed. "So after we explore everything, what then?"

I patted him on the shoulder. "We take things one step at a time. For now, we should be patient." We waited, not speaking, until Robert emerged.

Robert straightened tall as he strutted around us, showing us his clean clothes. "That is an amazing experience. Before you wash, put your clothes in the box on the right."

One by one we entered. Next was Jean-Luc, followed by Cat, Diane, and then myself. As Diane exited, she winked at me, brushing past me as I entered. Her light perfume stirred memories of my childhood crush.

After entering, I stripped off all my clothes and gathered them in a heap. Opening the clothes wash cabinet, I tossed them inside.

I entered the box in the corner and closed the door. Even though I expected the water, I was still a bit surprised when it flowed over me. Its warmth eased my tense muscles as it cascaded over my back and through my hair. I rotated a few times before placing one hand on the wall and leaned into the stream. I closed my eyes and remained motionless. Once I felt sufficiently clean, I chuckled. *Now J.D., how do you get it to stop?* As if by magic, the water stopped and a warm wind blew over my body. Within seconds, no traces of water remained on me. *How in the hell did I manage to trigger that?* I opened the door, left the 'wash box,' and emerged near the privy.

The privy was strange to me. I debated for a while, until the urge hit me, but still I felt a bit uncomfortable going indoors. After using the strangely-shaped device, I jumped off the seat when the thing sent a jet of warm water at my underside and saw the waste washing away to be replaced by more water.

I stretched and dried off. Passing in front of the wash basin, I looked in the mirror and nodded approvingly. I shifted to my side and flexed my muscles, chuckling and feeling silly. Moving to the clothes box, I opened it to get my clothes and received a shock. The clothes were clean, but had a very light fragrance about them that was identical to the aroma I had smelled on Diane. Picking through my clothes, I noticed the handkerchief Diane had given to me the night before. Its perfume must have mixed with my clothes. I debated whether I should try to wash the clothes again, or live with it. Since I was not sure a second wash would eliminate the scent, I decided to forget it, and got dressed. I rejoined the others.

We were all ready to tackle the world with newfound strength.

"Can we take it with us?" Diane asked, and we chuckled and nodded.

"Sure," I said. "I'll put it on the back of my horse. I am sure he wouldn't mind."

Diane came close to me. She winked and whispered so that only I could hear. "My, you smell nice."

I blushed red from embarrassment, and Cat, the nearest person to us, asked, "What did you say, Diane?"

"Oh, nothing." She grinned. "Are we going to examine some more? If J.D. is right, the three against this wall should be small chambers, and that door should be another large one." She alluded to the end of the corridor.

Cat opened the next door on the right, and to no one's surprise, it was as we'd suspected. A large bed took up virtually the entire space with a narrow path to get around one side of it. Cat tried to glance under the bed, but it was built on a solid metal frame that went to the floor.

We opened the next door and discovered a completely empty room. From the ceiling to the floor, there was nothing to see. It occurred to me that none of us had seen any insects. No flies, spiders, or anything else that could crawl, burrow, or fly its way in. We seemed to be the only living creatures in this strange enclosure.

The next door opened into a plain, though not barren, room. It contained a bed with a thin, orange covering with a nightstand beside it. There was nothing else. Cat checked under the bed again beneath the bedding, but came up empty.

We assumed the last door was a larger bedroom like the one where we'd stayed. Our suspicions were confirmed. Against the back wall directly opposite the door was a large, canopied bed. The deep, royal-purple drapes flowed all the way to the corner. The floor was covered in a weird, deep-brown fur, and an emerald-green gown lay on the bed. This was the first piece of clothing we had discovered that was not ours. The dress buttoned up the back. Picking it up, I gave the dress to Diane to examine.

"Well," she stated, "it has not been worn much. It's very soft and sewn for someone my size or possibly a bit thinner, but somewhat taller than me." She carefully folded the garment and set it back on the bed. She spotted something in the corner near the bed. As she passed a certain spot, a door opened, revealing an entire closet of various fancy and plain dresses and other women's garments. After admiring half a dozen of them, Diane looked at us. A sly, acquisitive grin crossed her face before she stepped out of the doorway, allowing the door to conceal it again.

"One last one," Jean-Luc said. Not waiting for the rest of us, he approached the door. It disappeared. As we caught up with him, we noticed it was the mirror image of the room with the sticky pegs and tables.

Pointing to the door on the left, I said, "That leads to the foyer room. Do you want to go check the horses before exploring a bit more?"

As if we were of one mind, our hands went to our grumbling stomachs. Opening the door, we entered the first room. Nothing was out of the ordinary here, contrary to some of our dreams, so we proceeded to check on the horses and retrieve our food. When we exited, however, we found a layer of snow on the stairs.

Dismissing the alarmed expressions on their faces, I spoke up. "Well, it did feel like it was going to snow yesterday. Hopefully the horses are fine."

We ascended the stairs, surprised at the scene above. Snow was still lightly falling, covering the trees in a wintry white blanket. The soil, however, did not have a bit of snow on it. It was slightly moist, but otherwise unaffected by the weather. The horses huddled together in one section of the field. Based on the appearance of the trees, it had snowed quite heavily, but the horses seemed fine. I paused at the threshold and huffed. When I did not see my breath, I shrugged it off as another mystery.

My friends and I gathered our supplies and got out the horse blankets. We sewed all but one of the blankets together. I gave an end to Cat. He climbed one of the trees a bit more than the height of the horses and tied it off. After gathering up the other end, he jumped to the next tree and tied it off as well. Repeating the process, he constructed a temporary shelter for the horses.

I ran my hand up and down Cinnamon's muzzle. "Should we picket them now?"

Cat shuffled his feet in the snow. "Well, I was hoping that, since we are out here, we could just leave and get to Reading."

Robert nodded. I agree. Let's go now."

I scoffed. "And if we ran into the magistrates on the road, what then? It appears they didn't find us the first time. We may not be as lucky the second time with fresh snow for them to follow our tracks in. Besides, I'd like to explore. I have a feeling we were meant to find this."

Diane took my hand into hers. "I agree. We should allow more time to pass, and perhaps we can find something to aid us."

Jean-Luc folded him arms over himself. "I said it before, I trust you, John. But let's at least get out of the cold."

Satisfied with the discussion, we returned to the foyer with our gear.

After settling down, we ate our dried food and discussed various things.

"So, now that you've had time to think about where we are, have you any ideas about the meaning behind it all, J.D.?" Robert asked. His mouth was half full of breakfast.

"To tell you the truth," I began. "I have no idea what all of this means. Some things are normal, like the bedrooms. Living underground is not unheard of and has its advantages. The lights are a mystery. As for the doors, well, a door is a door. I remember reading once that the ancient Egyptians used elaborate stone weights to counter-balance doors so one moment they would open with the slightest push, and the next moment, ten horses could not budge them. It is possible that these are something similar. For all I know, this whole enclosure could be the product of witchcraft. But until I know for sure, I am not about to panic or jump to conclusions."

We finished our meal and decided to explore the room straight ahead of us. With customary efficiency, the door slid up to the ceiling without a sound. Peering inside, we discovered a long corridor running right and left. Directly across from the open door, the light in the hallway revealed a spiraling staircase leading down. Looking right I could see two doors; left revealed the same.

"So, in your grand scheme, we should leave the downstairs for last and go this way, J.D.?" Cat bounded to the doors on the left. The rest of us followed silently. "This door," he began, "should lead to the peg room." He paused and opened it to confirm what we already knew. He darted to the right. "And this door leads to..." He stopped as he opened the door to see what it revealed.

The light brightened, and we saw a very large room that must have been an armory. Along the back wall were rows of weapons. Swords from all over Europe adorned the walls. Along the right wall we saw different types of armor, from sparring leathers, to ornately etched plate. Everything was in perfect condition. Even the leather was like new, without any of the cracks aged leather would normally show. In the middle of the floor lay a strip of padding about the width of a long sword with a white line across the middle, dividing it exactly in two parts. The rest of the floor was wood, so brightly polished we could see our reflections in it. There was only one exit, directly opposite the wall where we had entered. After searching a bit more, we left through the unexplored door.

We stepped into a hallway, equally as long as the previous one, but with many more rooms to explore. In the first, we discovered a room with a stone floor that reached about ten feet before becoming earth and remaining that way for about another ten feet. Scattered throughout the dirt were different types of rocks and some uncut gems.

"This seems suspicious to me. Let's not touch anything yet. I'd rather not take something that looks too easy to take. I know that sounds weird, but it is almost like someone is testing us."

Robert patted me on the back. "You heard J.D., everyone out."

The next room was like the previous one at first, with a stone floor, but in the center of the room burned a pure column of flame. I stared at it for a while, entranced by the patterns of brightly banded, dancing reds, yellows, and oranges. "That is amazing. How does it burn so cleanly without smell or source?" Tilting my head back and forth, I could have sworn that there was something inside, but the intensity of the flames kept us at bay, so it was impossible to confirm. Closing the door, we explored the next room.

Again, we discovered the half-stone floor, but the far end this time seemed to be carved from wood. Since nothing else was in there, we left.

When we reached the next door, we found a single word etched into the metal: EXPERIENCED. Inside, we saw a floor like the rest in this wing, but beyond the stone was cloaked in dense shadow that the light did not penetrate. We stared at the blackness, debating whether or not we should enter.

Cat inched up a bit. "Let me try this." From his belt pouch, he pulled out a stone, and before we could stop him, he chucked it into the darkness.

A sickly, hissing voice spoke from the shadows. "Sssstepsss insssidessss."

Robert stepped in front of Cat and backed up with his arms extended, forcing us out. Once outside, he spun sharply at Cat. "Don't ever do something like that again. Get it?"

Cat nodded and shied away from him.

The following room was a mirror of the wood one, except this one had bluish metal instead.

"Nothing in here," I said, still unnerved by what we had heard. "Only two left to check."

The next one contained a glass box of water with fish and some type of seaweed. It was hard to tell if the water was fresh or salt, but it did not matter. The motions of the swimming fish fascinated me and I found myself counting all the types of fish contained within.

"So peaceful." Cat traced the paths of several of the fish with his hand.

Cat's action caused me to grin. This would be any cat's fantasy. I thought of our Cat acting like a cat, which put me even more at ease as I chuckled at the notion.

The last area on the left was similar to the rest, but did not seem to contain anything. The floor beyond the stonework was bluish.

Cat inhaled deeply. "It smells so fresh in here, but other than that, it is empty."

I scratched the side of my head. "I am not so sure, Cat. The first room had the gems in earth. Then, in order, we had fire, wood, shadow, metal, and water. So it appears these rooms have something to do with the elements, and that means this would be air, based on everything else we have seen and what your nose tells you. The question now is, do we want to try to figure out the meaning behind why someone would put these here, or do we want finish our search?"

Cat glanced down the hall. "I wouldn't mind checking out those gems again."

Robert scoffed and shook his head. "And I suppose you'd be the first to check out those voices in the dark room too?"

"Are you calling me a coward, Robert?"

"I don't question your convictions, just your impulses. I would like to explore all of our possibilities before deciding on one."

Diane nodded in agreement. "That sounds like the best plan."

Leaving the rooms behind, we opened the first available door to reveal an elaborate library, with more books than I had ever seen before.

I motioned to the only other door. "That probably leads to the corridor."

Directly to our right, a large, metal framework of crisscrossing bars blocked all access to the books. Beyond the metal fence, several large, wooden chairs surrounded half a dozen tables. Since the books were all on shelves that ran perpendicular to the path created by the metal fencing, I could not read any of the titles.

Looking at the tables, we did see one book left in the open. The bound book was ornately decorated. Lying on top of the book was a white parchment that had the following written on it: *The Canterbury Tales, by Geoffrey Chaucer.*

I knew the name, but never thought I'd ever see the book. I stretched as far as my arm could go, but the metal bars were relentless. Running back to the armory, I lifted a Scottish claymore from one of the racks. Returning, I held the sheath and carefully hooked the table's leg with the cross-guard of the sword.

Robert stopped me from pulling. "What are you doing? What about, 'don't touch anything'? That goes for you, too."

I pushed his arm aside and yanked anyway, but the table was heavier than I'd thought. Instead of shifting it, the sword pulled out of its sheath, and I fell on my arse with my back against the wall.

Robert huffed and shook his head a few times before offering me his hand. "You and books, J.D. I sometimes think you'd love to be locked away in vault somewhere with only books as your friends."

I took Robert's hand, and he pulled me to my feet. "I wouldn't say I'm that bad, but I do love to read. Is there anything wrong with that?"

Diane brushed off my backside. "I am sure there are many things he loves, Robert." She winked. "Isn't that right, J.D.?"

I nodded and blushed. "Of course. But let's not discuss that now. We have another floor to explore."

# CHAPTER ELEVEN

With caution, I tiptoed down the spiral staircase into the darkness with my friends close behind. Only after I stepped into the corridor at the bottom did the light illuminate the hall and stairs. "It's odd the light waited until I reached the floor."

Robert stepped down and in front of me. "Indeed. This hall is like the one above, so we should start over there." He went to a door on the far left. After Diane, Cat, and Jean-Luc had stepped into the hall, Robert continued, "Jean-Luc, stay to the rear."

Jean-Luc nodded and shifted a quarterstaff in his hands.

I glanced at the weapon. "Where did you get that?"

"When you got the claymore, I picked this up. My parents taught me when they did shows on the ship from England to Boston. Didn't you ever wonder why I liked big pieces of wood to use as walking sticks?"

"It never occurred to me. I guess it seems natural in your hands."

Robert tapped his foot. "Are we done talking? Can we go now?"

I sighed and continued down the hall, not responding to his question. Entering the next room, I stopped abruptly, and Robert nearly pushed me over.

I gawked at the space until I regained my senses. "Look at the size of the room! I bet this takes up a quarter of the floor space that we explored above."

Robert stepped up beside me. "It's like Isaac's tavern, but there are more benches and tables in here." He nodded to the far wall. "I bet one of those doors leads to the kitchen." Along that wall, an opening ran nearly door to door. The opening was about waist height and ran to the ceiling. On the bottom part of the opening was a flat wooden surface that resembled a tavern's bar, but without anywhere to sit.

To our right, taking up the entire wall, hung an array of various coats of arms. I asked Robert, "Do you recognize any of these?"

Robert marched down the length of the wall and back, glancing at each coat until he stopped at one with three crows and a broken line. "This one is my father's. I've seen it in his study." He indicated the coat of arms next to his that had a thick "x" on it. "Diane, isn't that your family's crest?"

Diane examined the shield. She reached out carefully, as if avoiding a hidden thorn, and touched it. "I don't know—I don't remember much of that from living in Paris." She pondered for a moment. "J.D., didn't you learn about this?"

I joined my friends. "My father wanted me to, but I was more interested in the heraldic symbols and… everyone, step back."

Robert and Diane eyed me curiously, but stepped behind me.

I pointed to the wall. "Did you notice those five shields, starting from Robert's family's crest and going to the right, are slightly set apart from the others? I think these are our crests."

Cat backed up and glanced around. "I don't like this. I say we get out of here. Why would they have our crests?"

"Be calm, Charles. I am sure there is a reasonable—"

"To hell with reason!" Cat stomped his foot on the floor.

Diane went to Cat and gently placed her hands on his shoulders, staring into his eyes. "Cat, have we ever failed one another when we stick together?"

Cat lowered his head and shuffled his foot in small circles. He meekly replied. "No, but…" His voice trailed off.

Diane lifted his chin. "And no matter what this is or what we discover, as long as we are together, that is all that matters, right?"

Cat's tension eased, and he gathered her into a hug. "You are right. I am sorry."

I patted him on the back as I continued to one of the far doors. "There is nothing to be sorry about. We are all unnerved by the things we are discovering. Let's finish exploring."

Jean-Luc joined me. "What if there is no end?"

"All things end. Even Dante had limits to the layers of Hell. I am confident that, by the time we finish, we will discover the true meaning behind everything we have found here."

"I hope you are right, J.D."

"Come, let's go to the left."

I stopped, hardly believing what I saw when I entered. "I can't imagine how long it took to build it all. There are rows of cabinets and workbenches everywhere. And what is with the air? It smells fresh—clean, like scented water has been used everywhere." I navigated between the tables to the last row of benches. "Everyone fan out and take a row. Search everywhere. If this is like a tavern, we might find some fresh food, so this time, take what you think is important."

After a while we huddled to view our discoveries. Four of us had armfuls of fruits and vegetables, while Cat returned with knives, spoons, plates, and bowls.

Picking up a large round, pink fruit, I sniffed it. "There is a hint of citrus." I cut it down the center then took the halves and cut them in half. I brought a wedge to my lips, but before I could take a bite, Robert took hold of my wrist.

"Do you think that is wise?"

I tried to pull away from his grip, but I couldn't budge him. "There would be more efficient ways of killing us than poison."

"Why invite the risk?"

"Robert, I was only going to take a quick sample to see if it's edible. So, if you don't mind…" I glared down at his hand.

"Fine!" He released his grip.

I took a small nibble from one of the quarters, stuck out my tongue, and squinted. "It is sweet and sour at the same time."

Robert and Diane each took one of the pieces. Jean-Luc took one and broke it in two, handing half to Cat.

Cat gobbled his piece down. "I love the difference in taste."

I was examining the other choices to sample when Jean-Luc spoke. "I need to show you something." He led us to a window, which had devices like the metal pieces from the washing room. Placing a glass under one of the five extensions, he filled it to the brim with a foamy liquid that, by the smell, was some type of ale. He downed it, shocking the rest of us. "I have already tested it," he explained with a wink.

One by one we each tried an extension and received a different reward. Most of the brew was a bit on the cold side, but it was surprisingly pleasant. After completely filling a glass, I suggested, "We should finish exploring. We can always return later."

Cat's mouth and chin were covered in foam. "Do we have to?"

"Yes, Cat. Like I said, we can come back."

He wiped the excess on his sleeve. "Sure thing." He filled his glass again, took a quick gulp, and put down the glass.

We left the way we had entered and emptied into the hall. Without stopping, I hurried over to the next door on the opposite wall and opened it.

This chamber was about as big as the eating room we'd left. It extended longer than it was deep. A few rows of upholstered chairs were set up in front of a large white cloth hanging from the ceiling. The light seemed eerie. Although it bathed everything in the same pale light as all the rest, it seemed to be a focused on the cloth.

We shuffled in different directions. Diane and I examined the hanging cloth, while Robert, Jean-Luc, and Cat examined the chairs.

Robert placed his hands on the back of one of the plush chairs. "These are fastened to the floor and to each other in the rows."

Cat, who was in the last row, sat on the center chair and bounced up and down. "The cushions are at least soft."

Out of nowhere, a strange voice echoed around me so loudly that I could feel it my body vibrating. "Please, be seated. Important information is to follow." The voice sounded neither male nor female.

"It's haunted!" Cat cried, bolting for the doors as I stepped in front of Diane to protect her from the unseen speaker. Robert sighed in disgust, looking up, while Jean-Luc spun his staff in his hands.

"Wait!" Diane commanded. "Cat, where you going?"

Cat had reached the door and stopped. He addressed Diane. "I do not like it. Strange fire lights, strange dreams, and now strange voices. I say we stop exploring and leave. I want to go back home—back to the trees I love, the familiar sounds. Even the unusual odors of the forest would be welcome after the strangeness of no odors in rooms that should be full of them."

Diane extended her arms. "Come now, Charles, remember those talks we had about discovering the unknown together? What fun would this be without a bit of fear to get our hearts pumping?" She took his arm and led him back to me. "Do you know what you've done now?" She smiled at him.

Cat hovered over a different chair. "Diane?"

"Oui?"

"We what?"

"No, silly, 'Oui' is French for yes."

"Oh... Diane, are you afraid?"

"If I was alone, I would be. But when I am with all of you, I am never afraid. Now then, what did you do?"

"I sat down like this."

Again, a voiced echoed, although it did not seem as harsh the second time, "Please, be seated."

Exchanging nervous looks, we cautiously approached the chairs and sat, a little disturbed by the disembodied voice. Once the last of us were seated, the light dimmed, and a moving painting appeared on the white fabric. The painting showed someone dressed in all white with a hooded cloak obscuring the person's face.

I was distraught by the sight, as it reminded me of my dream the night before. I wiggled in my seat. "It can't be..."

Diane entwined her fingers with mine, which put me at ease.

The moving painting spoke, in the same neutral voice we had heard before. I found it unsettling that the voice never changed pitch, never changed pace, and never displayed any hint of emotion.

> Greetings to you who have discovered what we call experiment one-six-six. You are the first explorers to reach us. I am sure you have questions about the things you have seen, and perhaps feel apprehensive about all it has to offer. Let me assure you that you have nothing to

*fear. When we first built this habitation, it was because we had discovered a means of …looking differently into other realms. You see, fire, to a primitive man, was a ritualistic thing, until they learned how to use it. It fascinated them. This in turn generated new ideas about how to use the 'fire sticks' to their advantage. When the Egyptians discovered how to move the stones to create their pyramids, they, too, used it to their advantage. Over and over again, civilizations demonstrate how inventions, whether accidental or researched, can bring tremendous change. And yet it is also true that, in some cases, discoveries have destroyed the very cultures that spawned them. It was with great caution that we peered into the discovery that fate had bestowed upon us.*

The white scene behind the man changed to match the story he described. It showed a room containing some type of shiny metal. An individual, dressed like the one telling the story, worked behind a glass wall, his focus on some kind of table. After a quick glance, I returned my attention to the storyteller.

*One of our scientists had been attempting to travel quickly from one spot to the next, without the need for horse or vehicle. During one of his experiments, another scientist accidentally introduced himself into the experiment. This less experienced scientist had not been paying attention. Since the procedure required a sterile environment to work correctly, the young scientist's presence, and the half dozen books he carried, produced an unexpected result.*

*Nothing was left of the scientist but a wisp of smoke. We initially assumed he was destroyed as a result of his carelessness. As we began to more thoroughly examine the failure and what exactly went wrong, we discovered we could, indeed, reach a destination more quickly, but it was not the one originally planned for in our research.*

*We observed with fascination what this altered experiment had caused. Imagine, if you will, opening a shaded window and seeing the ocean bottom, or opening the shade to reveal the Aztecs building their great pyramids and golden city. As a scientist, your natural instinct would be to watch and learn from what you saw. When we realized what window the experiment had opened, we watched like children at Christmas with our eyes filled with wonderment.*

*As we viewed the new location, we came to understand more and more about it. We were drawn into the mystery and radical nature of what we were watching. This fascination resulted in our blindness to clues that should have been signals to us—signals that something was drastically wrong. As the days and weeks passed, each of us took turns observing the new life. We eventually learned a way to manipulate our window, so that more of the world could be seen. It was at that time we discovered that the window did not show another world, as we had initially thought, but was showing us our own world as it became contaminated by the very beings we had been observing. We found it increasingly unusual that, by observing the spots the window showed us without the aid of the "viewing portal," but by traveling to the locations ourselves, it revealed nothing out of the ordinary. It was as if the two places co-existed.*

*After debating for several days on the proper course of action, we determined that we needed to seal or repair the contamination. Once we reached that conclusion, it took several more weeks to determine how to accomplish what we intended.*

*At that time, we concluded that if the accident in the experiment was re-created, but without the additional elements of the books, reality as we knew it would be repaired. It was during the height of these debates that one of our scientists observed the test subject who had caused the accident initially. He had not been destroyed, but instead had somehow taken over this alternate dimension. By observing him, however, we inadvertently caused a chain reaction that washed the other world into our own.*

*The contamination spread rapidly, and if it were not for the quick thinking of some of our brightest people, we surely would have succumbed to that artificial world. It is for that reason I stand before you today. It was determined that the scientist had become a part of that world, and in doing so, gained power from being its creator. The scientist was the key to the alternate universe. Whether it was a creation of the contaminated elements, or an alternate universe that he easily dominated, is not certain. We discovered that he had no intention of stopping the contamination and even less conation to give up his mantle of control.*

*We needed a team to become part of his world so that, ultimately, they could defeat him, and the fissure between the two realities could be sealed. Once closed, it is our belief that it will instantly return our world to the time before the experiment went terribly wrong.*

*Since this is only hypothetical, we needed to find people who could readily adapt their own nature to that of the new world. The Crossing, as we have come to call it, will incorporate those people into its reality, while maintaining their identities. If that party failed, or was successful yet unable to seal the damage, we needed to be able to try something else. For that reason, we chose certain locations, and established habitations such as the one you have found.*

*You might be asking yourself, 'Why should I risk myself for something or someone I do not know?' All we can answer is that the contamination will eventually replace your reality with its own. Everything you know, everyone you love—everything—will be erased and replaced by a single, warped individual bent on taking over everything.*

*Strength is the key. Having come this far shows the strength you have as individuals and as a team. I hope you understand the importance of this task, and what exactly it means. Also, I hope you can understand that, in order to make certain an attempt will be made, we must force you into the situation.*

*For that, I am sorry.*

The moving painting faded to nothingness, revealing the blank white cloth. The light which had burned dimly during the presentation went out. The only clearly visible thing was the cloth. Like a mist rolling in at dusk, a strange, purplish light covered the floor and enveloped each of us. Alarmed, we rushed frantically to the door. Cat managed to arrive first and waited for the rest of us. When he saw we were close, he tried to open the door, but it refused to budge.

From behind me, coming from the white fabric, I heard various sounds: the clang of a blacksmith's hammer, the holler of someone selling fresh fish, and the voices of many people talking at the same time. I spun around. In front of me was a small community, busy at work. It was a clear day, and I was mesmerized by how real everything appeared. The sky darkened, and I could tell it was getting windier. Then I felt the wind in our room pick up, blowing over my back. The wind swelled and picked up speed, until it pushed us toward the moving painting. We tried holding on to the chairs, but our fingers were wrenched free. A force pulled us in. Despite our best efforts, each of us was thrown at the cloth and into the blackness of unconsciousness.

# PART II

### Nesh'tirai, "Jes Ja'hard mes Pani'a Garn'denia" Elilith

**In the Score of Rebirth, Year of Rebirth, Month of Rebirth, Day of Rebirth**

# CHAPTER TWELVE
# CONCEPTION

It is hard to explain how different I felt waking up in a strange bed in a strange land. Have you ever visited an exotic, far-off land? That doesn't even come close to the sensation of being part of a place—tied, if you will—to something you've never seen, felt, or even smelled before. And yet, for all the foreign nature of this place, deep down, it felt as real as my old home.

I awoke on a soft bed, with a damp cloth pressed to my forehead. I squinted as a ray of sunlight struck my eyes, blocking the person administering aid from my view. Moving my head to the left and right, I could see all my friends lying on beds set up around the perimeter of the round chamber. It was spacious, with furniture built from unfamiliar wood spaced evenly along the wall. The wall, floor, and ceiling were composed of this wood, carved with patterns and scrollwork. The robust aroma of fresh pine and something I couldn't identify filled the room. Small windows set near the top of the domed ceiling allowed the sunlight in. It was very peaceful, and I felt at home, which calmed my nerves. Looking back at my helper, I finally saw her face.

Seeing me awake, she greeted me with a cheery expression and nodded. "Kib nar'tartis oot lak artus jes?"

I shook my head and blinked my eyes. "What did you say?"

"Oh! Excuse me, I assumed you knew our language since you were in our woods. Nasty hits to the head you and your friends took," she said. "We've managed to treat your injuries. Did the brigands who have plagued our forests assault—oh, how rude of me! My name is Ki'Leana." She extended her hand, holding it downward at the wrist while she curtsied. She was tall— almost as tall as Robert—lightly built, and very graceful.

Still a bit shocked, I took her hand, holding it as someone would expect to do to royalty, and replied, "My..." I paused and sat up in bed. Leaning back into the soft pillows, I tried again. "My name is John Dent. What forest? Where are we?"

"Oh, they must have hit you pretty hard for you to forget which forest you're in. You are in the hamlet of Nesh'tirai in the Terestai Forest. Our scouting party found you and brought you here."

I studied Ki'Leana closely. Her complexion was pale as milk, and her thick, fair hair fell in waves nearly to her calves. Her clear-cut features were accented by arched, sweeping eyebrows, and the lush curves of her feminine body held my eyes—perhaps too long—before she spoke and broke my trance.

"Is there something wrong?"

"I'm sorry, but it's that, we were in—"

"—in a hurry and did not think we'd have time to stop here," Diane continued, having approached Ki'Leana from behind.

I gawked at Diane, shocked. She was clad in a dark green dress. The rich, frilly material of the puffed sleeves drew my attention. Around her waist was a tan cinch drawn taut. Her dress fell to her ankles, revealing brown leather boots. Her hair, no longer in a bun, flowed down her back. There was a shine about her, as if she were bathed in sunlight, even though, where she was standing, it would have been impossible for sunlight to reach her.

"We thank you for you hospitality, Ki'Leana," Diane said. "You are very kind to have helped. Is there any way we can repay you?"

"Well, once your friends have recovered, we can talk about it. We do need help, but first, we want to wait until you are all well. I see your friends are stirring. I will leave so you may talk. I will let the others know to speak your tongue." With that, she left the room, and I stared after her. Her every movement was so graceful, and I had to consciously stop myself from gawking.

I gingerly climbed out of bed, making sure I didn't have any other injuries. When I glanced around at my friends, I noticed we all had changed. Our usual clothes had all been replaced with traveling clothes and leathers, much like those worn by Luke, the scout we had seen on the way out of Salem. New thoughts ran through my head: of places I shouldn't know about, of skills I knew I'd never learned, and of memories I'd never experienced. The new knowledge weighed uncomfortably on my mind. I already knew this world was called Elilith.

"Perhaps we became part of the land the moving painting spoke of," I said, trying to rationalize as I'd always done before. "Maybe we passed through the window, and this new world incorporated us as part of it. Do you feel different in any way?"

"Yes," Jean-Luc calmly offered. "I feel much stronger." He flexed his arms and everyone could see muscles straining the sleeves of his new shirt. Additionally, his girth had slimmed a bit and his body was more defined than I'd seen it. Without saying a word, he did a few backflips and then bent backward until his hands touched the floor.

"That's interesting," was the only comment I could offer. I was too surprised at my friend's new talents to say more. "Anyone else feel anything?"

Robert strode over to me until he was only inches away. "Perhaps, but this is *not* the time to discuss it."

I felt intimidated by Robert's mere presence. He had never caused such feelings before, but he seemed more dangerous now. He straightened, folded his arms across his chest, and scowled down at all of us. I was about to say something about it when Cat interrupted.

"I definitely feel different, J.D. I can't say how. I agree with Robert. We don't know where we are. We don't know who is watching. Let's not say anything. But let's partake in some food." He indicated an alcove I had not noticed before. His speech was quickened, and like everyone else, he had been indefinably changed. He was thin and a bit shorter, but strong.

Carved into the wall was a closed cabinet with glass doors. The patterns in the wood caught my attention because of the strange star patterns in the grain that should have been impossible. The shelves held vegetables, fruits, breads, and pastries. Tall, slender, ceramic decanters of wine waited next to them. A note on one of the shelves read: "Eat as much as you like."

Cat flung open the door. "Food!"

We consumed the food and wine voraciously.

Jean-Luc wiped his mouth on his sleeve. "So what's the plan, J.D.?"

All eyes shifted to me. I swallowed the last pieces of a succulent vegetable dish. "I think we shouldn't mention where we actually came from and pretend we belong. We need to discover exactly what has happened to us, and how we are going to fix the problems mentioned by the moving painting."

Robert slammed his fist down on the table, causing Diane to jump. "Whatever we do, we can't show weakness. We should flex our muscles."

Diane patted her lips with a cloth. "Robert, please be civil. These people helped us with our injuries. Surely if they were evil, we wouldn't be having this conversation or this wonderful meal."

Robert quaffed the last of his drink and belched. "Agreed. I nominate J.D. to do all the talking." He banged his cup on the table, laughed loudly, and burped again.

We finished the final remnants of the meal and approached the room's only exit. I sighed with relief when I noticed the door had a simple wooden latch like the ones we had at home. "Perhaps they are not so different from us after all," I murmured. I lifted the latch, and everyone followed me out of the room.

We entered a gathering room. Hand-carved banisters wrapped around the perimeter, guarding stairs to a second floor. In the center of the room was a massive oaken table, so large that all of us could have lain end to end and not touched the edges. Sitting on one side of the table was Ki'Leana. Across from her was a man who strongly resembled her.

"It was a good thing we found them when..." the stranger was saying, but stopped when he saw us.

Ki'Leana rose when we approached the table. "Greetings to all of you. Welcome to my home. May you always find peace here. Let me introduce my brother. This is Jal'rean. It was his scouting party who found you and brought you here."

"Greetings." I stepped forward, extending my hand in friendship. "I am John Dent. My friends call me J.D., and I would be honored if you would as well."

"The honor is mine, J.D.," he replied clasping my wrist.

"May I introduce Robert, Jean-Luc, and Cat?" I led him to Diane. "And this is Diane. We are all in your debt."

"'Tis an honor and pleasure to have had a part in saving a vision of beauty such as yourself, Diane." Jal'rean took Diane's hand, bowed, and kissed it. "If you ever need my assistance, or would like me to show you around our fair town, I'd be happy to do so."

I was about to comment on his over-familiarity when I heard a knock. I saw a door beyond Diane and Jal'rean that was so perfectly melded into the wall that I might never have noticed it.

Ki'Leana's hips pivoted gracefully, her dress covering her feet so she seemed to be gliding. She opened the door and bowed to the woman at the doorway. This visitor was about as tall as Robert and her beauty illuminated the room. I found it very hard to break away from her gaze. As she approached us, all the men bowed in unison, as we knew by her very presence it was the correct thing to do.

"This is our leader, Amilmadra," Ki'Leana said reverently.

Following Jal'rean's lead, I took the leader's hand. Kissing it I said, "It is an honor to meet you. We are all in you debt. If there is any way we can assist you or your village, it would be an honor and privilege to do so."

"There is, indeed, something your group could do for us that would be mutually beneficial. For many cycles of Luna, we have been plagued by a band of mercenaries who have some way of sneaking up on us unseen and leaving no trail when they depart. They rob travelers in our woods. If they find any of my people, they kill them. Our searches for their hiding holes have eliminated all but one part of the forest. We cannot enter that part of the forest, for a foul magic covers the land. This cursed magic kills my people if we so much as brush against a leaf infected by its taint. We ask that you search to see if you can discover their hiding place, and, if possible, stop them. If you could accomplish this, we would be in your debt. My people are not wealthy with Empire gold. The works of our hands might be of interest to you. We would be pleased to give you equipment to replace whatever you lost." She paused for a moment, holding each of us with her powerful gaze. I could have sworn that I saw a white glow coming from her eyes. "I see strength in your party," she continued, "and I am certain that strength will overcome any obstacle. You do not

90

need to answer me now, though. There is a celebration tonight, and you are all invited."

Diane strutted over to Jal'rean, trying to imitate Ki'Leana's glide, but failing so horribly that I had to suppress a chuckle. She beamed warmly at him as her hands wrapped around his arm. "Would you do us the honor of showing us around?"

"The honor would be all mine," he replied, waiting for Amilmadra to exit before leading Diane behind her.

We followed Amilmadra into a town square shaded by large oaks and bustling with activity. She stepped onto a path bordered by colorful flowers that resembled hummingbirds, robins, and other colorful birds. Greens and yellows, oranges and violets all blended together into their own painting of the landscape. The beauty of the scene was unlike anything I had seen before. We strolled for a few minutes down one path, then took another that wound through the trees. We changed directions several times before we stopped in front of a great, spreading birch guarded by two of the largest individuals I'd ever seen. They towered over Robert, making him look like a child.

The men were dressed in armor that covered them almost entirely. The metal parts were polished to a mirror finish, and though the armor resembled plate, it flowed like fabric. Each of them carried a curved long sword and a tower shield with an emblem. The design was—*something*—soaring over a pair of trees. As Amilmadra approached, the guards sidestepped away from a massive door.

Amilmadra faced us. "I have things I must do before tonight's festivities. If you need anything at all, ask. My people's generosity is legendary."

She said this, not proudly, but as a simple statement of fact. She entered the tree, her movements even more graceful than Ki'Leana's.

Jal'rean retraced his steps with us until we reached a new trail. His steps, I noticed for the first time, were light, as if the light breeze that caressed our faces pushed him along. Everything was as beautiful as a painting. Even the birds seemed to perfectly match the trees they perched in. The fragrances of the flowers, which should have been overpowering, blended so elegantly that their scent left me lingering for more.

As we rounded one bend, the land ahead dipped down, revealing a horseshoe-shaped amphitheater nestled in the trees. Instead of benches, however, thick roots jutted up from the sod in the shape of stools around the freshly tilled circle of earth that formed the stage. In the front row, along one edge, five chairs had been arranged over the root seats. Vines teeming with white and purple orchids hung from high branches of the nearby trees, bisecting the circle and acting like a curtain. In the back of the stage, the land dipped out of sight.

Jal'rean pointed to the stage. "This is where the play will be performed."

I wanted to say something, but Diane spoke for me. "You planned all this for us?"

Jal'rean was solemn. "Not exactly, but let's say we've enhanced the original plans. This is the start of the Ar'tol'Va, the end of the last cycle of life."

We all looked at each other with puzzlement and concern. "Last cycle of life?" I asked.

"Do you not know of the elven cycle of life we practice?" he said with a bit of surprise in his voice.

"No, we don't." Robert demanded, "Tell us of it."

Jal'rean arched an eyebrow at Robert's rudeness, but replied graciously. "Our year is broken into twenty periods of twenty days. Each of these periods has a name. For example, the first is called 'Conception,' and the last is 'Rebirth.' Years are also grouped in twenty year segments. Years one through twenty would be 'Conception,' twenty-one through forty would be 'Birth,' and so on. And that cycle follows a score of twenty with the same naming principle. Tonight, marks the start of last day, of the last month, of the last year, of the last score. It is the day of Rebirth, in the month of Rebirth, in the year of Rebirth, under the score of Rebirth. It has been four hundred years since this last occurred. After this ceremony, Amilmadra will hold a private vigil to determine who will be worthy in twenty days."

"And what will happen in twenty days?" Diane asked politely, trying to take the edge off of Robert's discourtesy.

"Something most extraordinary, I assure you. It is something beyond the power of mere words to describe."

Our guide led us away from the stage, back to the center of town. Stands had been erected here to hold a variety of produce. As Jal'rean's people wandered by, they took something from each stand.

"Do they not need to pay?" I asked.

"We do not have those philosophies here. Members of our community contribute in their own ways, and we all benefit from the sharing." We followed him over to one stand that had round, dark-purple fruit. Picking up five, he brought them to us. "Here, try this, but be careful, it has some kick. We call it 'Mak'ra.'"

"Thank you." I took one from him. I sniffed the fruit then took a small nibble. A bittersweet taste burst in my mouth, and the texture reminded me of an apple. Pleased, I took a bigger bite, but something powerfully hot set my mouth on fire, and my eyes watered.

We all coughed, and Jal'rean immediately motioned us to another table, which held slender decanters of dark-blue liquid. "Drink this," he said, "it will ease the sensation for you."

The drink instantly put out the burning sensation, and my racing heart eased as calmness and euphoria spread through my body.

We each drank some of the liquid, feeling better with each sip. The rest of the morning and afternoon was a blur, and before we knew it, it was time for the event.

# CHAPTER THIRTEEN
## BIRTH

As we approached the amphitheater, we could hear everyone's chatter. Normally, with this many people all talking at once, the noise would have been unbearable. This, however, was like a light band of traveling musicians. Even though we couldn't understand what was being said, their language had a soothing effect on most of us.

"How the Hell are we to understand what is said?" Robert rumbled.

Diane poked him in the ribs. "Quiet, Robert! Don't insult our new friends."

Jal'rean shook his head. "I understand, my friend. Few understand our language, but fewer still outside our race have actually witnessed what you are about to see."

Diane stepped forward. "I apologize. He meant no disrespect."

"And no apologies are needed. Here." He extended his hand. "These are your seats." He grinned, bowed gracefully, and disappeared into the crowd.

As we settled in, the murmurs died down. Even the forest seemed to fade to an eerie quiet, and the wind fell still.

Amilmadra emerged from the center of the flowery curtain, stepping so lightly that the flowers didn't part as she passed through them. As she reached the edge of the stage, the area beneath her feet ignited with a golden shine. A nimbus of fireflies floating around her head completed the warm, unearthly radiance that surrounded her.

She began to sing. Her voice was perfectly pure as it rose and fell. The melody contained no words, only a wonderful blending of notes. She sang and glided to the left side of the stage. An elderly man emerged, followed by a female about his age and several younger people. They spread out in a "V", with the man in the center. There was a silvery glitter about him that wasn't present on any of the others.

Amilmadra's voice softened, and the old man began to sing, his voice blending with hers. The younger ones danced what appeared to be an allemande around the pair while butterflies and birds flew above the stage. The song was filled with strength, and I felt a sense of passion from him.

From behind the curtain, a female elf came over to our seats. "I am Aeri'Andi. I will explain what is going on."

Through nineteen acts, we watched the performers tell the life story of the oldest elf. We were captivated by the show, and didn't notice the passage of time.

The elves continued to dance, and the youngest of them came over to me, gently urging me up. I refused at first, but her youthful exuberance won over my reluctance, and I stepped onto the stage.

"Huzzah, J.D.!" Cat called before Diane silenced him with a stern glare.

Once I was close to the elves, I felt compelled to dance with them, caught up in the moment. I felt a sense of accomplishment and pride. A large, bird-like creature about the size of a cat emerged from the darkness and flew around me. At first, I was unsure what to think about the creature, but when it brushed lightly against me, I no longer cared. A wave of peace washed over my body, and I simply danced with it and with the elves. During the performance, I again brushed against the flying creature, and felt a sudden surge of strength course through my body.

The song of the eldest male faded and Amilmadra's voice picked up again. The man lay down on the stage, and the dance slowly stopped. All the creatures flew into the branches of the trees while we surrounded his body. The dancers' expressions changed to ones of sadness as the shine ebbed from his body. I too, was flooded with sad emotion. Amilmadra's singing also faded, matching the dimming lights of the stage, until only silence and darkness remained.

After a short time, soft glows emanated from everyone on stage. My body tensed up, and I shook in fear, but as I glanced around, the now peaceful expressions on the elves' faces help me calm myself. That is when I noticed the body of the aged elf had disappeared.

One by one, the elves came forward and sang about the man. The words blossomed in my mind like strange flowers, and somehow I understood their meaning.

When the youngest—who had pulled me on stage—finished her song, all of the elves stared at me.

I began to panic, but almost immediately a strange calmness again washed over me. I stepped forward and sang:

*We dance and sing praise to all life has to offer.*
*Each cherished moment we take and fill our coffer.*
*Death is part of the process that we need not fear,*
*So we sing of our loved one's deeds for all to hear.*
*Twenty by twenty is what we believe.*
*So although now we must grieve,*

*Twenty days thus will remove the pain.*
*With great joy we will see him again.*

I had no idea where the song came from, but the performers seemed to enjoy it. They hugged me, and then we bowed to the crowd. I returned to my seat as Amilmadra took center stage and ended her song. She passed back through the curtain as gracefully as she had emerged.

Applause erupted, and my companions and I joined in celebration. I was in awe of what I'd witnessed and experienced.

Cat slapped me on the back. "That was amazing! When do you learn your lines?"

Before I could answer, Diane took my hand. "I see you can dance. Now you won't have any excuses the next time I ask."

Jean-Luc nodded to me with his habitually neutral expression. "A job well done."

Robert scoffed at Jean-Luc's comment. "Now, maybe we can get on with what needs to be done."

My head whipped around trying to catch all the comments from my friends. Amilmadra came over to us.

"Thank you for a wonderful time," Diane told her.

"You are most welcome," she replied. "Before you settle down for the night, I would request you please come with me."

We followed her to the entrance of the tree where the two individuals still guarded. This time, I examined the tree more closely.

I could see traces of gold running in a scroll pattern around the perimeter of the pear-shaped door. As I stared at it, I noticed there was no latch, no hinges, no familiar way for the door to open. The leader leaned in and whispered something so softly it was barely a whisper on the wind. The metal around the door momentarily illuminated with a pale, bluish-purple light, then faded back to gold as it gently pivoted in the center, allowing entrance to the interior from either side. Amilmadra proceeded in, glanced back to us, and said, "Come." We followed without question.

The vestibule opened into a sunken room. Around the circumference of the tree's interior, at the same level as the floor, was a narrow catwalk, no more than two feet wide. The walkway was supported by rope netting attached to the opposite wall near the ceiling. Directly across from us, two more individuals dressed in green and brown leathers watched us. They had bows in their hands and full quivers slung over their backs. I could also see swords at their sides. On the wall between them hung a small brass bell, no bigger than a handspan in diameter. A small wooden staircase with a delicate, airy banister ran along the wall. The banister was carved with vines and various woodland birds so lifelike, I half-expected them to take flight. It reminded me of the carvings from the bedroom on our first night underground.

We descended to another floor perhaps twenty feet below the first. There, around the landing, were many doors, each of them designed in the same fashion as the main entrance. Amilmadra approached one of the doors and whispered to it in the same fashion as before. Inside, the walls were lined with weapons and armor of all types—truly an armory to inspire a king's jealousy.

She called to Jean-Luc first, beckoning him forward. "From the way you handle yourself, I can see that you find your strength within. For that, I offer you this." Her manner was wise and gentle. She stepped deeper into the room, and took something from the recesses of the treasure trove. She returned to the doorway with leather armlets, a quarterstaff, and some type of ring that I could not see in full detail.

"How do you know that I am as you say?" Jean-Luc asked, frowning at the items in Amilmadra's hands. "How is it that you know I do not want a sword or armor to protect me?"

"Do not fear. My people have the innate gift of seeing a person's true nature. As leader, my gifts are the strongest. This inner sight tells us much about the person—it allows us to know things that are otherwise concealed. It's one of the reasons my people brought you here to have your injuries tended. They saw goodness in you. As leader of my people, my abilities, allow me to see even deeper, to see things that even you may not know. Take this ring. Its name is Elorath. Speak it as you put it on, and it will offer you aid when you face your foe." She handed him the other items and motioned gracefully to the exit. Jean-Luc inclined his head in a half bow and left the room.

"Please come here, Robert," she said, and waited for him to approach. After ducking though the archway, Robert towered beside her. "To you," she said reaching into another recess of the alcove. "I give this armor, shield, and sword. When you need to find your mark, the sword will guide your arm." She picked up the items, one by one, and gave them to Robert.

Robert carefully examined each object. The first piece was the suit of chain mesh. "This is as light as cloth," he said. The shield was nearly tall as he was and shaped like an inverted teardrop. It bore an etching of the sun rising over trees. Last, he received a keen, long sword, etched with marks. "And these writings? These items feel—these items feel so light?" His face held a puzzled expression.

"Yes," Amilmadra said. "We have discovered a way to craft items to feel lighter and still retain the necessary weight to be used effectively."

"This is wonderful. Thank you, m'lady. I will use them well." Robert put the mail shirt on over his clothes. "I am surprised this fits so well." Withdrawing the sword from its sheath, he slashed through the air with sharp, purposeful movements. "Impressive. It glides so easily. This sword feels like an extension of my own arm. I can feel where it is moving, before I know where I am going to swing it."

Next to approach Amilmadra was Cat, who seemed eager to see what gifts the lady had in store for him. She held out what appeared to be the worn pelt of a large cat, perhaps black cougar or panther. "This is for you, my woodland friend. I am sure it will serve you well. And I have this also." She handed him a pair of thick gloves that had seen their share of use. They were crafted of thick, brown leather, cracked with age.

Taking them, he raised an eyebrow in surprise. "They feel so soft and comfortable."

Amilmadra reached to her right, disappearing from view for a moment. From somewhere, she pulled out a pair of brown boots and a short sword and handed them to Cat. The worn boots matched the gloves. The sword was in a somewhat torn, black sheath with what appeared to be claw marks from the tip of the sheath to the bottom. The crossguard appeared to be ivory claws, as if something tried to climb out of the sheath.

"Thank you," Cat said, with a bit of disappointment in his voice. It was noticeable enough that Amilmadra spoke.

"Often, Cat," she said, "the best things are in the simplest packages."

Cat bowed. "I meant no disrespect, kind lady. Thank you for the gifts." I could tell by the way he held himself that he was still a bit disappointed. However, he grinned and examined his gifts more closely, putting each of them on, one by one.

Diane was next. She did a full curtsy in front of Amilmadra, tilted her head, waiting for permission to rise.

"You may rise, child." The elf extended her arm to touch Diane's head.

Diane looked into Amilmadra's eyes, clearly fascinated by the power she saw in them.

"There is no need for formality here," Amilmadra stated. "I have chosen some special items for you as well. Take this mace, for it will undo those deeds that the evils of others have begun. Take this mesh armor, to protect you from the mightiest of blows. Take this talisman, for it will strengthen the talents that are strongest within you." Diane smiled and inclined her head.

"Thank you. You are most gracious with your gifts, and I only hope that I will have a chance to repay the kindness you have shown my friends and me." With that, Diane withdrew to examine her items. The mesh shirt was much like Robert's except that it was very obviously shaped for a female, being fuller in the chest and smaller at the waist. The symbol Amilmadra had given Diane was a small piece of metal, a bit smaller than her hand, poured from liquid silver, polished to an unbelievable shine, and embossed with the outline of an unfamiliar fish attached to a long silver chain.

"Please come forward, J.D.," Amilmadra said. "I have thought hard about your items, and I have decided that you should have these." She presented me with a pair of arm bracers, a ring, a small green pouch, and a dagger.

I took the gifts with a nod of my head. "Let me restate what Diane said, that my friends and I appreciate your hospitality and gracious gifts. We only hope to rise to the occasion so you will be proud of our accomplishments in your name." It felt weird for me to hear such words from my mouth. I had never been part of any royal functions, although that is what it felt like. Still it felt natural enough, and I dismissed it for the time as part of the nature of Nesh'tirai.

"I do have one more thing for you," Amilmadra added. "I will give it to you outside."

We gathered again in the sunken foyer, she turned to the door directly below the guards, and in the same fashion, opened it with a soft phrase. Inside the new alcove were what appeared to be ordinary supplies. We gathered up some bedding, blankets, dried fruit, wine skins, and other things to survive for a time in the forest. Once we had what we needed, we all left the storehouse tree.

Amilmadra was the last to step outside, speaking to us as the door closed silently behind her. "One moment, J.D. Let me summon your other gift." With that she scanned the trees, and called out a name: "Lumadian." Almost instantly, a creature appeared from the branches, flew down to her, and landed on her slender shoulder.

"Lumadian," she said again. "I want you to meet J.D. You and he will have to get to know one another. You will show him what you know, and he, in exchange, will keep you safe." She faced me and continued, "Isn't that right, J.D.?"

The creature glanced from Amilmadra to me and flicked its forked tongue a few times. Its eyes were wide open, and its tail twisted behind it like a serpent.

"Of course I will." I examined the creature a bit closer, trying not to surprise it. It was about two feet long and reptilian. The barbed tail was nearly as long as the body, and it had a long and skinny head. It had leathery, bat-like wings on its back, the same colors as the rest of its scaly body. I could see that its teeth and claws were very sharp; sharp enough to rip Amilmadra's clothes if it had desired to do so. The colors of its scales were like copper leaves, with veins of red throughout. Its eyes were a bright emerald green. When I was finished with my examination, it flew over to my shoulder and perched.

"*It is about time. Hello there!*" I remained perfectly still and upright. "*Hello, anyone home? I am Lumadian. I am a he, not an it!*" It was as if a tiny voice whispered to me.

"Hello?" I said aloud, with great apprehension.

"Anything wrong, J.D.?" Diane questioned me. "Do you expect the little fellow to return your greeting?"

Amilmadra nodded, and I somehow understood to be silent.

"Just felt like saying hello to the little guy. His actions startled me a little." I laughed and everyone else chuckled a bit, taking the nervousness in my voice as my reaction to Lumadian landing on me.

"Well now." Amilmadra gestured. "There is no time to delay. The longer we wait, the more this gang torments my people. I bid you peace and safe journeys. Su'nard, come forth please."

A man stepped from the trees. He was tall and lean, but like the rest of the elves, he carried himself with great poise and presence. As he approached, I noticed for the first time his ears were slightly pointed and his eyebrows swept upward.

*"Of course his ears are pointed. They are elves, you know."* I heard whispering again, although it did not sound like it was in my left ear where Lumadian perched. It seemed to come more from inside my skull—a very strange sensation, indeed.

"Well met." I extended my hand to the newcomer. The elf was dressed in dark leathers and carried a bow on his back, much like the guards in the armory tree.

"It is I who is honored to meet you, who would rid us of our tormentors. The journey to their lair takes about a day and a half, so we should start immediately. Are you all ready?"

We all nodded. With that, he strolled down a path out of the village. We followed close behind.

# CHAPTER FOURTEEN
## INFANCY

We followed Su'nard out of his village and deep into the forest. As we traveled, I felt uneasy about everything that had happened since we left home. *Where were we headed? Why? Why were things happening so fast?* My thoughts were broken, however, by my small companion.

*"Everything will be fine. After all, you have me to protect you!"*

I chuckled at his voice and boast, but the laugh did not last very long when he shifted on my shoulder. His claws squeezed my shoulder ever so gently, but enough that I sensed his level of displeasure.

"I am sorry," I said aloud. "I did not mean any insult."

*"It's fine. Most humans underestimate my strength, and end up regretting it. And one more thing—"* His voice rang clear in my mind. *"Just think your response, and I will be able to hear it. And you are not insane, either."*

*"Do you mean like this?"* I thought to him. The idea of doing so seemed foreign to me.

*"That is great! We will get to know each other very well. Oh, and although I like sweet berries now and then, I love meat."*

I suddenly had a strong desire for some fresh, raw meat. It was an unpleasant feeling, since I usually preferred my food cooked. Before I could dwell on it, I sensed more from my companion.

*"And another thing, I love an occasional scratching and some rubbing, but there will be time for you to pamper me later."* I heard him chuckle, and it put me strangely at ease.

We followed Su'nard for most of the day without seeing anyone. At first, the paths were like roots of trees, spreading out in many different directions, and I would have been lost in the first ten minutes if it weren't for our guide. The further we traveled, though, the options became fewer. As we were about to find somewhere to camp for the night, we noticed a hunched and cloaked figure limping in our direction. In his right hand was a carved staff, taller than he was. He used it for support as he faltered along. Through brief glimpses of his face under the hood, I could see he was very old.

A feeling of apprehension ran through my body. I grabbed the hilt of my dagger. Su'nard raised his hand when we were about thirty feet from the old man, and we stopped behind Su'nard.

"Greetings, old man," Su'nard said with a hint of apprehension in his voice. "What do you seek in the forest this day?"

The man slowly lifted his head, allowing us a clear view of his aged face. "I journey to the elves to bring them news of something that has recently plagued them." He inched to Su'nard and our elf guide mirrored the man's actions.

I could see my companions' uneasiness. Their hands went to their weapons. We watched as Su'nard marched up to the man, his bow low in his right hand.

"What news do you have for us?" Su'nard asked.

The man struggled to straighten and look Su'nard in the face. He yelled, "Just this!"

Immediately, I heard a voice scream in my head, *"Look out! To your left!"*

Without thinking, I fell to my right and brought my hands up. "Let my mark hit its target!" From my fingers, a white light grew into a small ball and zipped to a cloaked figure lunging at me. As I watched the light, things seemed to slow down like a bad dream, and mass chaos erupted around us when bandits attacked, and we responded. My ball hit its target square in the chest, knocking him back for a moment. That was long enough, however, for Lumadian to land on the attacker's shoulder. He sunk his barbed tail deeply into the man's neck. The figure gasped and fell forward onto his face.

Meanwhile, the old man had swung his staff at Su'nard with speed that defied his age. Su'nard raised his bow and was able to partially block the blow, but the strength of the old man's strike was such that he still made contact with our scout's head, sending him to the ground. Blood oozed from the elf's wound.

Robert, who had drawn his weapon, cleared the distance in an instant. Catching the man off guard, Robert sliced at the foe's arm. With amazing grace, Robert spun his blade around, and returned the flat part of the blade to the man's skull, knocking him unconscious.

Another man emerged from the trees and slung a stone at Jean-Luc, but my friend easily dodged. Jean-Luc ran forward, seized the assailant by the shirt, and threw him down. The man jumped to his feet, drew his sword, and dove, but Jean-Luc merely sidestepped, knocking the attacker off balance. The man swung around and brought the sword over his head. Jean-Luc caught the sword at the pommel. With a twisting motion, Jean-Luc disarmed the man, sending him into the dirt. The man attempted to flee, but Jean-Luc intercepted him, kicking him in the head so hard, I thought he would take it clean off. The man slumped motionless to the ground.

Cat darted off to the right, disappearing silently and swiftly into the wood, with a grace I had never seen from my friend. Moments later, I heard screams of agony and terror. Meanwhile, Diane knelt at our elf guide's side and touched him on the forehead. A soft, bluish light flowed from her hands to the elf, and his injuries disappeared. Su'nard blinked his eyes a few times.

An arrow zipped past my head, narrowly missing me. Sitting high in a tree were two more people. I watched as an assailant fired an arrow that hit its mark squarely in the center of Robert's shoulder that normally would have taken down any man. But all that did was infuriate Robert even more. He spun around to find the source of his pain. I snapped my fingers at the tree, and another ball of light emerged from my hand. It struck the tree limb, cracking it at the base where the trunk and limb met. The limb broke, sending the two men sprawling to the dirt.

Both the assailants drew short blades and rushed at Robert. Robert met one of them head on, blocking the attacker's blow with his sword. Diane was trying to pull Su'nard to his feet. I watched Robert dispatch that attacker with a slash of his weapon that sliced the man's throat. He sneered evilly at the other man, who backed away. My friend shifted his blade, and another bandit suddenly appeared behind him. I could see the assassin's blade dripping with green liquid as he tried to sink the blade into Robert's neck. Some type of large, black panther sprung from the bushes and sent the assassin sprawling to his belly. In an instant, the cat was upon him, pinning the man under its weight. I watched in horror as the panther took the man's neck into his mouth and with a crunch, broke it.

The remaining man dropped his blade. He began to say something, but Robert cut a deep gash into the man's chest. The man staggered back and touched the crimson fluid staining his black clothes. His face drained of color as he fell to his face.

The panther guarded its prize. When we approached, it darted off into the forest. We gathered ourselves.

Diane rushed over to Robert and stared at the embedded arrow. "How are we going to get this out? Where is Cat? He'd know the best way. Robert, sit down so I can see the wound better."

Robert dropped down and panted, "Diane, I-I-I'm having trouble breathing." He gasped and wheezed.

Jean-Luc and Su'nard joined Diane. Su'nard had a knife out, but Jean-Luc took it from him. Jean-Luc dug at the wound, opening it wider. Robert grunted and fell forward as Jean-Luc wrapped his fingers around the base of the arrow and yanked back, removing the entire head of the arrow from Robert's body. Blood fountained from the opening.

Diane chanted so softly that I couldn't hear the words, but the symbol around her neck and her hands glowed a soft sea-blue. I watched as tendrils of her spell twisted around the damage and poured into Robert. The light bathed his body, and his torso expanded as if he had taken in a deep breath. The wisps withdrew, closing the gash as they left his body. She grunted and closed one eye. "Robert, you feeling better?"

Robert nodded and staggered to his feet.

"I'd still like to know where Cat is. Has anyone searched for him?"

Before I could respond to Diane's question, we heard Cat's voice. "I am right here." He emerged from the trees dragging a bloodied and lifeless body. "They have horses and a camp over there." He indicated somewhere in the woods. I took a few steps and scanned the forest in an attempt to see the camp, but the thick vegetation obscured any chance of seeing more than a few feet ahead.

Robert wiped his blade on this last victim's back. "Well, we should search these bandits, tie up the one I knocked out, and take them all to the camp, so that no one can tell what happened here."

Without questioning him, we all gathered the bodies and piled them deep in the forest away from the camp Cat had discovered. As we picked up the man, who originally appeared to be old, we discovered that he was actually younger than Cat. We covered the traces of combat on the road as the sun disappeared over the horizon. The forest was dense enough to hide any traces of a campfire from the road, and I thought, *Cat was extremely lucky to have discovered such a concealed location.*

Just as we settled down I heard, *"I didn't mean to kill him,"* in my thoughts. *"Everything happened too fast!"* Lumadian landed on my shoulder. Instinctively, I reached up and scratched him under the chin, which produced an effect very similar to a cat's purr.

*"Nothing to worry about,"* I thought to him. *"You did well."* I could feel his pride as he coiled up around my neck.

As the light of day disappeared, the man who had confronted us in the road stirred. Su'nard had bound him up in ropes with knots I'd never seen before. The man panicked as he beheld his captors. His eyes darted back and forth between Robert and me.

"What do you wish of me?" There was obvious tension in his voice.

Robert pulled his armor off and inspected the damage the arrow had done. The metal seemed to have repaired itself. He strode over to the man, a hint of glee in his eyes. "You will tell us where your associates are quartered, and we might consider letting you breathe another day." I was surprised by his words, and from the expression on Su'nard's face, I suspected he was equally shocked.

"What...what do you mean? It appears you have bested my party. We were all there was."

Robert leaned into the man, pressing on the lump on the side of the man's head. "I have no patience for the stupid, so you'd better gain some intelligence quickly. You were obviously the leader of this band. You are in no position to barter. Wouldn't you like to live?"

I could see the fear in the man's eyes, and even I felt intimidated by Robert's presence until Lumadian managed to calm me down again with his slow breathing near my neck.

"We thought we could take advantage of the situation. If we got away with it, we could always blame the other bandits. I'd never got to their hideout. It's…" He stopped, as if realizing he had said too much.

"It's what?" Robert loomed over the man.

"It's haunted!" He screamed, sounding panicked.

I spoke up, trying to break the tension. "So, you do know where it is."

"I-we happened across it in our travels. It is how we found out about them. They had us join—I mean they wanted us to join. We figured we could get some coin, then abandon them. We were going to…" He clutched his throat and gasped for air. His body twitched and I noticed a trickle of blood from his mouth. Robert called Diane over to see if she could help. She knelt beside the man and closed her eyes. The soft radiance enveloped her hand, but did not flow to the man's body.

*"He is dead,"* my companion relayed. *"It appears he was under a command not to betray those brigands."*

*"What do you mean?"*

*"It's a spell that…"* He stopped for a moment, and collected his thoughts to better explain. *"What you did to the bandits with the light is a spell. Spells are forces that one can control without the need for sword or bow. There are many types of spells. One of them is a guarantee that you will complete a task. Complete the task, and nothing happens. Break your word, or do not fulfill your promise, and the other part of the promise takes effect."*

"There is no hope, Diane. His treachery was his undoing. He is beyond your aid." I approached the man's body. "It is a pity, but greed does that to people. We should bury the bodies, though." When I noticed the concern on their faces, I added, "They might attract the panther we saw earlier." With that reminder, everyone agreed to my suggestion. With a little work, we dug shallow graves.

Jean-Luc carefully lowered one of the men into the hole, then ripped off a strip of cloth from the bottom of his shirt and covered the man's eyes. "May you fare better in the afterlife."

Robert carried two men—one in each hand—tossed them into the graves face-down, then ransacked the bodies and took some items. He managed to toss some bows and quivers to the side before Diane reacted.

Diane stomped over to him. "Robert! What are you doing?"

Robert glanced up and sighed loudly. "They aren't going to be able to use them now, are they?" He continued his search and pocketed two rings, a small pouch that jingled, and a few vials of greenish liquid.

Diane knelt on the fresh dirt beside him and looked him in the eyes. "Please stop, Robert…for me."

Robert stared into Diane's eyes, nodding. He jumped to his feet and stood next to Jean-Luc and me. While Diane said a prayer, Robert slipped Jean-Luc and me each a ring, then pocketed the small pouch and vials. After Diane was done, we covered the graves and returned to camp.

Cat brought the dying embers of the bandit's campfire to a roaring blaze.

We sat in a silent circle around it until Su'nard spoke up. "Your party seems strong in its bonds. How did you all meet one another?"

I cleared my throat and thought about the best time to start. "It started about thirteen years ago, when four of us—Jean-Luc, Cat, Diane, and I—met as children on a boat trip. Since it was a very long voyage, and we were the only children, we bonded.

Jean-Luc's family entertained the crew. Cat explored the boat, getting into all types of mischief. And I talked to Diane all the time. There was something about her that was so relaxing. Shortly after we arrived, my father was *summoned* to Robert's father's mansion to create custom-carved furniture, and he brought me along. Mr. Twinholm suggested that Robert and I spend time together after learning we had arrived on the same boat. The five of us would get together and explore. Robert was a very vainglorious child back then, but one day while exploring in an unfamiliar part of the forest, Cat tripped over a ravine and snagged his foot on a root, otherwise he would have fallen a good fifty feet down on his head. Robert managed to wiggle far enough down on his chest to grasp him and pull him to safety. Ever since then, whenever one of us got into trouble, Robert always was there for us."

Robert sat up a bit more, puffing out his chest. "That is what friends do for one another."

I bit my lip and didn't reply. "Enough about us, though. Let's get ready for the night."

Jean-Luc took the first watch, then I, Su'nard, Cat, and finally Robert. During the time I guarded the camp, I heard several noises that I could identify, and some that I could not, but none came within the circle of the fire. The rest of the night was uneventful.

Morning came, and we awoke to a cold, crisp day. Lumadian was cuddled under my chin, lying on my chest. His little body generated a great deal of heat. When I began to stir, he shook, stretching his wings.

*"Good morning! What's to eat?"*

I chuckled. *"Well, I do not have any fresh game in my sleeve. Perhaps you can find some."*

Without hesitation, he flew out of my sight. *"Wait! Please be careful!"*

*"Stop being a mother hen,"* was the reply I received.

I ran my hand down the neck of one of the horses the bandits had, patting it to calm it down, and examined the scoundrel's bags, but all they had was food on the brink of being spoiled and some sour mead.

As I finished my inspection, unusual flavor flooded my mouth and a sense of glee filled my body. I tasted a mouthful of something gamey that both delighted and repulsed me. After wondering for several moments, I spotted Lumadian sitting on a fallen tree eating a rabbit.

"Enjoying yourself?"

Lumadian chuckled and dug into the rabbit with a renewed fervor. The taste left my mouth.

*"Sorry,"* he said. *"I sometimes forget about that."*

After the rest of my friends had gotten up, we ate breakfast and broke camp. We decided to ride the horses, so that we would be fresh. Lumadian flew to my shoulder, a good deal messier than when we woke up. I wiped his muzzle clean. *"Am I going to have to teach you how to eat more cleanly?"*

*"Only if you hunt with your mouth,"* he replied.

I did not respond to his comment, but mounted the horse, joining my friends on the path. We rode on for a short while, and I noticed a change in the trees. The bark on the trees was darker, and they were much closer together. Many of the trees were bent in strange angles, drooping over the path. The songs of the birds became less and less frequent until they were nonexistent. The wind picked up, and there was a noticeable change in temperature that sent a chill down my back. When we proceeded down the path that would ultimately take us to our destination, the horses refused to budge.

"We should continue on foot from here," Su'nard said. "We are very close to the spot where I cannot go any further."

"How will you know?" Cat asked him.

"You will see. It is very easy to perceive."

We continued down the path with weapons drawn, not sure what we were going to encounter. After a short jaunt, we stopped and gawked. Ahead of us, were two massive trees, their very size dwarfing anything else around them in both height and girth. I could not see their tops. They guarded either side of the path, branches intertwined. The knotted trunks looked like they had many faces, twisted in horror. The trees created an archway over the path that appeared black from the lack of sunlight.

"This is where we must part ways. I will be waiting when you emerge. Be cautious, and do not always trust what you see."

"What would happen if you entered there?" Cat asked curiously.

"The land is poisonous to my kind. I would perish almost instantly."

Taking a moment to reflect on Su'nard's words, I asked Lumadian, *"Is it safe for you?"*

*"I am not an elf."*

"Be safe Su'nard. Stay out of sight, and we will see you soon." Diane leaned over to kiss him on the cheek.

Blushing a bit, he said to her, "Keep them safe and well."

She smiled. "I will."

I patted my sides and inhaled deeply. "Is everyone ready?"

Everyone nodded. I looked at my companion and felt his uneasiness. He replied, *"I hope they have good food."* I chuckled and scratched the side of his muzzle as we stepped onto the forbidden path.

# CHAPTER FIFTEEN
## EARLY CHILDHOOD

We passed the massive oaks that framed the entrance, and I felt out of order—as if something surreal had slipped over the actual forest. Everything cast weird shadows. Even our own shadows resembled hunched imps. The path ahead of us twisted, making it impossible to see more that twenty feet ahead of us. We inched down the path, not sure what to expect. The trees here were all black as coal, bent at strange angles, as if they fought a pitched battle with one another. A strange mist dragged on our feet and I felt as if I trudged through snow.

We soon came across a murky, slow-moving stream that was foul with an odor I could not identify. Cat gestured that he noticed movements ahead. We hurried off the path, trying to get a better glimpse of what was there.

As I pondered, Lumadian flew off my shoulder into the branches for a better view. *"There are four humans standing near an old wooden bridge across the stream. Behind them is a necromancer—a person who deals with the animation of the deceased. He wears the symbol of Tumar, the God of the Dead."*

I relayed this information to my friends.

"How can you communicate with him?" Robert asked.

"I don't have time to explain it now. We need a plan."

"I have an idea," Cat offered. "Have your friend distract the necromancer as we rush the others. With any luck, we can get there before they know what hit them."

"Let me ask him." I stretched up to Lumadian.

"Ask?" Robert said. "He is only a pet. Tell him what to do or we can have some lizard soup after this."

I felt anger and disgust at Robert's comments.

*"Would you help us do this, please?"* I asked my companion, trying to ease my feelings about asking him.

*"Sure,"* he replied in my mind. *"Just keep the troll out of my way."*

I began to question what he meant until I realized he was referring to Robert. Lumadian flew off through the higher branches and perched in a tree behind the necromancer.

Through Lumadian, I could hear exactly what the man said, which I relayed to my friends.

"Be on guard." The necromancer had a gravelly voice. "The group the elves hired will be here before nightfall. They were on foot according to our last reports."

A man in a midnight-blue cloak nodded. "Are we meant to kill them, Azen?"

Azen scoffed at the man. "Why? Do you think they would be of any use, Pinser?"

Before Pinser could answer, a man with a huge scar on his face stepped forward. "I can think of some uses for the woman."

While all the other men chuckled, Azen scowled. "Just keep it in your pants, Rodden. That goes for all of you. Zulden and Gothmore, stand guard at the bridge."

We skulked closer with Robert and Jean-Luc in front, followed by Diane and myself. I did not see Cat, but continued onward, trusting my friend's abilities. We kept low to the ground, letting the mist hide us as we scrambled blindly forward. When the bridge came into view, we stopped and waited, whispering to one another so softly, I barely heard the conversation.

I examined every position, trying to determine each cause and effect. "Jean-Luc, do you think you can cross in time?"

Jean-Luc gauged the distance. "I should be able."

I nudged Robert. "Don't let them sound any alarms."

Robert smirked. "Oh, they won't. Trust me."

I nodded to my friends. *"Go!"* I thought to Lumadian, as I whispered to my friends, "Now!"

We jumped to our feet and dashed at them yelling loudly, surprising the enemy with our bold attack. Azen gestured, waving his hands in a silly, circular fashion. Blackness surrounded his hands for a moment and then disappeared. Lumadian bit him hard on the neck, but the man managed to elude my companion's tail with sudden jerking motions.

Jean-Luc cleared the bank in a single, colossal leap. He threw a jumping kick at Rodden's side that knocked the wind out of him.

Robert ran across the bridge, but the bridge was rigged somehow and broke apart. He plunged into the black water, getting covered entirely in muck. The liquid clung to him as he shook in the waist deep water.

Pinser swung a mace at Jean-Luc, hitting him square in the back. Instead of crippling my friend, the mace shattered like shards of glass.

Diane teetered on a remaining segment of the bridge. I reached out to her and pulled. We both tumbled back to the side where we'd begun, safely down but separated from the rest.

Zulden and Gothmore, both with swords, advanced on Jean-Luc. Zulden swung his sword, but over-balanced when Jean-Luc side-stepped his attack. Jean-Luc was not as lucky with Gothmore, and received a deep cut across his arm.

Jean-Luc held Zulden and used him as a temporary shield. The two struggled, and Jean-Luc barely managed to hold on with his good arm as Rodden got to his feet.

"Help us, my friend!" Azen screamed. With another quick circular motion of the hands, he spoke a few words. A strong gust of wind blew from him, flattening Diane and me. I felt a small cry of pain in my mind as I saw Lumadian blown into one of the trees. His body plummeted. I tried to communicate with him, but did not get a reply.

Robert strode over to us. His face held a blank expression, and he drew his sword.

Without thinking, I held my hands out and screamed with surprise as words flowed unbidden from my lips. "Dancing lights be in your eyes!" I saw multiple colored lights flash in Robert's face. I could tell he could not see. He emerged from the brook, his whole body dripping muck from the stagnant water.

Diane held her symbol above her and spoke. "Let your body be refreshed." She pointed at Robert. Water fell from the trees and drenched Robert, getting rid of nearly all of the slimy liquid. He seemed to have recovered from his daze and rushed me.

Blood gushed from Jean-Luc's wound, as the men surrounded him. The captured man freed himself from Jean-Luc's grasp, pushing him into the dead foliage. Zulden raised his arm to deal the death blow. Instead, he screamed in agony as his arm flew off into the mire. The panther had returned. Gothmore, paralyzed with fear, stared at the beast.

The necromancer chuckled and cast another spell. I watched him, drawn to him by the spell. I could see the colors of everything around him, except for the panther, fade. The colors blended like paint and wrapped around the necromancer's neck. The wound that Lumadian had caused healed.

Robert lunged at me, swinging his sword in an attempt to decapitate me. Luck was on my side, and I managed to duck.

From behind Robert, I heard Diane incant the same spell as before, bringing even more water that washed the rest of the slime from his body. Robert blinked. "Where am I?"

I simply yelled, "Get them!" and attacked our remaining foes.

"Help me!" Rodden, confronted by the panther, screamed.

With a giant leap, the panther sprang over him. Rodden sighed as if he thought the beast had misjudged its jump. It was not until we heard a muffled cry that the henchman seemed to realize the necromancer was the panther's mark.

Zulden fell into the water. Ripples of water seemed to speed to the blood, as if they had minds of their own. From his arm, I could see the skin swell where the water pumped into his body. With horror on his face, the man was carried away by the current.

Rodden fled down the path, but ran directly into Robert. I wasn't sure how Robert suddenly appeared there, but one thing was clear: he was very upset. With one hand he pushed the man away from him. With the other, he swung his blade, successfully removing the unfortunate man's head from his body.

The panther stalked Gothmore, the last remaining man, growling and licking its bloody muzzle. The man threw his sword at the panther, hitting it with the tip of the sword, but the blade didn't stick and fell. In a blur, the panther was on the man, pinning him down with its great weight. It raked its back claws and bit the man while he wailed in agony.

I hugged Diane and floated us both across without touching the unusual water. Only after we reached the other side did I wonder how I'd done it. We fell back in a defensive posture in front of Jean-Luc, blocking the panther. Robert returned and swiped at the feline, but it darted off with incredible speed, running across the water as if the surface was solid.

With the threat gone, I rushed to Lumadian, while Diane administered aid to Jean-Luc. She managed to repair his injury. I carefully picked up my little friend and put my ear to his chest, trying to hear a heartbeat.

Diane came up behind me and looked at the tiny reptile. She pressed her hands against him and chanted softly. Moments later, he blinked his eyes.

"*Did we win?*"

"*Yes,*" I replied, "*but only barely. How are you?*"

"*What's to eat?*"

I chuckled and sighed happily. "He is fine."

We heard the trees rustling as Cat emerged with his bow in hand. "I am definitely going to need to practice this."

We examined the bandits, but discovered nothing of interest. Before I could comment on what to do with them, Robert tossed two of the bodies into the water. I was about to say something, but decided against it, seeing the expression on Robert's face. Once the rest of the bodies were disposed of, Diane approached him.

"Just what were you doing attacking J.D.? You could have taken off his head!"

"What do you mean, Diane?" he asked, with another blank expression.

Diane enunciated each word. "You attacked J.D."

Robert rubbed his forehead. "When did I do that?"

Diane was about to say something when I intervened. "Perhaps the water had some type of effect on him. You saw what it did to the man who lost his arm. I know Robert would not intentionally attack me."

Diane nodded. "We should continue on."

Without any further discussion, we followed her down the path. I put Lumadian on my shoulder and he wrapped himself around my neck again and drifted off to sleep. The path was more open than the entrance to the corrupted forest. Eerie, luminescent moss lit a path deeper into the woods, since sunlight did not enter through the thick web of branches above. We could not tell for certain how long we ambled down the path, not wanting to misplace a step. After several hours, we saw a large stone building. The mortar was cracked with age, and dark gray vines grew up the walls. We quickly crouched down when we saw two guards at the entrance. They wore white and silver armor.

"What do you suppose is in there?" Cat motioned to a building.

"I am not sure," I replied, "but we should check it out."

# CHAPTER SIXTEEN
# LEARNING

We crept to the building, crawling on our hands and knees below the tall plants and the same strange mist that seemed to come and go, trying to reduce the chance of an alarm being sounded. We watched the guards carefully, but they never faltered, never swayed—never even moved an arm to scratch themselves. The closer we approached, the more pronounced the oddity became and with it, the smell of death and decay.

Their white armor did not reflect anything. As I narrowed my vision, I saw that it wasn't metal, but bone. I tried rousing Lumadian, but he was still fast asleep. We got right up to the building and saw that it was surrounded by a moat of the same mucky, black water. A wooden plank led from one of the paths to where the guards stood. The protectors of the building were more like statues than anything else. We advanced to the front of what seemed to be a bastion or small fort, and yet the figures did not flinch.

Robert drew his sword. "Why aren't they reacting to us?"

"Maybe they are only statues." I joined Robert. The building was about three stories high. Large cracks at the base crept up the sides like vines, diminishing the higher up the surface they crept until they disappeared completely by the third level. The large, square building only had one visible entrance: a massive, wooden door behind the two guards.

Cautiously, Robert shuffled to the plank. "I don't want to take another swim in these possessing waters." He prodded the boards with the tip of his weapon. The moment he touched the wood with the tip of his sword, the figures animated and rushed at him with amazing speed.

The first figure swung its massive two-handed sword at Robert. Robert raised his blade to meet it. Clanging metal sparked in the air. The force of the blow knocked Robert off balance, sending him to one knee.

Jean-Luc and Cat met the other guard as it crossed the plank. Cat, in an attempt to mimic Jean-Luc, did a jumping kick, but it looked like he hit a wall. He simply slid to the ground. The figure was seemingly unaffected by the blow. It swung its blade at Jean-Luc, but my friend was able to deflect it. With his other hand, Jean-Luc punched the side of the foe's head, but the blow only seemed to hurt his hand. He shook it back and forth.

Robert recovered from his stumble and swung his blade at his foe's neck, but the sword skipped off the shoulder and hit the helmet. The force of the blow sent its helm into the moat revealing a skeletal head. Robert, flabbergasted at the sight, remained still, which gave his adversary enough time to toss him nearly twenty feet across the path.

Diane rushed forward and held her symbol in front of her again. "Light, banish the darkness!" I squinted as a blinding light shone from the symbol, hitting the skeletal foe that had tossed Robert. Its body rattled as it fled Diane and ran right over the edge and into the deep moat, disappearing from sight under the pungent waters.

Cat attempted to kick his opponent again, this time making contact with the hilt of its sword. The force sent the weapon skimming across the dirt path. Jean-Luc swung his palm at the foe again, causing bits of the bone to shatter and fly from its jaw.

I wondered what I should do, trying to calm my fluttering heart by taking in deep breaths. My mind raced, and the image of the bandits came into clear focus. I lifted my hands tentatively and summoned a ball of light that hit the guard square in the chest, drawing its attention to me. Leaving Jean-Luc and Cat, it bolted to me with speed and grace, claws extended. I stepped back, not wanting it to touch me.

Robert recovered from his throw and was in the process of coming to my aid when Diane stepped in and hit the thing squarely in the chest with her mace. The skeleton staggered back and fixed its empty gaze on Diane. Seeing her symbol, it froze. That was more than enough time for Robert. He barreled into the skeleton. The force pushed the thing into the murky moat. The weight of its armor yanked the abomination down under the ebony water.

With the two guards dispatched, we approached the gate with caution, alert for any surprises. The door was wood, heavily reinforced with crossing steel bars. There was a metal latch on the right side of the door.

Etched in the stonework above the door was what appeared to be English lettering, but it was worn so badly with age that I could only read out part of the last name. "Von B"

As I examined the writing, Robert lifted the latch and pushed in the door. "Well, we won't figure it out with you gawking at a few…" Robert began to choke and wheeze.

I went to help, but was stopped when a wave of stench flooded over me, making me sick.

Cat covered his mouth with his hands. "Ewwww, it smells like rotten meat on a summer's day."

Inside, the stone was even in worse condition than on the outside. The walls, ceiling, and floor were all webbed with cracks with pieces of the walls on the floor. All of the interior doors were marred and blackened.

Jean-Luc opened the door to the left. "So, J.D.'s method of exploring, then."

The floor had scattered debris, but something in the far corner caught my eye. On the right wall was another door of warped and aged wood. That door was heavily barred with planks. Against the door was a massive bookcase and desk. There was more wood propped against the desk and the wall diagonally across, making it virtually impossible for anyone to move the desk without first removing the debris.

Trash that had long-since decayed to unrecognizable piles cluttered all of the corners. Dirt caked the cobwebs. The wood suffered from dry rot and age.

"I wonder why they would block this door. Should we take a look?" Robert asked.

"Perhaps not," I offered. "We do not have any way of knowing what is beyond. Why would they barricade the door from the *inside*?"

Robert examined one of the beams supporting the desk. "Normally you'd do that to keep someone or something in. Whatever it was, though, it is surely dead by now. This wood would crumble at a touch."

"Well, we could explore the rest of this floor, and if we find nothing else, come back here."

"That sounds like a plan," Cat said.

I noticed Cat was prancing back and forth, like a small child needing to visit the privy, but I shrugged it off as nervousness.

We returned to the main room and flung wide the door opposite the entrance. It opened into a long hallway. There was a door about midway down on the right. Across from this was a recently bricked up archway. We continued down the hall past the door to an intersection. The left passage led to stairs going up, and the right led to stairs going down. Instead of leaving the floor, we spun around and tried the only door in the hall we had not yet explored.

I stepped inside what appeared to be a study. Shelves lined the walls, filled with scrolls tied with red ribbons. In one corner of the room was a desk and simple bed, and in the other was the only other exit. The floor had a moldy, rotten fur rug.

I faced my friends. "I will check through the bookcases along this wall. Robert and Jean-Luc, each of you take a wall. Diane, why don't you examine the desk, and Cat, you the bed?"

Everyone quietly went to where they had been assigned.

Cat stripped the bed, tossing blankets and pillows on the floor. "Some animal must have used the bed. It reeks of old urine and feces."

Diane opened the drawers, but found only aged parchment and dried ink. "I don't think anyone has used it in a while. Everything seems so old."

I went to the scrolls, but each one either disintegrated in my hands, or was so weathered with age that the ink was unreadable. "I can't understand anything. The scrolls crumble to dust."

Robert chuckled as he swept along the surface of the wall. "Nothing useful here."

Jean-Luc was on the other end of the bookcases when I saw him pull out a scroll that was different from the rest. It was much newer than anything else we had found, and it was like someone had purposely placed it in such a manner that only careful observations or blind luck would let someone find it. "I found something."

We all gathered around as he unrolled the scroll and read it aloud.

*4<sup>th</sup> Moonsday of Gelidrown*

*Our plans against the elves go well. Their foolish adherence to tradition will be their undoing. Enough people travel the lands that we are well supplied without using any of our own resources. Additionally, we discovered a site not far from here, with an abundance of minerals that will make us wealthy beyond our greatest expectations. Your plans for vengeance against the elves are flawless, and when we are done, none of them will survive. Your hatred for them is our hatred for them. I have ordered more attacks upon the remote parts of their forest. Your spells greatly aid in that regard, although some have mentioned some side effects like lethargy and loss of appetite. Their complaints are insignificant.*

*I should mention though, that one of our more powerful fighters, Hastidor, has come down with some sort of illness. It began soon after he entered the mine. He was exploring the deeper alcoves of one of the passages when he emerged in a fit of rage and covered in a strange, white powder. As time passed, he grew more prone to fits of anger. During his next assignment, an argument erupted in which he cut down one of his own men, then proceeded to chop his man's limbs off one by one. I attributed it to his harsh nature, but he remained extremely belligerent even when he returned. His level of hostility rose to where anyone in conflict with him became either wounded, or dead. When I and a score of men confronted him, he defeated most of them before I could put him to sleep. We had to confine him to one room. Once he awoke, he destroyed the door into the hall across from my study, going through it as if it was mere parchment. Again, I managed to subdue him with sleep and had him dragged to the same room. We bricked up the doorway, and instilled a magic ward on the door.*

*I know we should dispose of him, but I wonder how he got so incredibly strong, and if we could use that strength to our advantage. I will keep you informed of my progress. I have included a map to the location of the mine with this note.*

*Lastly, if you could send an additional ... motivator... for the guards, it would be greatly appreciated. Lately, they have been preoccupied with something they found in the cellar and insist I check it out personally. My time is precious here with the planning and I need someone who can snap the men into order so they don't bother me with these petty things. I will let you know what I discover there as well.*

*May your purse always be full of gold,*
*Zalikan*

I examined the map and scrollwork. "Interesting. Perhaps Zalikan met his demise at the hands of his men. Perhaps the effect of the mine drove them all mad. That notwithstanding, we will have to determine if the risk of going into the mine is worth the possible benefits. We could use some type of currency here. It seems gold is as valuable here as it is home. I am hoping we can discover more about it after we finish exploring here." I rolled up the map and tucked it into my pack. "One door left to try on this floor before we decided to go up, down, or open the blocked door."

"Sure thing." Cat calmly went over to the door and opened it.

I saw the swinging blade wielded by a skeletal creature come at Cat. It would have sliced him in two if it were not for two things. One, the doorway was narrower than the creature's swing, and although the stonework was weathered with age, the blade could not slice through the solid stone. Two, Cat reacted by jumping back at least ten feet, landing perfectly on his hands and feet, then drew his sword.

Robert went to intercept the creature, but not quickly enough. Jean-Luc reacted first. Running at full force to the skeleton and then sliding, Jean-Luc delivered a punch directly to the hideous creature's backbone, separating the top half from the bottom. The thing still took a swipe at Jean-Luc, but he was able to roll out of the way.

"There are more inside," Jean-Luc called, as he backed away so the creatures could come into the room single file. Robert went to crush the skeleton that was entering as the one broken in half clawed its way into the center of the room. With a swing of his sword, Cat cracked the skull of the half skeleton and with a continuous motion, struck another one that was attacking Robert.

The noise of combat woke Lumadian, and somehow, he sent a wave of strength into me, and I knew what to do. My fingers outlined the opening between the rooms and I called, "Let our oppressors be languid!" A greenish liquid spewed from my hands. The liquid hit the archway and a web-like surface appeared across the door. I was surprised by my own action.

Diane held her symbol at the creatures, trying to summon the essence of her power. This time, however, nothing happened, and she tried over and over again.

Jean-Luc came around Robert's right side. Cat was already on his left. The three of them dispatched the skeleton in the room while they waited for the next. They did not have to wait long. Armed with two long swords, the skeleton tangled in the greenish web and tore it free. Robert, Jean-Luc, and Cat attacked the thing at the same time. The force of all their blows shattered the bones to powder. As it fell another came to take its place. This one held a spear aimed at Robert. He easily dodged the thrust. The trio dispatched this monster with efficiency.

From the room, I heard chanting in a language I could not understand. As it finished, the web blasted into the room, covering my three friends. I watched as my spell slowed their bodies.

*"How do I get rid of it?"* I asked Lumadian.

*"You just do! Just get rid of it!"*

As I tried to eliminate the effects of the spell, a large skeleton entered the room. It resembled that of a human, but the skull was grossly large. Its huge build even towered over Robert. It had a blackened mace that did not reflect any light. "Death to the living!" It swung the mace in the direction of Robert, and then stopped. It fixed its gaze on Diane and her symbol.

Robert tried stepping in front of it, but was too slow.

The skeleton grappled with Robert and hurled him into Jean-Luc, causing them to crash to the floor. It swiped at Diane with its skeletal hand, barely missing her as she dove for the floor. It bent over and pinned her to the floor with its free hand, lifting the mace.

I rushed to Diane's side as Lumadian flew in its face. "Stop!" I called.

I saw a flash of black out of the corner of my eye, and a large creature hit the skeleton with such force that it crashed into me, sending us both flying. I was dazed, but I thought I saw the panther. It jumped on the skeleton's back. With its powerful jaws, it broke the skeletal neck, sending the skull flying. The panther stayed on the skeleton's back, cracking bones one by one. I stared into the beast's eyes, gasping for air as it crushed into me. The cat slipped aside and tossed the remaining part of the motionless skeleton into Jean-Luc and Robert, who were still trying to recover from the spell. It ran out the door and down the hall.

I staggered to Diane and helped her to her feet. Together, we stumbled to Robert and Jean-Luc. Another creature blocked the door.

Standing about my height, the creature was dressed in black. The robe had a symbol of the sun being blocked completely by the moon, with only the ring of light around it. The creature had pale, pasty skin pulled taut against its body, and the bones were clearly visible. It cackled at us and scanned the room. Raising a bony finger, it chanted something. From its weathered digits, a grayish, sickly vapor flooded over us. The mist burned our eyes and skin. We gagged at the stench.

An evil grin emerged on the creature's face as we choked helplessly on the noxious fumes. I was nearly unconscious, still gasping for air after nearly being crushed by a panther. I watched the creature circle its hand in the air. A sphere of fire shimmered over its head, the heat of which increased the temperature of the room. It tossed its hands back as if about to throw the fireball into the room, when I saw a blade emerge from one of its eye sockets.

The creature did not cry out in pain, but leaned forward to pull the tip of the weapon from its skull. This momentary delay worked in our favor, and the ball fell on the creature. Fire consumed it almost instantly, charring the figure beyond any recognition. From the doorway stepped Cat, with only a few cuts and bruises. He rushed to Diane and helped her into the room, and then assisted all of us.

"Is anyone injured?" he asked.

"I'll be fine," Diane replied. "I need to get that smell out of my nose." She opened her pack and rummaged around until she pulled out a small bundle of cloth. Carefully, she pulled away the cloth to reveal a small, fancy glass jar. She pulled the glass stopper and sniffed the end of it, closing her eyes. Dabbing behind her ears and on top of her wrists, she smiled at me.

"What is that?" I staggered a bit closer to her since I was still coughing the fumes out of my system.

Tilting her head to one side, and moving her hair out of the way, she grinned widely. "Here, smell."

Leaning in, I inhaled. My sense of smell returned as my nose took in the wondrously pleasant scent. Gently cupping the back of her neck, I leaned in closer and barely touched it with my nose. I closed my eyes and inhaled again, imprinting the aroma in my mind.

Diane giggled and stepped away, touching the end of my nose with the glass stopper. "There," she said. "Now you can smell good, too."

I was reminded of the wash room incident and was going to say something, but decided not to mention it. I rubbed my nose in an attempt to wipe away the alluring effect of smelling Diane all day, but my actions caused it to worsen by spreading the scent around. Still, it was better than the cloud of noxious vapors.

Looking around the room, I saw that this was some type of garrison. Rows of weapons lay strewn on the floor with some still in a rack. All the metal weapons were rusted and in bad disrepair. The floor was also littered with a few more of the skeletal corpses, but their lifeless husks had been badly broken. In one corner, was a large wooden chest that defied everything else we had seen. It was clean and without any signs of age.

"How can these things do what they do? It has to be some type of witchery!" Jean-Luc spoke out, which surprised me a bit more than animated corpses, since he was usually the quiet member.

"*Animation of the dead is a common practice, and it does not cost anything much,*" I heard from Lumadian. "*And now that we are safe, I want to say that I did not enjoy the tactics before. You need to protect me more!*" I could feel his muscles tense a bit, claws holding my shoulder in a tight grip. "*And another…*"

"*I agree,*" I interrupted him. "*You are more important than menial tasks.*" I could feel him hiss a chuckle into my ear, as he relaxed.

"*Next time let Cat go ahead, and I'll stay in the trees.*" Lumadian put an extra emphasis on the word 'trees.'

"*I will do better,*" I replied. Focusing my attention on my other friends, I said, "Lumadian told me the beings here use the power of this land to animate the dead. As we explore further, we should be ready for anything. Clear your minds of anything we might have known in our previous lives. We need to be ready for anything from dancing piles of bones, to rabbits in vests with top hats."

"Or possibly talking reptiles?" Diane asked.

"Yes," Cat agreed, "for all we know, there could have been witches in Salem. Who is to say that the 'window' that brought us here did not work two ways?"

"Well, it is possible, but I would imagine it would be harder to go from a world that has magic to a world without it," I replied. "Remember, we got changed into what we are when we got here. One could reason that a being from here crossing over to our land would be changed equally. So their concepts and ideas would remain, but most of their abilities would be lost. Unless…"

"Unless what, J.D.?" Cat asked.

"It is possible the lands are contaminating each other because of our intrusion."

"Should we discuss things in front of it?" Robert pointed directly at Lumadian.

At first, I thought he was kidding, but looking into his face, I realized he was very serious.

"*It? Can I sting him just once, please?*" Lumadian stretched his neck and adjusted his position on my shoulder.

With his voice in my head I chuckled out loud.

"What did it say to you?" Robert's hand slid down to the pommel of his sword.

"He was insulted at being called 'it,'" I said. "You should be more polite, especially to the one who is helping us on our journey. Size and appearance is not important."

Grumbling, he pushed past me and inspected the chest. He wiped his hand over its surface. Lust crept into his face as he gazed at his fingertips for traces of dirt and didn't find any. "It has not been here long. No dust has settled on it." He attempted to take the chest, but it resisted his best attempts. Jean-Luc took a position next to him, and together they strained to move the chest, but their efforts were in vain.

I leaned to one side to get a better view and examined the chest more closely. The wood of the chest felt like a type of pine, rounded at the top, with a hinged lid that would swing open. On the front was a brass lock. I tried to open the lid, but the chest refused to be tampered with.

I left the chest and waited next to Diane, while Cat joined Robert and Jean-Luc at the chest. The three of them explored different means of getting inside. Robert tried slipping his sword under the chest, but he could not get any part of it to go under the box. He duplicated his effort with the lid, seeking to slide any portion of his sword under the rim, but the lid was so tightly sealed nothing could penetrate it.

"Stupid thing, I know how to get inside." Robert drew back his sword, with the obvious intent to strike it.

Jean-Luc reacted first, simply imposing himself between Robert and the chest. "Let me do this, my friend. You might damage what is inside when you slice the thing in two." The words calmed Robert, and he sheathed the sword.

Jean-Luc closed his eyes and brought his hands up in a prayer like fashion, except the tips of his fingers shifted away from him. He took a couple of deep breaths, moving his arms back and forth, keeping the hands together. He opened his eyes and was about to strike when I heard a scream in my head, "*Stop him!*"

I jumped at Jean-Luc, yanking his tunic. "Stop!"

Lumadian explained, "*There are protections on it to stop thieves.*" He flew over the chest and landed on its surface, looking at everyone. I could feel him doing something as a small part of my strength flowed from me to him. He reached down, grasping the lid in his tiny claws, and flew up. The lid gently opened to reveal the contents. Once the lid was fully open, he let go and returned to my shoulder. "*Had 'it' sliced the box, I would not have warned him.*"

The three around the chest peered inside. Lining the bottom of the chest were a fair quantity of gold coin and some gems. On top of the gold were a few rings, a stick, a folded brown cloak, and two brooches.

"*May I have one of the gems?*" Lumadian asked me.

"Of course you can!" I replied. Inching closer to the treasure, I reached inside and pulled out a bright shiny green one bigger than one of his tiny claws.

"Why are you giving him one?" Robert asked. "How can he use it?"

"He stopped Jean-Luc from getting hurt. He opened the chest. He's already helped us in fights. That entitles him to a share, too. He asked for a gem, so I gave him one. What is the matter with you? Ever since we entered these lands, you have been edgy and angry. We are your friends, remember?"

"Yes, you are my friends, but it is not." He indicated Lumadian again.

Lumadian had ignored the yelling since I had given him his prize, taking the gem and rubbing it on his muzzle over and over again. As Robert glared at Lumadian, my little companion swallowed the gem whole, sending a warm, pleasant sensation through my body.

Robert stopped talking and I could see the fire of anger in his eyes. He advanced on me, but Diane intercepted him.

"Robert, take a deep breath. J.D. was right. Lumadian is entitled to his share. What he does with his things is his business and his business alone." With that, she hastened over to me and scratched Lumadian under the chin. He produced a low rumbling hum as he rubbed his muzzle against her hand. I could feel something stirring inside me as a feeling of pleasure filled my body. I glanced at Lumadian, and the feeling stopped, but not before I heard him chuckle.

*"Did you have to eat it in front of him?"*

*"Do you always stop and think what you are eating before you eat it?"* He replied in my mind. *"Also, it gives me strength and allows for my growth."*

My friends and I divvied up the rest of the loot. Jean-Luc took the cloak, Diane took both brooches, Robert took two rings, and

I took the last ring and the stick. Each of us got four gems—they wouldn't include Lumadian in the division—and we let Robert carry the coins, which he had put in a sack. We formed a line down the hall with Robert and Jean-Luc in front, Cat behind them, and Diane and me in the rear. We slowed a little to give the others a chance to reach the end of the hall first. While we walked, she gently nudged me then slipped me the gems from her share.

"Don't feed all of them to him at once," she whispered. "We do not want to slow down his fighting prowess."

I could feel Lumadian swell with pride as I felt my strong attraction to her build. *"She is very nice for a human."* The feelings I was receiving from my companion diminished slightly, but not entirely.

We joined the rest of our friends, checking down each corridor and wondering which way we should travel. After a bit of a discussion, we decided to go up first, since we were sure there were floors above. With that decision made, we went to our left and climbed the stairs.

Lumadian glanced over at Robert. *"Just be sure,"* he continued, *"that power doesn't go to his head."*

# CHAPTER SEVENTEEN

I think it is important to point out to you, my reader, whoever you may be, that Lumadian wasn't a pet. He wasn't a good friend. He was an extension of me. He was as much as a part of me as the hand that writes this journal. He was my eyes when I couldn't see. Through him, I found courage I never knew I had.

\* \* \*

A loud noise off in the distance drew John's attention. The wind outside his cave whipped strongly, blowing the falling rain in through the opening, when a second thunderous boom reached him. Taking care to get out of the rickety chair, J.D. summoned a floating viewing ball that resembled a cat's eye. The sphere zipped out the entrance, stopped at the end of its maximum distance it could be away from its summoner, and hovered. He peered out through it into the night's gloom and saw a fire at the borders of his vision near the city of Port Haven.

"What have you done, Robert?" John asked in shock.

"This world is ours for the taking," The memory of Robert's voice echoed in his ears.

*I should have listened to Lumadian's warning then*, he thought as he reflected on the last words he had written. Scanning his home, he wished that things were different, but knew Fate still had not completely unfurled its complete path to him. He thought of his friends and the simple times and allowed himself to once again feel joy for the briefest of moments. He examined the text he had recorded thus far and murmured aloud, "Interesting. Even the way I recorded things changed from the time we were in Salem to the time we arrived here. So many things changed that day. In a way, I felt as if it was fun." Stopping for a moment, he rubbed his eyes, trying to remove the moisture there. "I cannot be distracted this way. I need my strength." He sat back down to gather his thoughts again. "I need to finish, and there is so much more to record." Finding the spot where he had left off, he continued.

# CHAPTER EIGHTEEN
## LATER CHILDHOOD

The staircase opened into a small viewing room with low benches against the wall. There was a door across from the stairs, next to the outer wall, and one on the opposite side. In the center was a large, gray stone statue of a human dressed in fancy etched plate mail.

I circled the statue. "He exudes a sense of menace, even for a statue. Why would the sword be carved in black stone?"

Robert scoffed and dismissed me with his hand. "They are exaggerating his features. Why else would they craft a sword with a four foot wide pommel on a seven foot sword?"

Cat stared into the eyes. "Leering down the stairs with his arms folded over his chest, he reminds me of you, Robert."

Robert side-stepped around the statue to stand next to Cat. "What?"

Diane glanced at them both. "Now, boys…"

Cat looked down for a few seconds before bouncing back. "Which way, J.D.?" His head swiveled from one door to the other.

"We go to the left." I maneuvered around the statue to the wooden door. The stonework here was in better shape than that on the previous floor, but there were still cracks, mainly on the walls and floors. We piled into a long hallway that disappeared around a corner. A single door was in front of us. With no other door in sight, we went in.

The room was spacious and well-decorated. There was a door on the left wall all the way at the end. Near us were two rows of two benches. At the far end of the room was a raised platform with a wooden podium in the center. Draped over the front of the podium was a black cloth trimmed with purple strings. There was a pattern of some kind on it, but it was too weathered and old for me to determine what it depicted. As we scanned the room, we noticed a few bodies slumped on the floor in front of the first row of benches.

Diane solemnly went over to the bodies, removing her symbol from under her blouse, but before she reached them, Robert stomped over and cut off their heads, even though they were lifeless.

"No use in taking chances, I say." Robert wiped his sword on one of the corpses' tunics and replaced it in his sheath.

Diane blinked her eyes several times, dumbfounded for a moment, before blasting him. "How dare you! How dare you, you ignorant dunce! How did you know they were not injured? How do you know what condition they were in?" She poked him repeatedly in the chest with her finger. "If you ever do anything like that again, you will have to deal with me! What's wrong with you? Even if they were those *things* that we encountered, they still deserve burial with their bodies intact." With her piece said, she did not wait for a reply, but simply knelt at the decapitated figures' sides and chanted softly.

Robert glared at us, but we all avoided his scornful gaze, trying to look like we were examining something in the room. Out of the corner of my eye, I watched the tense muscles in his neck and face ease from anger to sorrow. "All I was trying to do was avoid a conflict," Robert said meekly, before trudging out the room into the hall.

*"It's about time someone told him off,"* Lumadian said in my mind. *"You need to watch him closely."*

*"He'll be fine once we are out of here. He's a little jumpy. We all are. Robert likes to be the center of attention, Lumadian. And he is trying to adjust to all the strangeness we have encountered."*

Jean-Luc and I readied ourselves before the door we had yet not opened and tried the latch. It opened easily, revealing a deep closet filled with rotting robes that matched the banner adorning the podium. The smell of the moldy clothes and the stench of death were heavier in the confined space. In the far corner, we saw another body, huddled in a crouch, with her arms clutching herself. She had a few robes around her, as if in an attempt to conceal herself. At her side was an empty scabbard. To her left on the floor were a book, a vial, and a quill.

Jean-Luc called to Diane. "Diane, there is another one in here. She was hiding from something."

"Merci, Jean-Luc." Diane said to him as she surveyed the closet. Knocking the robes to the floor, she approached the huddled body. "Poor thing," she said as she knelt before the woman. We both saw the fright etched on the woman's face. After saying a few words, Diane picked up the book and brought it out into the room where Cat and Jean-Luc waited.

"Robert has not returned yet?" She asked looking around for him.

"No, he is still in the hall, I think." Cat came away from the podium with a sparkling gem that he closed his hand around.

Diane cautiously entered the hall. "Robert?"

"In here," was the distant reply.

Diane poked her head back into the room, calling us to join Robert. While we had searched the room, he had gone back and tried the door we had left behind when we arrived on this floor. It was clearly some type of bedroom. In the center of the room against the back wall was a huge bed, still draped in rotting covers. On the left of the bed was a wardrobe that went from the floor to the ceiling; the wood had rotted around whatever remained inside. On the outer wall was a narrow window slit that only revealed the darkened forest.

"Did you find anything?" Cat asked Robert. The object that had been in Cat's hand was gone.

Robert looked at Cat with an odd expression, as if he was trying to determine whether or not he should answer. After a moment Robert said, "No, there is not anything to find here."

After his reply I asked, "What about you, Cat? What did you find?"

Everyone watched Cat as he reluctantly pulled out a round, shiny, yellow gem.

*"That is nice,"* I heard in my head. *"He should be careful with it though. It is meant as a weapon."*

"Weapon?" I asked him, saying it out loud.

*"It is meant to be thrown at a target to hold them fast for a long time."*

"How do you know that?" I continued, speaking so that everyone could hear.

*"I know my gems!"* he said proudly, shifting his weight on my shoulder.

"Lumadian," I said, glancing from my companion to my other friends, "told me that this is a weapon to be used when we need to hold someone. All you have to do is throw it at your target." I looked at Lumadian for confirmation. He simply nodded.

With an even more pleased expression on his face, Cat put the bauble back into his pouch.

"Very well," Diane stated aloud. She seemed to be making sure her voice would get everyone's attention. "We need to get things straightened out. I realize the situation is weird. I will not deny that I have a bit of a problem with what has been going on.

We need to stick together, though." She held up her hand to Robert, who was about to say something, stopping him. "Whatever we have to do, it is best we do it so we can undo what was done and go home."

"I have a question, Diane," Jean-Luc said, as he stared forlornly out the window. He slowly spun. His face lost all expression. "What if we—or that is—if someone does not want to go back?"

Everyone peered at him a moment, pondering his words.

"What do you mean, Jean-Luc?" she asked.

"What if we want to stay in this world, after we help do what it is we need to do? I have never felt this way before. I have never been as athletic as I am here. The talents I have now far exceed anything I had before. We already have money. I have not even used this!" He retrieved the quarterstaff from his back and twirled it around in front of him building speed until the staff was a mere blur. Stopping the quarterstaff instantly, he continued, "I am not sure that when we are done, I would want to go back. This world seems so much more interesting." He petted the top of Lumadian's head. "Look at him! Lumadian is fascinating and incredible. Who knows what other objects of grandeur are out there to behold?" He stopped for a moment for it to sink in.

I was speechless, not knowing how to reply to my friend's statement. It was not like him to carry on with fiery zest about anything. After a moment I spoke up. "If any of you might be considering this, all I can say is we should continue doing what we can first. Once the time comes for us to decide whether to go back or not, it would be up to each individual to decide. Even if we all decide to stay here, we need to rescue our land and the people we love. Even though it might not be something we volunteered for, it is now our task to complete. Also, we should have no more petty arguments. We need all of us to be successful. We are, after all, friends. We need to remember that little detail.

With that in mind, we should tell each other everything that has changed about ourselves so no one is surprised by anything. Any trinkets you have, and the gifts you have figured out... everything you know, even if you think we already know it. Agreed?" I waited for my friends to nod before I continued. "Alright, I will go first. I have this bracer from the elves." I held up my wrist. "This ring and dagger are also from them. I also received from the elves a pouch of spell components for my spells. I have this ring from the chest and this stick."

"*Wand,*" Lumadian corrected me.

"Wand," I restated, holding it back up. "I have no clue what any of it does. Diane?"

"I have the two brooches from the chest, this armor, mace, and my symbol. The armor is nice, and with it I feel great. The mace is light. The symbol seems to help against these animated dead things, and it somehow lets me heal you, but I do not know how."

Nodding at her, I continued, "Who wants to go next?"

Jean-Luc spoke first. "I have this quarterstaff. I have not had a chance—no—I have not wanted to use it yet. These leather armlets protect me as if I was wearing leather over my whole body." He extended his arm to Diane and asked, "Feel my arm above them." Diane complied and told us that it felt as though the arm was protected by leather. "I also have this ring, which allows me to move with greater agility. This cloak allows me to stick to walls. Watch this." He put his hands against the wall and went right up it. Jumping to the floor, he then put his foot on the wall and strolled up to the ceiling, then across the ceiling. Once he was over by where he had been sitting, he jumped, did a flip, and landed on his feet in front of us.

"How—" I floundered. "—did you know it did that?"

"Well, the funny part is, when I put the cloak on, I knew what it did. I can't explain it."

"Well," Robert began, "I have this armor, shield and sword. I have not noticed much out of the ordinary about them. I still get hit, although I do not have to repair the armor. It does it on its own. I do not even know if the other items are anything special. I have no idea what this ring does. But the other ring—" he took it off to show us. It was a gold ring twisted with silver. "—gives me even more strength."

"Do you have anything else, Robert?" I asked.

"No, that is all. If I had anything else, I would have told you," he replied with a scoff.

"Great," I replied. "Cat?"

Cat's gaze darted around the room at all of us, then at his own feet before speaking. "These gloves give me strength in my hands, and these—" He pushed the center of his hand. Instantly the glove contracted around his wrist becoming one with his body as five small hooked, sharp blades extended from all of the digits. He pressed again and it became a glove. "These boots allow me to jump far and land on my feet, as well as having claws on them, too. This pelt allows... This pelt allows me to do this." His clothes melded onto his body, darkening to black. His body enlarged and he fell to all fours. His fingers melded together like a fist, then into a paw. His face shifted as fangs emerged from a muzzle. The entire process was extremely quick and when it was done, a black cat replaced our friend. He was huge, possibly three or four hundred pounds. Although I knew he was my friend, his yellowish eyes brought fear to my heart. He shifted back and joined us.

"Why did you conceal this from us, Cat?" Diane asked. "And are you still... you... while you are a jaguar?"

"Yes, I have the body of a cat. I can still think, but it feels like I was always a cat. I have senses and what I would guess as the instincts of a cat. It's weird to explain. I did not know how I felt about it, and I did not know if you'd consider it witchery."

Lumadian spoke to me. "*Amilmadra explained that everyone got things based on what she saw inside. It was not by chance he is known as 'Cat'.*"

Trying to calm my friend I said, "It's not that unusual, and it fits you well."

"I got an idea," Jean-Luc offered. "Put this cloak on over your other one."

Cat did as he was asked, donning the cloak. Once on, it completely concealed the pelt underneath.

"Now," Jean-Luc continued. "Try changing—you can understand us while you are a cat?"

"Yes, Jean-Luc." Cat shifted again, replacing himself with his black cat.

"That is good, Cat." Jean-Luc said. "Now, try going up the wall."

We all watched as Cat approached the wall and gingerly put his paw against it. The wall cracked against his weight but held up. Cat gingerly tried moving up the wall, and was able to advance straight up it without any difficulty. He jumped down, landing on his feet. Up until that time, I had never thought I'd ever see a cat grin, but I swear I saw him do so.

"Come here, Cat, before you change," Diane told him. Cat complied moving over next to her. She reached out and touched his muzzle, running her fingers along it. She continued feeling his face, moving her fingers to his ears, as she gently scratched between them. We were all a bit surprised when he closed his eyes and purred. She continued her fingers down his back, letting her nails run over his back. When she reached his tail she softly pulled it, causing him to open his eyes and look back at her. She smirked at him, then lifted his tail and said, "Well at least you are still male." She let go and smiled.

When Cat changed back, he was deep red in color. Then all of us broke out in laughter, breaking the tension that had been building for some time. It felt good to be able to laugh with my friends again.

"Well, we should get to exploring again." I started to rise.

Robert held up a hand. "Wait a moment. What about Lumadian?"

"What about him?" I asked.

"You said everyone had to tell everything, so what about him? *He*," Robert took the time to emphasize the pronoun, "is part of us now. He should have to tell us about himself."

I stood there for a moment before I asked my little companion, "*What do you say?*"

"*I am still mad at him.*"

"Just a moment," I said to my friends and had a discussion with Lumadian in my mind.

"*I realize you two got off to a bad start, but we should all try to get along.*"

"*I do not trust him. He would be a nice snack for a Husuniak.*"

Ignoring the fact that I did not know what a 'Husuniak' was, or the fact that I probably did not want to know what it was, I pressed on. "*Everyone is curious about you, including me, and could you blame them for wanting to know about such a fascinating and intelligent creature like yourself?*"

Lumadian puffed out his chest. "*I suppose not. I cannot blame you for being a human. What do you want to know?*"

"He wants to know what *interesting* facts we want to know about him." I exaggerated the word 'interesting' with a bit more stress, hoping my friends would pick up on the clue—like they had always been able to in the past. I also hoped Lumadian would not.

Diane was the first to speak, sitting right next to me, almost shoulder to shoulder. I felt her hand brush against mine again, and her fingers danced on mine. "Well, first what else does he eat?"

Lumadian ran from my shoulder to hers, startling her a bit. I could see her stiffen. "*She is a good one. Are you going to mate with her?*"

"Lumadian!" I shouted aloud, making everyone jump a little.

"What did he say?" Diane asked me.

"He said that he wanted to give you a kiss." I waited to see what each of them would do.

Diane caressed his muzzle, gently kissed him on the nose, and smiled at him.

Lumadian shook his head back and forth a little and ran back to my shoulder. After he settled down, I asked him, "Why did Amilmadra ask you to come with me?"

"*She did not ask me to come with you. She asked me to teach you and for you to keep me safe.*" Lumadian thought back to me as I started to feel a bit hungry.

"*Alright then, what are you going to teach me?*"

"*I will teach you how to control the energies and how to use them against your foes. I will also share all my intelligence with you bit by bit as you are ready. We are now Se'da'tais.*"

"*What does that mean?*"

"*I do not know the word in your language, but the closest meaning would be 'one from two.'*"

I cleared my throat and I felt another hunger pain. I held my stomach. My other hand still held Diane's. "Lumadian likes fresh meat and some berries. He gains strength from eating an occasional gem." I stopped to hear a complaint from Robert, but it seemed like he was honestly trying to listen, so I continued. "Lumadian will be instructing me on how to use the energies of Elilith to do various things. He communicates by speaking in my mind." I stopped for a moment.

"Is your tail poisonous?" I asked him verbally so that everyone could hear the question.

*"Yes, to a certain degree. A little sting and you go to sleep, a big sting and go to sleep much, much longer, possibly forever."*

"He said that the sting could put people to sleep, from a little while to permanently."

"Thank you Lumadian. If no one else has anything…" I paused a moment.

"What does the book say, Diane?" Jean-Luc asked.

"I have not even checked it out yet." She retrieved the book. The tome was a bit aged, with its pages yellowed and the leather binding worn and cracked. Painted on the cover of the leather book was a rose with purple petals. Carefully she opened the cover, which read:

Merial of the Black Fist
My Journal to Supremacy

"Interesting way to start a journal," Diane commented before flipping a page and reading aloud.

"Second Metalday, in the Month of Martel

"I passed my initiation today without a problem. My task was simple: steal from a band of thugs we encountered on the road without my companions knowing I did it. It was child's play, really, and I acquired not one item, but two: a long sword and an ornate brooch. I say, always exceed what is expected of you.

"First Freeday in the Month of Leafburst

"Today, our mission was to hit someone who had gotten close to discovering us, and kill Zachary, a person traveling with us, so it would appear like the other party did it. It was so easy. Zachary had cut his adversary badly and stood gloating over his foe. They were in such a position that they were out of sight of the rest of the combatants. I crept up on Zachary's blind side and tapped him on the shoulder. When he spun around, I stabbed him through the groin and made it look like his opponent had done it."

Diane flipped through the book. She did not see anything of note until a certain entry caught her eye and she read it to us.

"Third Fireday, in the Month of Hearth-Fire

"I have finally reached a position where I am happy and comfortable in the guild. The seasonal rains started today, and the wind picked up. The guild was progressing with its battle with various towns when we came across a stranger dressed in black leather armor. He was dazed, but there was strength in him. He recovered and immediately dominated everyone, somehow giving us inner powers. I was jealous that someone who had only arrived a short time ago could instantly become our leader, but I was silent, lest I feel his wrath. I must say, though, that he did give us focus, turning our attentions to the elves. I tried to discover who he was, searching through prophecies until I found:

*The land will be forever once the stranger in black appears,*
*New directions, new times all due to him,*
*The banded hand arrives to stop him,*
*A judgment determines the Fate of the land."*

"That must be him!" Cat said excitedly. "What else does it say? What is the last entry?"
"One moment, Cat." Diane flipped through the journal. "Here is the last one."

"First Clouday, in the Month of Twilight-Freeze

"We were all deceived by the man. I discovered where he came from and what his actual plan was for us. We are mere puppets to him. He has released the death upon us. The dead do not argue with him. I cannot believe he sacrificed our base. If this journal survives for someone to view—since the dead care not for things like this—I will say that you must first stop the attacks on the elves. The stranger somehow gains strength from that fight. Disguise yourselves as members of the clan. You will find cloaks with patches on the lower level. Leave Master Erik Von Breinenhouser's home and follow the path deeper into the woods, past the mine. The road will fork. Take the right path no matter what it resembles. You will see a small hut. Go to the door and speak these words, "The stranger gives me strength." That will give you access to their base of operations. You need to defeat Grazalian. Doing so will shatter their will and will cause strife as others attempt to take his power. I hear them coming. I do not want to die. I hear them coming. I do not want to be among the undead.'"

"That is weird," Jean-Luc said, after Diane finished the reading.

"What is weird, Jean-Luc?"

"I feel sorry for her, even though she was not a nice person."

"Whatever one reaps, they will also sow," Robert sneered. "You should not feel compassion for someone as evil as that woman obviously was."

Diane raised her hands and closed her eyes. "You shall love your neighbor as yourself."

"If these were my 'neighbors' I might, but for things here, I do not," Robert countered. "I suppose I could feel *compassion* because she became one of those undead things. It was a sad way to meet her end. I would even feel sorry if it happened to Lumadian. It is a terrible way to go."

*"Was that his way of complimenting me?"*

*"That is his way,"* I replied.

After the awkward silence passed, we all got up. I asked, "Do we want to finish our explorations, or go get what we need and continue?"

"If there is a chance to save anyone here, I think it is important to explore this keep first," Diane said. "If we manage to save one person, the extra time will be worth the effort."

We all agreed and left the room to search for the stairs leading up.

Cat stopped us when we passed the statue. "Look!" He shouted and nearly jumped up to the statue's face. We all gathered around, wondering what Cat had observed.

"I do not see anything," Robert said.

"I do not see anything either," I said, although it seemed familiar.

"It is the scientist in the moving painting. The one who created—what did you call it J.D., Elilith? The one who caused the accident." Cat sounded excited at his discovery.

"You are right, Cat," Diane confirmed.

"Is that so?" An evil grin came across Robert's face.

"I am positive," Cat confirmed.

"He is right, there is no doubt," I acknowledged.

"Great. That is all I need to know." Robert plowed into it with his shield, completely separating the figure from the pedestal. The statue toppled and crashed on the stone floor shattering it into pieces that flew across the floor and down the stairs. A booming voice echoed in the chamber.

"How dare you destroy a tribute to me? You shall all be punished!"

The voice was so loud, that my ears rang, and I stumbled. Cat jumped back to the wall, sticking to it. A blue mist seeped up from the base of the statue. It flowed to us, and I heard chanting in my mind coming from Lumadian. The vapor washed over Robert first, as my companion's chanting stopped. Lumadian's protective spell covered Robert's body in a soft red light, as if he were silhouetted by a dying campfire. The mist continued to Diane, but again a red glow covered her body. Next was Jean-Luc, and then me. I felt the mist pass over me, but felt no different. Finally, the mist reached Cat. I expected to see the same red light, but the vapors swirled around him.

*"Cat leapt out of range of my ability to aid him! I am sorry!"* Lumadian squealed in panic.

I watched my friend's human body transform, much like before when he demonstrated his ability to assume a panther form. He got bigger, as big as the feline form, then continued growing. His clothes seemed about to be ripped to shreds when they merged into his changing body. His skin coloring went from pale to white, with large brown spots. His fingers merged together and blackened into something resembling hooves. So, too, did his feet, merging toes into hooves instead of paws. A mop of a tail grew out from his backside. His mouth elongated to a muzzle. Within a few moments, he wore a shape I had seen in many pastures back home. He was a cow. His moo sounded like painful wailing. I turned away, trying not to laugh. I did not know which was funnier, seeing him as a cow, or seeing him as a cow standing on a vertical wall.

*"Cat was out of my protection radius. I only could protect those very close. I am sorry."*

"It is fine. You did your best. I notice you saved Robert, too. Was that by choice?" I asked.

*"Yes, I made sure he was in it first. Even though he caused it, I could not—I wanted to start over and try for your sake to not hate him."* He chirred to me, disappointed that he could not help Cat.

I reached up and scratched his chin softly, then withdrew a small fruit I had gotten from the elves from one of my pouches and gave it to him. He took it reluctantly, eating with care.

"Cat," I called, trying to see his expression.

The cow gingerly stepped forward until he reached where the floor met the wall; then cautiously stepped off the wall and onto the floor.

"Can you understand me, Cat? If you can, nod your head once."

Cat cocked his head to the side, as if puzzled, then nodded his head once and mooed painfully.

"Cat, I am so sorry. I did not mean to hurt you." Robert seemed to be feeling terrible in light of our recent talk about supporting each other.

Diane spoke. "J.D., you said Lumadian speaks in your mind. Could he do the same with Cat?"

I nudged Lumadian, who was finishing his berry when I heard his answer. *"I could try, but you do not want me to contact him."*

*"Why would I not want that?"*

*"If I cannot contact him that would mean his mind is blocked. I can only communicate with one human at a time. It is hard to explain, but think of it this way: If I could have communicated freely with all of you, wouldn't I do that instead of making you repeat everything like a parrot? I can, however, contact an animal's mind. It is sort of like probing something that cannot defend its mind. All intelligent creatures immediately block it—that is—all other intelligent creatures with whom I have not bonded."*

*"We need to talk about that later. For now, please try."*

Lumadian closed his eyes and concentrated on my friend who had wandered near the window. We waited for his response for what seemed like an eternity before Lumadian spoke in my mind.

*"I have good and bad news, I'm afraid. Part of him is blocked from me, which means he has part of his mind. The other part, though, is an open book. That part is basically how to live and function as a cow. It will take him time to answer or sort things in his mind since basically, as a cow, it is an automatic response to his environment to live with any concerns. Does that make sense?"*

I nodded and was about to respond when Jean-Luc stepped over to me. "Could I speak with you for a moment, J.D.?" He gestured at the door. I followed him out into the hall.

"I did not want to add to Cat's troubles, but look at him again," Jean-Luc told me.

Curious, I took closer note of my friend. My position allowed me to view him from the side. His head was a typical shape with the ears and tufts of hair. His body shape was that of a healthy specimen of what he was. He had a tail like a rope whip, and his udder hung deeply under him. "I do not see what you mean," I told Jean-Luc.

"He has an udder," Jean-Luc whispered.

I suddenly realized what my friend was hinting at and shuddered, thinking what the mist would have done to us had Lumadian not protected us. "Come back, and we will not mention it. I will tell everyone what Lumadian told me."

I summarized my companion's words. "While Cat is not paying attention, he will be as any cow that would graze in a field. In fact, you would not be able to tell them apart. When we have his attention, he will be himself, but that instant will always be in check, since the spell wants him to exist as a cow. I have no idea on how to change him back or what we should do. Does anyone else?"

Diane stepped forward and scratched Cat behind his ear. "Oh, Cat, how do you always get to be the one who ends up in situations like this? Cat, can you hear me?"

All the response she got was a pitiful mooing from our friend.

I approached Diane and whispered softly in her ear. I asked Jean-Luc to run downstairs with Robert and fetch the drawers from the desk and return with them. Without questioning me, they both left and returned as requested. I asked them to put the drawers in the bedroom and come back. They had inquisitive expressions on their faces, but did as I asked. Once they did, Diane led Cat into the room and shut the door. We waited for a while before we heard the door open. Diane emerged with Cat, who was back as his black panther.

"Is that you, Cat?" I felt stupid after I asked, since I knew it was him.

The panther nodded and stretched, crouching down and back on his front, then stretching up and forward on his back. He rubbed Diane's leg and paced back over to me, doing the same.

"I think he wanted to thank you for the idea," she said.

"You are welcome, my friend. I did not expect it to work this well though."

"What idea did you have, J.D.?" Robert asked.

"Well, Robert, he was a cow with an *udder*, so the mooing we heard was a plea to be milked. Once he was milked, he could concentrate on Diane. I suggested that by taking his panther shape, it might restore a better portion of his mind. It worked. The question now is: should we have him try to go back to human? Remember that his 'human' form is currently a cow."

"How did you know it would work?" Jean-Luc asked.

"Well, when he transformed into a cow, he did not fall off the wall, but stepped off it, which suggests he still had the cloak that allowed him to do those things. It was reasonable to assume he could change if we could get his attention."

Diane came over and held my arm. "I do not think we should risk it right now. Perhaps we will find something to change him back. Who knows what portion of him we might lose if he goes back to a cow?"

"Cat, are you comfortable staying in your cat shape for now?" I asked him.

He nodded and showed his teeth as I chuckled.

*"Lumadian,"* I thought. *"Try to contact him again, please."*

Lumadian only took a brief moment to report back to me, *"I cannot contact any portion of his mind."*

"We should continue exploring, and after we are done in this building, we can determine what the best course of action is." With everyone in agreement, we went into the corridor and down the unexplored region.

As the hall wrapped to the right, we saw a set of stairs leading up. Peering up the stairs, I noticed the cracks in the walls diminished even more. Without discussion, we climbed the stairs to the floor above.

# CHAPTER NINETEEN
# HOPES AND DREAMS

The corridor followed the outer wall before disappearing around a corner to the right. In front of us was a sturdy, oak door free of wear. I tapped the tip of my dagger along the wall. "There are no signs of age up here. Whatever happened did not reach up this far."

I tried the door, but discovered it was locked. I asked Lumadian to open the door like he did the chest.

*"It is not held by a spell, but by a simple lock."*

"Lumadian said it is held by a normal lock. Should we try to force it?" I asked my friends.

Cat solved the problem by leaping on it, sending the door crashing. The room was another fancy bedroom. There was a bed and a wardrobe. At the foot of the bed was a large, empty bucket. I could see Cat sniffing the air. He bounded over to the drawers and rubbed them.

Diane edged into the narrow but long room and opened a drawer filled with feminine clothes, still fresh as the day they were put in the drawer. Opening all of them revealed the same thing. "Interesting," Diane said. "These are all silk. Cat must have been able to smell the *scent*, if you know what I mean." She winked at

Cat as she went to leave, but not before she palmed a few pieces and hid them in her supplies.

We continued down the hall to a trio of doors, one on each wall. I noticed the floor here was polished marble.

Without a word, Jean-Luc tried the door on our left. It opened without difficulty. Oil lamps hanging from the ceiling illuminated an even more spacious room. A definitely feminine bed took up the entire back wall, with a large picture frame above it. The frame, however, had pitch on it, obscuring whatever was underneath. The pelts of two very large black bears covered the floor. Along one wall was a bureau, and the opposite side had a monstrously large desk. We began searching the room for anything we could find.

I bent over one of the rugs. "Well, at least they have the same type of animals here, so that is good. Maybe the two worlds aren't as different as I thought."

Robert chuckled. "And how do you know the bears aren't one of those bleed effects the man told us was occurring?"

Before I could reply, Diane spoke from the desk. "There are notes here in the same penmanship as the person who wrote that book. She was in a position of authority for sure, since some of these are her plans on how to extend her power evenly. Also there is no ink well or quill here and some of the ink is streaked as if someone snatched it off the desk, suggesting she left in a hurry." Diane got up from the desk and closed the door. "Look," she continued. "She could have easily barred the door from her own room." Diane's fingers traced an elaborate metal bar that extended beyond the doorframe and latched into place to lock. "Why would she not stay in her room?"

With a sarcastic tone, Robert replied, "I do not know, but why would she wear an over-sized shirt like this?" He held up a thin, pale blue dress that was extremely short, like it would barely cover the thigh.

Diane smirked at Robert. "That is a dress."

Robert scoffed. "Who could endure a temptress, then, who would wear something like this?"

Diane giggled. "I do not know, but with the woman being in power over men, it would be an excellent way for her to motivate them. Isn't that right, J.D.?"

I jerked my head away from the bureau drawer I had been searching and gave my attention to my friends. I had heard what they said, but my mind was elsewhere. "I am sorry, what did I miss?"

Lumadian instantly suggested, "*Say the phrase, 'why not put it on'?*"

Without thinking about it I repeated the words. "Why not put it on?"

Diane laughed and took the garment from Robert. She sashayed over to me and whispered, "Only if you agree to do anything I say."

I felt my face redden as I put the pieces of the conversation together. I glanced at Lumadian, then Diane, then back to Lumadian, who only nodded.

"That would also go for Lumadian," she whispered, wiping the grin from his face.

"This is unusual though," I said, trying to change the subject. "This isn't a picture. It is a mirror. In the corner here you can see a part that isn't covered up."

Just as Diane was about to add the garment to her supplies, Cat tried to pull my pants, and got my leg instead, biting me. I yelled in pain and he promptly released me, as if realizing what he'd done. "What is it, Cat?" I rubbed the slightly bleeding wound with my hand.

He dug his nails into the bedding, and hopping partially up on the bed so his forelegs rested on the bedding and legs were on the floor, he attempted to pull the covers, but his claws shredded the cloth and he knocked over another bucket.

Robert pushed the covering aside to reveal a thin, tapered blade with a wavy end. The blade was so blackened that it did not reflect anything. Robert patted down the bed, but did not find a scabbard. Rolling the blade in the bed sheets, he tied the bundle to his back.

While Robert had been examining Cat's discovery, Jean-Luc searched around the armoire. "Hey, I think I've discovered a hidden compartment." He pressed down on an irregularity in a floorboard and uncovered a compartment holding a belt with vials of yellow liquid attached to it. There was also a miniature sword that fit easily in the palm of Jean-Luc's hand. It was designed like a long sword, with gems and writing etched on the side. Handing the belt to Diane, he put the pin sword in one of his belt pouches.

We were about to leave when Cat ripped one of the bearskin rugs aside. Inlaid into the floor was a mosaic of a humanoid face with demonic features. Instead of eyes, there were balls of flames. The skin was a deep orange. Cat looked up at us, then back to the painting and snorted loudly.

I stood and stared for a moment before I asked, "I wonder how he found it?"

Cat, excited by the question, pawed the floor near the image without touching it. His tail went straight up and waved about with agitation. He seemed to attempt to talk in English by flexing his jaw differently, but all that came out was a growl, then a purr until he gave up.

"How can he communicate with us?" Diane asked.

I have an idea." I went to the desk and gathered the papers containing old orders. "Give me the vial of ink and a quill, Diane." Diane handed them to me. I sat at the desk to write something down. After I was done, I asked Diane to come to the desk and write down what I called out. Sitting in front of Cat, I held out the paper to him. On the paper, I had written the alphabet in nice big letters. I said, "Now, I will indicate each letter. When I get to a letter you want, nod your head. When you are completely done, let me know somehow. Do you understand?"

*"He is still himself, you know. You do not have to talk down to him,"* Lumadian reminded me.

"Well, when I departed my village, I never thought I would be speaking to my friend the panther. He will have to forgive me."

Cat nodded his head. I moved my finger from letter to letter. The first letter he selected was 'I,' followed by 'smellaholeunderthepicture'. Once I got to the 'e', Cat jumped up on me and licked me right on the lips with his tongue.

Diane giggled. "Oh J.D., I think Cat wants to baiser sur les lèvres with you. He says there he can smell a chamber under the mosaic."

Cat got off me, and I swore I could hear him chuckle.

"Question now is," Jean-Luc said, stepping to the picture, "is if we actually want to try to open the thing."

*"Remember what happened to Cat when Robert messed with something?"* Lumadian stabilized himself after nearly being knocked off my shoulder by my overreacting furry friend.

"Good point, Lumadian," I said so everyone could hear. "Lumadian reminded me of Cat's predicament—that we could end up with much worse than what happened to Cat by messing with something we do not understand. I do not know about you, but I do not want to end up that way. No offence, Cat."

"Perhaps, there is a solution in the woman's journal," Robert suggested.

"It is possible, but unlikely," Diane said. "I would not record that kind of information in my journal."

"Alright, we will search the rest of *Master* Erik Von Breinenhouser's mansion. When we are done, if we do not find a means of opening this hiding hole, we will decide at that time. That way, we do not take unnecessary chances."

We were about to leave when I heard Lumadian say, "*Why not try your vision sense spell?*"

"One moment. Lumadian has a suggestion, I think." I asked, "*What do you mean? What is a vision sense spell? How can I do something like that?*"

"*Concentrate on the object. Think that you want to see those things that are hidden. Oh, and for this spell, gesture with your hands in front of you. Not only does it clear the path from where you are to where you are concentrating of errant magical energies, but it plants ideas in people's minds that it does something much more. The more they believe in a spell, the better it will work. Personally, I have never needed to do it, but your kind usually does.*"

I shrugged and attempting to do as he asked, moving my hands back and forth with the index and middle finger together tipped away from me, and the rest folded in on my palms. I felt silly, but I looked at the face, trying to get my eyes to not focus directly on it. After a few moments I was going to give up when I saw something. The burning eyes had an eerie radiance coming from them. I could also see a shine from the snout of the demonic face. Without realizing it, I bent low and pressed the eyes and snout at the same time. The panel pushed down a little then slid under the floor.

Inside was a necklace of stunning beauty encrusted with gems I could not even begin to identify. I could also see the strange light coming from it that I saw from the panel. In fact, I noticed that my friends had glows around the items they were either given or found. Also inside was a jar of a thick, black liquid with a big cork. The stench coming from the jar was overwhelming even with the stopper tightly in place. Also in the small compartment were a dainty lady's ring with two pearls and a little bag. I pulled everything out and slid the panel back. I gave the bag and all its contents, plus the ring and necklace to Diane. Holding the jar up in my hand, I said, "I have a bad feeling about this, and I don't know why. What should we do with it?"

Robert responded first. "We should smash it and leave."

Diane shook her head. "Haven't you learned anything about smashing things? If John senses something from it, let's leave it."

Robert grumbled then sulked away.

I left the jar on the bureau. "If we discover what it is later, we can come back for it. For now, we should leave it."

Diane inspected the bag as we retreated and nodded her head. "It's a bag of cosmetics. There is a mirror, rouge, and a strange cylinder with a waxy red substance inside."

The room across the hall was also unlocked. As Robert entered, a man in heavy armor swung a sword at him, but Robert jumped back, plowing everyone into the hall. He snatched the shield from his back clumsily and barely deflected the second blow. Robert lunged forward with his blade trying to pierce his adversary through the heart, but his blade was deflected by another man who seemed to have been waiting just inside the door, hidden against the inner wall.

I scanned inside the room, trying to see around Robert, and saw five people, but did not know if anyone else was inside. A man in back dressed in a purple and black robe chanted, "Freeze them in their tracks!" Snow shot forth from his fingertips.

Acting mostly on instinct, I also waved my hands, and a warming protection surrounded us. The man's spell hit the protection and melted into nothingness. I countered with a spell of fire, tossing it right at the armed man in the doorway. He stumbled back, giving us the opportunity to rush into the room. Jean-Luc met the man next to the door; Robert squared up with the armored man; I confronted the man with spells; Diane went after a female in a long black dress; and Cat advanced on a man dressed in brown and green leathers.

Jean-Luc went to throw a punch at the man, but yanked his hand back. "He has something dripping from his sword!" With a monstrous leap, he jumped over the man and drew his quarterstaff. He whirled around to strike, but the man showed remarkable agility as well, dodging my friend's swing and grabbing the staff. Using Jean-Luc's momentum, he tossed him across the floor.

Robert continued to swing his sword, but his opponent laughed as he deflected the blow with ease. "Is that the best you've got, Robert? My ten year old page could do better. I, Darren the Bold, will show you how it's done!" Then Darren did a quick swipe with his blade, hitting Robert hard in his arm. I could see that he was deeply wounded even though there was not a lot of blood showing.

Cat stalked his foe, ignoring the combat around him. I could hear his target call, "I now take control of this beast to do my bidding." Cat continued to pursue his prey. The man shouted, "Hold this creature as if stone." Cat simply leaped on the man. I heard a muffled cry, then silence. Out of the corner of my eye, I could see Cat had crushed the man's neck with his powerful jaws.

Diane held her mace and pulled out the symbol from under her blouse and let it dangle in plain view as she advanced on the other woman. She, too, wielded a symbol. It looked like a coffin with a skull on the lid. The woman tossed what appeared to be a copy of one of those round marbles Cat had found earlier, hitting Diane square in the chest. Diane stopped and an expression of shock came over her face. She was immobilized from the effects of the bauble.

I carefully studied my adversary, watching his actions so that I could use them at some later date. His robes matched Azen's, with symbols like those the necromancer we had fought outside in the swamp. He gestured with his hands, but I jumped at him, cutting his movement short. He began to chant, 'Drain the life from the one I confront and give me all the…" He stopped mid-sentence. It was then I noticed that Lumadian had landed on his shoulder. I attempted to ask him what he was doing but received no response. I realized why the man's face had drained white as a ghost's. Lumadian's tail was touching the necromancer's neck, but not penetrating it.

*"Order him to surrender or your 'pet' will kill him."*

I pointed at Cat and his victim. "Order your remaining men to surrender, or you will know what it is to be one of those undead you command. I will order my pet to kill you."

"Lower your arms, now!" he commanded and they complied.

I did not, however, let my guard down. I gruffly issued orders to my friends, hoping they'd understand. "Take their weapons, but do them no harm."

Robert grumbled then spit in Darren's face as he sheathed his weapon. "We will finish this someday."

"Cat, come here," I said, hoping he would understand. He came over to sit next to me. "Why have you come here?" I asked the necromancer. "We are not the elves your band seems to loathe so much."

"Before we continue, do you mind?" He stared at Lumadian.

*"Please come back and sit on my shoulder for now. Be ready for anything."*

*"You are the boss."* He flew over to me.

"We normally only kill elves, but we also kill those who trespass on our lands."

"Your lands?" Robert exclaimed. "You are the ones taking their lands and attacking people on their lands."

"Silence your dog, or the conversation will not continue," the necromancer ordered. He seemed a bit more confident with Lumadian back on my shoulder.

I thought Robert was going to explode. Holding up my hand, I said, "Your time will come. For now be silent." I tilted my head to the side and put on my best serious expression, which I struggled to maintain when he replied.

"Yes sir, I was out of line. Please forgive my outburst," Robert said.

"You will be punished later." I shifted my gaze back to the necromancer. "Tell me what we want to know, and I will consider letting you live."

"Why should I tell you anything, since you will probably kill me anyway?"

"Had I wanted you dead, you would be so right now and I would get my information from one of your friends. Perhaps the woman would tell me what I wanted to know." I tried to sound ruthless, but did not know how well I was doing.

The necromancer spoke in a sly and cold tone. "You bring up a good idea. How about a show of good faith by allowing one of the members of my group to leave?"

I tried to mimic his tones. "Are you crazy? So they can go warn others?"

"So, you do plan to kill us? I mean, what do you plan on doing after this conversation is over? Are you so concerned that we will warn someone? It shouldn't matter when you would release us if you truly are going to keep your word."

"We will worry about that when we come to it." I touched Lumadian on the crown of his head. *"Go get that black jar for me."*

"What is it you want to know?" my prisoner asked.

"Who developed the curse on the statue and how can it be reversed?"

"The *woman* here did, and she is the only one who knows the answer to that question. Her name is Brendalynn."

I directed my attention to Brendalynn. Lumadian flew in and gave the jar to me. I watched my captives' eyes fill with surprise. I grinned and said, "I am waiting."

"You have to go on a quest for me," she replied, mimicking my expression.

"And if we kill you?"

"Then I hope the people affected by my curse will enjoy chewing their cud and giving milk," she said gleefully. "Oh, and I hope they were not male to begin with, otherwise they will have other unexpected joys as well."

"Well, that is senseless. How could a cow go on a quest?"

"Exactly." She sounded smug.

"So, give us a quest to accomplish."

"Why would you need to break the curse? None of you are affected."

"Are you questioning me now?"

She thought for a moment then cast a spell, moving her arms back and forth like a serpent. Our hands tightened on our weapons before she stopped and explained. "In order to fulfill your request, I must finish the binding of the curse. Your healer can confirm what I speak is the truth. All curses need their releasing element."

I coughed and peered at Diane. "Well, does she speak the truth?"

Diane was confused at first, as if unsure how to answer, but then simply nodded.

"Very well then," I said. "You may continue. Carefully."

I watched as she gestured, closing her eyes for a moment. When she was done, she opened them and said, "I want you to dispose of a problem for me. You need to defeat Almator. He controls the mining complex not far from here. Doing so will lift the curse. The cursed one must be there at Almator's defeat. I only hope you have not waited terribly long to seek me out. Oh, and if I should 'accidentally' die before you can do this, then whoever is effected will live the rest of their days in a pasture."

"What do you mean 'terribly long'?" I asked.

"You have seven days from the time the change occurred to deal with the curse, or the effects are quite permanent."

"And what do you think of all of this?" I asked the leader.

"What she does with her spells is her affair." He laughed for a moment. "But I must admit, I like the idea."

"Very well, we accept the challenge." I felt a slight tingle, and I knew that what I accepted was the completion of her spell. I asked Lumadian, *"Is there a way to erase us from their minds?"*

*"Of course there is a way, but this is a bit more difficult. Try to find out how long they've known about you."*

I asked the necromancer, "How long have you known we were here?"

*"Well, that was subtle,"* I heard in my mind.

"Once the statue was destroyed, Marla—was notified." He cursed himself, as if trying to cover up her name.

"Marla is it, and not Brendalynn? I see." I attempted to cast a spell on them while they were off-guard. I felt the energies flow easily from me to cover all of them in ghostly images of feathers. They lunged at us, but not quickly enough. Their eyelids drooped then closed as they fell unconscious to the floor.

"They are sleeping for now," I said a bit apprehensively, "but I still do not have a clue about what to do."

Robert suddenly collapsed on the floor, and I noticed that blood drenched his wounded arm.

She rushed over to him and clutched his good arm. With her symbol extended and a soft chant, I saw healing light flowing from Diane to Robert. Within seconds, he was completely restored. Her own arm trembled and she moaned slightly in discomfort.

*"I have an idea,"* Lumadian said. A mischievous feeling swept over me, and I shivered. *"Take what you want from them, pick them up, and follow me down the stairs."*

"Search the bodies, then carefully follow me downstairs. Lumadian has an idea." My friends and I loaded their items into a bag to sort later. Although it took a while, we helped each other carry the bodies to the room with the broken statue. Cat kept a lookout for anything else.

Once they were all set, Lumadian suggested, *"Imagine the statue whole again; let it be completely repaired in your mind then use your eyes to see it."*

I did as my scaled friend suggested, concentrating on the figure. An image appeared on the pedestal where the figure had been. I could see every part of it. I raised my hand and said, "Restore that which was destroyed." I saw a pinkish light lift a small piece of the statue's nose and set it into the ghostlike image. Bit by bit, the energy picked up pieces and put them where they belonged, picking up speed until the very last piece of its helm was placed. The light wrapped brightly around the statue from head to toe. When it faded, the statue was as if it never had been damaged.

"Alright, that was interesting," Diane stated. "Now what?"

*"Everyone but you and Robert leave the room. Stand next to him, and have Robert destroy the statue again."*

I cleared my throat. "Lumadian wants everyone to leave the room, and then Robert can destroy the statue again. Am I right if I assume that the curse will affect everyone in the room again?"

Lumadian nodded and added, *"Just to be extra safe, have them stay in the other room."*

"Everyone in the other room now!" I yelled, as I saw the first signs of one of the other party's members waking. Quickly, my friends piled into the room and shut the door. Lumadian used my energies to reinforce the protection spell around Robert and me.

Robert looked into Lumadian's eyes. "I am trusting you." He crushed the statue with his shield.

The same greenish mist materialized, harmlessly passed over us, and enveloped our captives. Marla sat up and screamed as her magic notified her of the destruction of the statue, but it was too late. I watched all their images twist into bovines. Each one was a little different, but there was no mistaking what they had become.

"Well," I said to the woman—now a velvety brown heifer—who had cast the spell, "I have kept my word. You did not die." I approached the door and called out to my friends, "Come out now!" All I heard was mooing from the room. "Oh my god!" I ran to the room and flung open the door. Diane and Jean-Luc sat on the bed, still in human guise, mooing. When they saw me they laughed. Cat was in the far corner, lapping the remnants of milk from a drawer. I wanted to be angry, but the scene was too much for me and I laughed out loud. "We should finish our task. We can push them in here for now. Before we go, we will let them outside to graze."

We returned upstairs to examine the only unexplored section on this level. The simple door opened into a small antechamber with the most elaborate door we had seen in the mansion. A beautiful blending of different metals made it appear like marble. It was gold, with designs of something like pewter melted into the metal so that it would appear as if the design was painted into the door. This arabesque design reached from the top of the door and wove left and right down to the bottom.

I reached to open the door, and a mouth appeared on the surface asking, "What is the password?"

I was puzzled, not knowing what to say and poked Lumadian for an answer. *"Don't ask me. I did not design this. I can say that it is a protection spell. If you know it, you say, 'the password is' then say the password. It could be anything, though. If you get it right the door will open. If you get it wrong, a number of 'bad' things could happen."*

"We need to search the rest of the keep, it seems, because if we are wrong, we will trigger a bad effect." I sighed at Cat again.

"And not to keep using Cat as an example, but you know what can happen when we are wrong. We can only tempt Fate so far."

None of my friends disagreed, but before we left Jean-Luc suggested, "We should divide up what we took from them, in case it would come in handy."

"None of these people's clothes have that strange touch, so I assume we have better. Put that all in a pile for now, and we will try to retrieve it later. There is this..." I held out the sword. "Out of all the weapons, this is the only one that has a magical shine. Does anyone want it?" I waited for a moment and when no one spoke, I continued. "The man Cat defeated wore two rings. This one has a wolf chasing his tail, while this one has images of different animals all around the band. Anyone want these?"

Diane said, "I'd like to see them, please." At the same time, Cat growled a bit in my direction.

"You want to claim a prize from something you defeated?" I asked.

Cat nodded then sighed heavily and sniffed at his paws.

"Don't worry," I said to him. "We will get you back to normal. Would you mind if Diane held them for you?" He shook his head back and forth.

Diane slipped on the ring with the images of animals first, gazing at her outstretched fingers and spinning it around with her other hand. "It is a very nice ring. I think I will love it."

Cat growled and sighed loudly.

"What did you say?" Diane asked Cat with surprise.

Cat made a sound then stopped as if he realized that Diane might have understood him.

Diane let out a weird sort of purring noise.

I never thought I'd see a panther do a complete back flip, but I witnessed it that day as Cat rushed over to lick Diane's face.

"Diane," I interrupted, "what is going on?"

"I can understand and talk to him now!"

"Is that so? That is great news. Cat, do you need anything?" I asked.

Diane, acting as the translator, said Cat was fine. She tried the other ring on as well, but it did not seem to do anything. The only other thing with any magic around it was the necromancer's belt. It had the brightest magical aura of anything I had seen.

"I would like to try this, if no one objects?" When no one spoke up, I buckled it on. I did not feel any different, but the belt was a comfortable addition. With the task of handing out the items complete, we gathered ourselves. "Well, I don't know about any of you, but I think Mother Nature is calling, and I could enjoy some food and a bit of rest now. What do you think?"

Robert stretched and yawned. "I agree, but let's go outside. I think I'd feel more comfortable, and besides, it would give Cat the opportunity to bury his droppings."

Cat initially gave Robert a dirty look, but when the rest of us laughed, he eased up, and I would have sworn he laughed too.

After our visit to the local tree, we returned to the first floor's hallway, had some food, then rested. When I felt enough time had passed, I got to my feet. "Well, time to journey to the lower levels of the keep."

Everyone nodded, and we continued on.

# CHAPTER TWENTY

The stairs spiraled down into darkness, hugging the exterior walls of the keep. We passed five platforms along the way, remnants of floors long since decayed. At the bottom was a large, root cellar. The stonework was full of large holes exposing open dirt. Cobwebs spanned virtually every corner of the room, and some even draped over the walls.

There was a thick layer of dirt on the clay floor. Cots and bedrolls were strewn about, rotten and decayed with age. The smell of death hung heavily in the air, and I could see bodies in the darkness. I fumbled with a torch and, with a bit of assistance from Robert, managed to light our way. With the new source of light, two things could plainly be seen. One, I could see another descending staircase in the far corner. Two, the bodies rose and lumbered over to us.

Robert and Jean-Luc jumped forward and out, to protect our front as Cat slunk between them. I began a spell while Diane held her symbol above her head and chanted. Robert cut into the first creature. I could hear the bones of the animated corpse cracking, but the thing seemed unaffected.

Cat leaped on one, crushing it. Cat's forward momentum kept him moving in the same direction until the creature he had trampled reached up and clutched his tail, its claws digging deeply. I heard a howl as blood dripped from Cat's tail.

Jean-Luc delivered a spinning kick to the head that would have knocked out or even killed a normal person, but his opponent moaned and shambled closer to him, trying to get a grip on his arm. Jean-Luc managed to avoid the attack, as another creature got closer.

I concentrated with all my might on something that would affect all the creatures, hoping to unleash unknown magic within me. I heard Lumadian chanting as well. Balls of light erupted from the two of us and hit everything that was dead. The creatures were all pushed back, charred by the spell, but still they continued to advance.

Diane finished her chanting with, "Let the light of day enter the gloom."

We heard a rumbling from all around us and tilted our heads back. The ceiling had melted away like snow on a warm spring day, then the floor above it, and then the next, until the dreariness of the outdoors was revealed. The clouds parted and shafts of light streamed down through the open ceiling and engulfed the room. As light impacted them, the corpses moaned and collapsed, becoming lifeless again. Sunbeams burned the bodies into ash. After the last creature was destroyed, the spell's light dimmed and the ceilings melded themselves back together. Everything was quiet, as if the room had never been disturbed.

"That was interesting," Jean-Luc said. "I wonder what other surprises were in store for us."

Diane gasped and caught her breath before joining Cat. She touched his tail and closed the wound. "I was not expecting something like that, but it worked."

I was about to ask Lumadian what he thought, but his little muzzle was wide open, which caused me to chuckle and shiver at the same time.

In the far corner of the room, we discovered an iron chest. Unlike the extreme age everything else showed, this chest was sturdy and new. I tried shifting my sight and noticed the box emitted the light Lumadian called magic.

"Lumadian, can you break the," I paused for a moment before choosing the word, "*magic,* so we can open the chest?"

"*Let me try.*" He flew over to the chest and landed on it. I watched with my altered vision as the light flowed softly from the box to Lumadian and dimmed until there was nothing left. "*There is a simple lock left, perhaps the…*" he paused, then I could hear him chuckle in my mind. "*… Robert can now get it open.*" He flew back over to my shoulder and settled in.

"Robert, it should be safe now to open. If you would do the honors, please."

Robert swung his sword at the lock, breaking it on the first try. Without hesitation, he flipped open the chest to reveal six heavy, woolen, hooded cloaks. Each of the cloaks had a weird symbol embroidered on it. The patch was in the shape of a shield with a dark blue background. Going from the outside rim to the center were four jagged, yellow lines that all met in the center. We each took a cloak. The one no one chose had a rose pin with purple petals that Diane immediately recognized.

"This must be Merial's cloak," she commented. Removing the cloak she had initially chosen, she put Merial's cloak with her supplies instead. She checked the chest further, but when she discovered nothing more she said, "We should continue down those stairs."

The stairs were heavily laced with spider webs that my torch easily burned. We cautiously descended the stairs. Unlike the crumbling stone stairs above, these were constructed of wood and we were unsure if they would hold our weight. Each footfall caused moaning from the ancient beams that echoed the narrow passageway. At one point, we almost decided to abandon exploring further and go back, but considering the distance we had already traveled, we decided to continue. After making our way past missing planks, we finally reached the bottom.

The floor was earth. The red-clay bricks had crumbled to mush. In front of us was a door so worn with age that there was gaping holes in it. I nearly choked on the aromas of death, urine, feces, rotting meat, and garbage all around us. Robert opened the door.

Before us was a mausoleum, with crumbling stone biers in lines on both the left and right. The decorative tapestries that had once adorned the walls were all but decayed away. In back of the stone room was a black marble throne. Sitting on the throne, was a human, perhaps twenty-five or thirty years old. He wore dark robes of the finest silk. He seemed strange in the room of death.

"Come in," the stranger said. "I have been expecting you."

"Who are you?"

"I am the," he paused for a moment, "lord of this manor. It has been a long time since I have had any visitors." He rose and descended the few stairs that ran down from his throne. My friends reacted by drawing their weapons. "Now, now," he said. "Is that necessary?"

Robert pulled his shield from his back and set it in front of him. "It is until you show what your intentions are."

"Ah, a cautious band, such a refreshing change. I am Master Erik Von Breinenhouser. I often come here to think and talk to my beloved wife Gretta. She brings me much peace." He stepped closer to the crypts as we readied ourselves. Both Cat and Lumadian growled.

I asked Lumadian, "*What is wrong?*"

"*He is not what he appears to be,*" Lumadian replied.

"Calm your pets or I will do it for you," the stranger said. "I am unarmed. What chance would I have against such *powerful* foes such as you?" He chuckled and took a step forward. "You will provide me as excellent servants." With that, he shot a blinding light from his fingers and we staggered back. When it dimmed, I could only sense fuzzy images.

"Where is he?" I heard the noise of a something slicing through the air where Robert had been standing. "Can you see?" I asked Lumadian.

"*Yes,*" he replied, "*he is attacking Cat with his fists.*"

At that moment I heard a flurry of blows and growls in front of me. It was hard to tell what was going on. "Sting him," I told Lumadian.

"*It would not affect him. The creature is not living.*"

"Diane, cast your spell you did before."

She began a soft chant. When it was complete, my vision had cleared up enough to see Erik pick up Cat's limp body and toss it on top of me. The force of the throw sent the two of us crashing through the entrance. Lumadian was barely able to fly out of the way in time. We hit the ancient door with such force that it splintered and rained down on us. I tried to push him off, but I was hardly able to breathe. My concern wasn't for me, however, but for my friends. I sighed with relief when I realized that Cat was still breathing, although barely.

Robert, having recovered his sight, swung his sword at the creature's head. As the blade was about to hit its mark, the creature bent over backward putting his hands on the floor right behind his feet until the blade passed harmless over him. When Robert pulled his blade back, the thing straightened.

The creature had incredible speed. He punched Robert in the chest before my friend could react to the attack. The attack pushed Robert backward, but he regained his footing and spat at the vile creature, hitting the foul thing with blood from his mouth.

Erik stopped for a moment to taste the blood on his face, using a sickly, black tongue. "Yes, you will be an excellent slave." The creature lunged for Robert again.

Jean-Luc used the hesitation to his advantage. With his quarterstaff, he swung with all his might at Erik's head, but at the last possible moment shifted the blow to the creature's legs, knocking him to the floor.

Diane rushed over to Cat and me, trying to examine his injuries. I gathered what strength I could to yell, "Cast that spell again! Heal our injuries later." I was having a hard time breathing until Lumadian landed next to me and touched my forehead with his own. I could feel his breathing, slow and unlabored, and mine eased. But with my problem eliminated came a new realization. I could smell the odors of the room with a new intensity that I did not like.

Diane spun around again to cast the spell, which drew the attention of our foe. With an incredible strength, he sprung up seizing both Jean-Luc and Robert by their throats. With one motion, he flung them across the room and into the wall, the force of their impact crumbling the walls. Moving with supernatural speed, he appeared in front of Diane, knocking her symbol from her hand with ease. He leered with a wicked glee, and I could see his fangs extending. He embraced her, pressed his lips against her smooth cheek, and kissed her down to her neck. I felt a weight leave my chest as Cat leapt at the foe, breaking the creature's grasp on Diane. They tumbled to the dirt. The monstrosity hissed at Cat. He rose to his feet, picking Cat up by the scruff as if he weighed nothing.

"No mercy for the animal. I will enjoy draining it as well." The monster's long claws snaked around Cat's neck. I could see him squeezing his hands closed in a malicious attempt to inflict all the pain he could before he killed Cat.

I noticed Robert behind the creature. He hit him with something that looked like a dart. As I saw his swing hit its mark, the object grew from miniature sword, to a full sized great sword. The weapon impaled the creature directly through the back emerging from the center of its chest. The creature changed to a misty vapor that disappeared into the ceiling with the same swiftness it had when it was flesh.

*"You will have to find his true resting place, or he will re-form and kill you all,"* Lumadian warned me as I regained my footing.

"We need to run as soon as Diane heals everyone." I went to the center of the room and gawked at the ceiling. "We need to leave this room, now!" Diane was a bit disheveled, but finished healing Cat of his injuries. She was tired after her spell, but waved me off when I offered to help. We ran up the stairs, which collapsed behind us. Up, up, up we ran until we arrived at the polished metal door. As before, a mouth appeared requesting the password.

"The password is 'Gretta,'" I said, sure that I was correct. The mouth disappeared, but nothing happened. For a moment I thought I was wrong, but we heard a clicking noise and the door swung open.

Inside was an elaborate bedroom. My eyes were drawn up to the raised portion of the room. Against the back wall were two beds. The wooden, four-poster one on the left, covered in clean pink bedding and many plush pillows, lay under a fresco of Erik's face, although with a kinder, gentler expression. On the right, the bed was covered in orange and brown bedding. Above that bed a fresco of a beautiful woman with raven hair, hazel eyes, and a mesmerizing air was surrounded by cherubs. My inspection of the room was cut short when my eyes fell upon a large coffin, its lid closed, set on a bier in front of the beds.

"Where is it?" I asked Lumadian aloud.

*"Open the coffin. You will need something wooden to plunge into his heart."*

"What are you..."

*"Do not argue. I will explain after!"* His voice was frantic.

"Get something wooden to plunge into his heart! He's in the coffin!" I yelled.

Flipping off the lid, Robert confirmed that the creature was indeed inside, with his eyes shut. "He's in here!"

The creature's eyes snapped open and focused directly on Robert. His bony, clawed hand held Robert's neck. The yellow, elongated nails pierced his neck with ease, producing a great deal of blood. The creature spryly sat up and lapped at the blood that spurted from the wound.

Jean-Luc shouted, "Enough!" and jumped to the bed. He broke one of the columns in two, jamming the sharp end into the monster's chest.

For the briefest of moments, the creature closed his fingers around Robert's neck, as if trying to remove my friend's head from his body. Then Erik closed his eyes and his arm went limp, releasing Robert.

Clutching his neck, Robert staggered back and Diane began to chant. In an instant, the roof opened as before. The light of a full day's sun flooded every inch of the room. As the rays of light hit the creature, they steamed like warm raindrops on cold stone. The beast burst into flame, producing a sickly smell. As the light from Diane's spell diminished, so too did the flames, leaving nothing but ash inside the coffin, which was unaffected by the flames. She stumbled and moaned from exhaustion, but managed to stagger to Robert and heal his wounds as he lost consciousness. When she was done, she collapsed on the floor, her face drained and white.

Lumadian nuzzled my ear, giving me strength. "*He was a vampire, a very lethal type of the undead. You are very lucky to be alive. Had he been able to rest here, he would have returned full strength and killed us all. The only way to even put him to sleep is with the wooden object in the heart. As you saw, sunlight completely destroyed him.*"

I was engrossed listening to Lumadian, and I did not notice Jean-Luc's approach until he asked, "How did you know the correct word, J.D.?"

"The tombstone below read, 'To my beloved Gretta: My accident caused this, and I will not rest until I undo the spell that took you from me.' I figured anyone with that much remorse would also keep his private bedroom locked with her name."

Diane questioned, "Couldn't anyone who knew the name come in here? I mean, any of his henchmen could have done so."

"True. But would you want his wrath if you were discovered?" I asked her.

"That's true. I wouldn't want that wrath."

Robert moaned and sat up. "I have a really bad headache."

Diane got to her feet and shook off our attempts at assistance.

I helped Robert up. "It is good to have you still here. Rest while we search around."

Jean-Luc, Cat, and I fanned out to search the room while Robert and Diane rested. Jean-Luc patted each of the beds. "Nothing in here, but they feel comfortable."

I stayed with Cat as he sniffed around. I glanced out the window and noticed the sky gradually changing from gray to purple and black. "Time sure does seem to fly here."

Jean-Luc searched a desk on the same side as Erik's bed and picked up an old leather book. "Hey, come here." He handed it to her.

Diane untwined the leather straps and opened it. After leafing through some of the aged paper, she said, "It appears to be another diary. Listen to this entry:

*"Today, I attempt to open a portal into other worlds. I am sure if I can find the correct world to plunder, I can greatly increase my wealth and power with little cost in men or energy."*

I coughed and gathered my thoughts. "You don't suppose Elilith existed before, and he happened to open the portal at the same moment the scientists created the accident?"

Robert spat on the floor. "That is absurd. That is like the chicken and the egg argument. How could this world have existed before it was created?"

Diane cleared her throat. "Before you jump to conclusions, listen to more:

*"With Gretta by my side, I created the portal, but something unexpected occurred and I was blown from the area. The spell should have been broken, but the negative energies lashed out at the nearest live target, my wonderful love. It changed her into the most disgusting and decrepit thing I have ever witnessed, before becoming wispy smoke and disappearing. I remained on my back, watching the portal, when a man dressed in white and carrying books stepped out. He grinned at me and disappeared also, dropping a book in the process. I stayed still until I heard a hum from the portal. I covered my body in a protective aura as the door erupted in a violent explosion. The energies shot out and contaminated the keep, dying as they reached away from the source."*

Diane flipped through more pages. "Apparently, he went insane searching for a way to get his love back. He even said the dropped book had information on the occult and he used that information to turn himself into a vampire in order to ensure he'd have enough time to find a cure."

Cat growled at Diane.

Diane looked at Cat and nodded. "It might have, we have no way of knowing."

"What did he say?" I attempted not to let my concern for my friend's condition show, but having been worn down by the day's activities, I am sure he saw the despair on my face.

"Cat wanted to know if it was possible that the book was the cause of the problems here."

"We may never know." I tried to bolster my friends' confidence. "For now, we should all rest. When we wake, we will go get Cat's ability to take human shape back. Anyone want to say anything?" I waited for my companions, but they produced no response. We went back to a bedroom. Without returning to the cellar, we gathered all the bodies on the other side of the room far enough away that nothing else would catch fire, and after retrieving some oil from the lamps, we set them ablaze and watched for a bit, to be cautious. We settled back into the master bedroom and planned watch shifts for the night, minus Diane and Robert. We let Diane take Gretta's bed, and Robert got Erik's. No one seemed to be in a talking mood, so I scooped Lumadian in my lap, leaned against the back wall, and closed my eyes for the night.

Cat nudged my side in the wee hours of the night, before he went to the foot of Diane's bed, circled around a few times, then settled down. In the distance, I heard the cawing of a strange creature greeting the approach of a new day. Disturbed by the previous day's events, I barely got any sleep. Once the darkness was replaced by the gray sky, I woke everyone up. We gathered our things and headed downstairs.

When we got to the room where we'd left the cows, Cat spoke to Diane. "Cat wants us to leave the cows here. If they should get killed, he'd never be restored."

"I don't have an issue with leaving them here in the room." I faced Cat as I spoke. "We should see if we could get something for them to eat and drink, though. Diane you and I will stay with them. Robert, Jean-Luc, and Cat, go see if you can find something."

They left to gather weeds outside the keep while we entered the room. Diane called out to Marla. The cows mooed at her, approaching her with earnest interest. Diane noticed they all needed milking. The room stunk of fresh dung. Ignoring their pressing need, Diane took a moment, but finally found the correct cow. It mooed sadly at her.

"What did she say?" I asked. "Does the ring work with these cows, too?"

Diane stroked the heifer's nose. "She said, 'What... you... doing...'" She gazed into liquid, brown eyes. "I came to see if you were fine. I can see you need milking. Should I assist?"

All I heard was a mournful moo.

"One second," I told Diane, as I ran upstairs and got the buckets. I returned to Diane and handed her one. "What did they say before I left?"

"Yes, milking good," Diane translated. "The spell is obviously clouding her mind."

"I can see that," I responded, hiding a grin. My amusement faded when I realized that Diane intended us to milk every cow in the room. Although I was glad my mother had insisted I learn to milk, I began to fear that I would dream of udders for weeks to come. As she milked the former sorceress she asked her, "What is the Almator?"

Diane nodded, and touched the next cow.

"Diane, unlike you, I do not understand 'moo,'" I said through gritted teeth. "That information is important."

"She said, 'Almator, the six-armed beast.'"

"Lumadian, can you try to contact their minds like you did for Cat?"

Lumadian shifted on my shoulder. "*Sure.*" He took a few moments as I watched him go from one cow to the next. "*For some reason, their condition is deteriorating fast. The woman who created this is barely human anymore, but like Diane, all I am getting is the six-armed beast.*"

"That sounds absolutely delightful. Do you know any creatures with six arms?"

*"Well, I know of many beasts, like the anivorax, a displacer beast, the ki're centaurs and even some dragons. Let me think—oh! There are some creations that have six or more limbs."*

"Creations?"

*"It is like taking a scarecrow and actually making it animate under its own power to do work."*

"This world really scares me sometimes."

*"You need not worry. You've got me!"*

I actually relaxed at that and handed him one of his fruits. He squealed in my ear and nibbled on the morsel slowly. I knew he was savoring the flavors, since I got to enjoy them too.

Smiling, Diane continued idle chitchat, trying to gather as much information from the herd as she could while we milked and tossed full buckets out the window. As we finished, Jean-Luc returned with an armfuls of weeds and grasses.

Robert carried in a water trough, placing it against the wall. "Cat found a small, overgrown stable close by." He motioned to Cat. "There is a pump there, but the water came out black. Jean-Luc and I are going to run back and get the hay bundles and some sacks of grain." He pulled Jean-Luc's arm, and they left. We finished milking the cows by the time they returned with more food.

I faced Diane. "Remember that water spell you hit Robert with?"

"Yes?"

"Think you could do it again in the trough?"

"I can try." Diane concentrated, her hands rising. Water appeared, and when she dropped her hands, the water fell into the trough. She did it a second time and filled it to the brim.

Shortly after that, Robert and Jean-Luc returned with the food. We tossed the furniture out and spread the food out over the floor.

Before we left I asked, "Diane, can you talk to all of them?"

"Yes, although they are slow to understand or answer."

"Inform the necromancer that, if he hopes to return to normal, he'd better offer some clues to what the Almator is, or I hope he enjoys remaining a cow 'til the end of days.'"

Diane took a moment to identify the correct bovine before speaking to it. I saw the particular cow she was addressing pace back and forth mooing with a painful call.

Diane shook her head. "It's no use. The necromancer's mind is too far gone to understand the question. All I get from any of them is 'six-armed beast.'"

"It was worth a try." I left the room. The others followed, closing the door behind us. Concentrating on the door, I heard the lock click. "Do we want to go into the barricaded room?" I asked.

A resounding "NO!" from everyone gave me my answer. We departed for the mine.

# CHAPTER TWENTY-ONE
## GROWTH

We followed the directions on the map for most of the morning. The deeper into the forest we travelled, the more chilling it became. Bone-colored moss hung from every branch, entwined like a giant spider web canopy. The gnarled bark of every tree appeared to have faces, some twisted in agony, others bent demonically. The path we were on was sometimes flooded with a black, thick liquid, but not enough to stop our progress. I know I should have eaten, but the putrid, acidic odor robbed me of any appetite. We travelled all throughout the morning and into what I assumed was the afternoon. I didn't see the sky until we rounded a sharp bend in the road and saw the mine in the distance on the right side.

Boulders so massive that they forced the trees near them to bend at unnatural angles surrounding the bases of the trees the entire way to the cave. The entrance was twice as large as Robert, about three times the width of Jean-Luc, and appeared unguarded. We cautiously approached the opening, making sure that no hidden creatures were ready to pounce from the trees, but arrived without incident. Gazing into the darkness of the tunnel, we were able to see traces of a passage that sloped sharply downward into obscurity. After searching through our supplies, I lit a few torches and handed them out before shuffling into the shaft. It grew warmer the deeper we descended. The air was pungent with a mixture of old scents that none of us could identify. The torchlight danced on the walls making weird shadows off the irregular walls. After traveling a while, the shaft opened to a chamber with many branches coming off of it.

Just stepping into this first opening revealed to me why people wanted the mine. Veins of purple, gold, and green minerals mixed with hundreds of holes where gems used to be. The veins themselves gave off an eerie radiance that intensified as we brought the torches closer to them. In a few spots around the chamber were bins that were obviously used to store the valuable minerals, but all of them were empty.

I addressed Cat. "Can you determine if you smell anyone or any... thing?"

Cat went into each passage, trying to smell them one by one. With each success, he told Diane what he could smell. Two of the seven passages had humans mixed with creatures, two had creatures, and two were empty of creatures, but had a pungent, earthy odor to them.

"Which should we take?" I asked.

"Since Almator is a beast, one of those is what I would guess," Diane said proudly.

Jean-Luc spoke up first. "How do you know that?"

"A woman to woman chat I had before we left," she said, as she brushed by me, purposely making contact with me and sparking the memory of the day before we left home.

Robert entered the first passage on the left. "We will use your style of investigation, J.D. Allowing Cat to follow a scent is fine, but we won't abandon your method of approach, since it has gotten us this far."

I was a little taken aback by his flash of insight and thought, *There is hope for him after all.* We decided to proceed down the first tunnel, having Cat lead, with Robert and Jean-Luc next, followed by Diane and myself.

We traveled cautiously down the twisting passage, trying to be as silent as possible. The path sloped severely downward about halfway down, and we all leaned way back to avoid sprinting down the rocky path. After a few minutes or so of travel, we saw a light at the end of the tunnel and heard noises in the distance.

Quietly retreating back up the passage a bit, we discussed our plan of attack.

I whispered, "Cat, I want you to slink down to the front of the entrance and see which creature you think poses the greatest threat. Before you attack, growl… then you, Robert, and Jean-Luc will rush in, and the rest of us will follow. Since the noises definitely don't sound human in nature, we won't take the risk of the creatures gaining any advantage—let the element of surprise work in our favor." With the plan set, we all got ready.

I could barely see Cat in the darkness. We had discarded our torches. He crouched on his belly for what seemed like an eternity before growling and leaping into the room, and we all followed him.

Stepping into the light, I blinked my eyes, trying to get them to adjust to the change. I heard a scream in my head, *"Duck!"* Without hesitation, I ducked as a pickaxe embedded itself in the wall above me. I fumbled for my assailant's leg and yelled, "Let your flesh feel the warmth of fire upon it!"

With my vision finally cleared, I watched with fascination as flames erupted from my hands and burned the creature in front of me. I could feel the heat, see the amazing colors, and smell fire, but the most impressive thing was that it had no effect on me. In appearance, the thing was human-like with the exception of being covered from head to foot in what only could be described as dried seaweed. The fire took the creature, igniting its entire body in a column of flame. With my adversary defeated, I scanned the room to see who I could assist.

*"Remind me to ask you more about magic,"* I thought to Lumadian.

*"Whenever you are ready to learn more."*

Jean-Luc had already defeated one creature—its decapitated corpse oozed greenish bile—before he chased after another that fled down one of the exits.

Around Robert, three of the kelp beings—as I decided to call them—attempted to bring him down. I could hear Diane chanting something about strength in the background, and Robert's muscles bulged to incredible proportions.

Peering down the other tunnel, I saw Cat pinning down a human female. His jaws were firmly locked around her throat. At his captive's side was a black whip with a spiked, metal end.

Robert swung his sword in a downward arc to slice the upper section of one of the kelp beings clean off. Continuing through his attack, he swiftly changed direction, catching the axe of another in one fluid motion.

The third, however, brought its axe squarely into Robert's back, digging the weapon deeply into his body, and then jiggling it as if still mining minerals. Diane went to intercept the third, but Robert yelled, "No!" with such anger that it froze her in her tracks. With one hand, he plucked the pickaxe from his back, implanting it in a new location, namely the head of the creature that had attacked him. With his other hand, he sent his and the creature's weapons to the rocky floor. He grinned as he picked the creature up by the neck and proceeded to use the kelp being's head as an axe, bashing it against the rocks over and over again.

I approached Diane, wondering if she was injured, when I felt a sharp pain in my back making me stagger forward. I looked over my shoulder at a human dressed in all black. He grinned at me, and I found my world spinning. I managed to focus long enough to see a blur pierce his neck from the back, emerging through his Adam's apple. I squinted. The sickness in my stomach caused me to fall to all fours as I gritted my teeth.

Sounds bled together, and I had a bitter taste in my mouth. My body shook; my own muscles were no longer under my control. I felt tiny claws on my back rip the dagger from my wound. I fell to my stomach as I felt Lumadian's teeth nip me in the spot the weapon recently occupied. My vision cleared as the queasiness dissipated, allowing me to survey the room again.

Robert was still bashing the creature's head against the wall, while Cat kept the woman pinned. She began to chant, but was cut off when Cat simply tightened his grip around her neck. Diane finally headed to me. I realized my whole encounter must have been much shorter than it had seemed to me.

*"Get up, slow poke, the poison is all gone,"* Lumadian told me.

Shaking my head, I got to my feet as Robert let the creature fall to the ground. My friend breathed heavily and spun at us with a fire in his eyes.

Just at that moment, Jean-Luc returned from the corridor dragging the body of a creature he'd defeated in one hand, and carrying his staff in the other. Robert lunged at Jean-Luc with his arms open in an attempt to strangle our friend with his bare hands.

Jean-Luc dropped the body and twirled his staff. Sidestepping Robert's attack, he hit behind Robert's legs and lifted, sending Robert to his back. Robert shook violently as if he had tremors. His hands were still in front of him, locked in the choking position.

"J.D., put him to sleep!" Jean-Luc shouted.

I concentrated on the spell, like I had previously done and, like before, ghostly images of feathers appeared. Robert's eyes fluttered for only a moment before he fell asleep, the tremors in his body still jerking. Jean-Luc bent down and touched him behind the ear, stilling him.

We huddled around Robert, wondering what had gotten into him, until we heard a growl and saw Cat with the woman still pinned beneath him. His jaws were locked in place, but not tightly enough to choke the woman. Hustling over to the pair, I took the whip from her side and threw it to Jean-Luc. Taking my dagger, I cut her belt and slipped it out from under her. I slipped her gloves and boots off to be safe, and was about to call Cat off when Diane spoke.

"Slice her pant leg and blouse a bit. That will destroy any magic either piece might have."

Looking at Diane with a puzzled expression, I did as she instructed, cutting both pieces of clothing without a problem. With everything either shredded or destroyed, I tried to remain emotionless upon seeing the woman's fear-filled eyes. "We can do this one of two ways. Either you help us, or my kitty cat will have lunch. It is your choice. If you understand, blink your eyes twice." I waited a moment before I saw her blink twice. "Cat, release now and get down!" With hesitation, he released his grasp and licked her neck a bit, cleaning up the slight trace of blood, before retreating to the corner of the room to lie down.

The mysterious woman leaned over, spitting blood at us. She brought her right hand to her neck feeling the traces of blood. An attempt to stand made her crash into the wall. She braced herself against the craggy surface until her equilibrium returned. I could feel the hate from her as she spied our party. When she tried to speak, nothing came out. Coughing some blood into her hand, she tried again. "My name is Miriele Xi'Syn. So you are them, eh? I did not expect to see you this far in."

"Does everyone here know who we are?" Diane asked.

"Probably not everyone," Miriele continued. "But then, I am not just *anyone*. We were given your names and a general description of you. What is it that you want to know, and how much will it cost for my release?"

I was about to answer when I heard a noise behind me.

"Oh, my head," Robert groaned. "What in blazes happened? Why is my head ringing like a Sunday bell?" Robert sat up.

Diane crouched next to him and tapped him on the shoulder, "You had a tad bigger dose of battle rage than you were used to, I'd say." She walked past him to Miriele. "Let me heal your injuries, at least."

Miriele was about to resist, but sighed and dropped her arms. Diane cast two spells: one that I recognized as healing, but the other was new to me. When it was completed, all traces of injuries were washed away from Miriele's neck, including the red stains. Diane didn't show any indications that the spells were affecting her as strongly as before.

Feeling her neck with her hand, Miriele cleared her throat again. "You do very nice work, m'lady. So, what is it that you wanted to know?"

I stepped in front of Diane. "What is your purpose here? What are these things you have working for you? What do you think we should do with you after you have finished answering our questions?"

"How refreshing. Someone who is direct, I like that. First, I was left in charge of the mining in this particular shaft. Everyone here has their own location and goals set for them. I do not know other people's locations or goals. This prevents wanderers because we also know some passages are trapped so they cannot be intruded upon. It also prevents us from revealing too much. We were harvesting the purple stone, pallaxian, which has unusual properties. Second, these creatures are summoned by the druid who runs this operation. He brings them from the outside. Few ever cross him. He is a dangerous individual. Lastly, since I value living, I want to travel with you to prove my worth."

"Yeah, prove your worth by stabbing us in the back," Robert stated coldly as he got to his feet.

"Interesting," I said, ignoring Robert's comments. "Let me ask my companions." I motioned for everyone to gather at the end of the hall.

"Can we trust her?" Jean-Luc asked, motioning over his shoulder at her.

"What are we supposed to do with her if we don't take her with us?" I asked.

"Kill her," Robert offered coldly, causing everyone to stare at him in disbelief. "What? I was kidding! Gosh, no one can take a joke."

"*I don't trust her, but she is better than 'him,'*" Lumadian added.

Diane looked contemplative with her hand on her chin. "It would be nice to have another woman to talk to for a change. And someone who knows the mysteries of Elilith could help us immensely. I say yes."

We broke our huddle and I addressed Miriele. "We accept your offer to prove yourself to us. When was your next pick-up scheduled?"

"Five days from now, they'll send a few trolls to pick up anything we've gathered and take it outside to where the giants would take over. I do not know where the giants would take the supplies, though. This shaft," she said, indicating a nearby shaft, "leads to sleeping quarters and supplies, while the other leads to further veins of precious gems and metals."

"Let's go get some food supplies and then explore some of the other shafts."

Jean-Luc asked, "Shouldn't we ask her about the creature, J.D.?"

"What do you know of the Almator, Miriele?" I asked.

"The beast below? Not much, actually. Everyone tends to stay away from the holding chambers and the entire floor, since those who haven't usually ended up as lunch. It cleans out a village's worth of troublemakers rather quickly. There are also *things* that worship and revere it."

"What if some troublemakers wanted to find this beast? Do you know a way to it?" I asked.

"The only way I know of is to fall into one of the traps. Why in the world would you want to confront the thing?" She pointed to the tunnel. "Come, let me get some of my remaining gear. Do you think I could keep my whip at least?"

Without answering her question, I tossed the whip to her as we proceeded down a passage lined with lit torches. The corridor opened into a larger chamber with many wooden doors. She crossed the room to a door that was the only one set with iron. After some quick movements with the latch, she pushed it inward and went inside. Diane followed her, striking up a conversation. I could hear them chatting about something, but the nature of the cave didn't allow me to hear anything coherent.

The two women emerged from the bedroom a short time later. Miriele had changed, replacing the cut clothes with practical traveling leather. She wore black, thigh-high boots, brown leather pants, and a weathered jerkin. She had a long, black cloak and carried two short swords at her sides.

"You are right," Miriele said to Diane, glancing at me, then back at her. The two women laughed about something.

I must have been confused and blushed.

"*What's wrong?*"

"*I guess I don't understand women, Lumadian.*"

"*Well, we can talk about that too.*"

I shook my head and chuckled.

Miriele started to walk. "Over here," she said, leading us to a food pantry. The sights there almost made my mouth water; the scents that hit my nose made it so. There were dried meats and cheeses, as well as bottles of all types of drink. We took what we could carry, and I happened to find a jar of sweetened fruit for Lumadian. Well supplied, we set off, back the way we'd come.

"So, Miriele," Robert said in a low voice, "those things comprised your whole force?"

"It is easier to maintain control, especially over Alghe."

"Is that what those were called?" I tapped her on her shoulder to get her attention.

"Yes. I am not surprised you have never seen them. The druid can summon creatures from elemental planes."

*"Don't ask about the planes, acknowledge what she said."*

"Interesting."

"Quiet!" Robert demanded. "We are almost there."

# CHAPTER TWENTY-TWO
## TRANSITION

Returning to the main passage, we decided to take the next corridor. Miriele advanced to the front, reached into an inner pouch, and extracted a long, thin metal rod that grew as she pulled it out. It extended to the size of a long cane, and she gently probed the floor ahead while Cat stayed at her side. Diane and I were next in line, with Robert and Jean-Luc bringing up the rear. We traveled, taking small half-steps until Miriele held up her hand. I strained in the darkness to hear anything, but the best I could come up with was a faint murmur.

"What is… " I whispered, but shut up when Miriele snapped her head back and gave me a stern glare.

We readied ourselves and inched down the passageway. After about a minute, the voices became clearer.

"You the stupid one," a voice yelled.

"Me smash you," cried another.

While we sat there listening, it sounded like others in the room began pounding the ground and chanting something. We heard a scuffle break out. We prepared ourselves to rush into the room, when Miriele suddenly faded to a ghostly outline of herself, then to nothing at all.

"Reveal all to us!" I bellowed, tossing my hands up. Pink dust showered from my fingertips, bounced off the curve in the tunnel, and covered all our bodies in a light.

"It's a trick," Robert huffed as he stormed around the corner of the rocky tunnel into the room.

Jean-Luc barged through us. "We will deal with her later. Right now, concentrate on the fight!"

I took a deep breath, held it, and then rushed in with my friends.

In the center of the room, two huge lumbering hulks stared into each other's eyes. They were about nine feet tall, with spotty leathery skin. Long, unkempt hair grew in various spots on their bodies, and from the smell, I could tell it had never been washed. Their heads were large and mostly humanlike, with grossly exaggerated jaws, noses, and ears. I wrinkled my nose at the odor in the room, which was worsened by the half dozen others that formed a semicircle around the fighting pair.

"*What are they?*" I thought to Lumadian in a panic.

"*Ogres—brutish giants.*"

All of us stopped in our tracks and stared up at the behemoths. They ceased their chants, remained motionless, and faced us. Even Robert waited, still gripping his sword with both hands. Scattered around the room, mostly at the feet of our opponents, were small piles of bones and half-eaten bodies that appeared mostly human.

One of the ogres lumbered a few steps toward us asking, "Who dat? Why dem glowing?" He asked his former adversary.

"Let's pound dem," was the reply.

Robert ran into the room. Using a stalagmite as a platform, he jumped up and chopped the head off of the ogre who had brought us to the attention of his compatriots. The remaining husk slumped forward, hitting the creature's former foe. The creature tossed the husk of his adversary off of himself, and pulled on the weapon still clutched in the dead ogre's hands. Robert hit the ground with a roll, barely dodging the attack of another ogre at the entrance.

Diane created a ball of light in front of her. The ball hovered for a moment until she smashed it with her mace. The ball of light shattered into rays, striking virtually all the ogres in the eyes. The only ogre who escaped the wrath of Diane's spell stepped back into the darker recesses of the grotto while all the others growled and stumbled around the room.

Cat leapt on the back of an ogre who was partially bent down, sinking his claws firmly into the creature's back. With his grip on the monster secure, he bit down repeatedly on the back of the ogre's neck, tearing large chunks of flesh, until the duo crashed down.

Lumadian flew to the left as I went right. I began to think of him as an extension of myself and could feel his actions as if my own claws landed on an ogre's shoulder; my own tail stung the thick, rubbery neck of the creature; and my own wings lifted me up as the over-sized mass fell, impaling itself on a stalagmite. I picked up a fist-sized stone from the rocky floor and threw it at the feet of the stumbling ogre. I mumbled a spell under my breath. The rock sailed to the spot I directed, but the behemoth's stumbling redirected its path, sending the stone to rebound off the same stalagmite Robert had jumped off of. It hit the ceiling where it bounced off a few stalactites before hitting an even larger one, cracking the cone-shaped harpoon at its base. It fell, crushing into the two unlucky ogres who lumbered underneath.

The two ogres who had been blinded shook off the effects at about the same time and blocked the back of the cave.

The remaining ogre clapped his hands with purpose as he stepped into the dancing torch light. The shadows moving across his face enhanced his demonic features. An evil laugh erupted from his misshapen face. The sound and nature of his laugh suggested a human male of a refined upbringing more than the gargantuan beast before us. "I must admit, I thought the clamor I heard about you was exaggerations of the lesser folk, but I can see now that you do not disappoint." He extracted a brilliant blue diamond the size of Lumadian from one of many pouches that hung from his bloated body. Tossing it, he crushed it under his boot. The temperature plummeted until our breaths were readily seen. We tried to get out of the way, but discovered we were frozen to the ground. "What are you doing here?" he asked Miriele, as she materialized. When she didn't reply, he grunted. "I am waiting!"

She strutted over to him. "I know that I am supposed to stay in my tunnel, but I saw them nosing around, and I could not resist the urge to follow them so I could gather information." She paused with an evil grin. "With the bounty on their heads, I also was thinking that I could get some of that lovely treasure."

"Why, you devious minx!" Robert tried to break the hold the spell had on his body to no avail.

"Go back to your assigned corridor. You will not get anything from their capture."

Miriele glided her hand down the hilt of her sword. The weapon's blade pulsated with a dull red light. The glow wisped off the blade to wrap around her feet. Once it had completely left the weapon, the light lifted her into the air until she was face to face with the ogre. "Come now, Mordic, surely there is something I can do for you."

*"What is she doing?"* I asked Lumadian. I sighed heavily. *"Were we fools to trust her so soon?"*

*"It is always interesting to judge humans. But what defines you is the fact you do not learn everything about another's essence from a simple smelling like some other beings do. Humans thrive on the discovery. You'd be lost if you knew everything about everyone at the first meeting. Although I do not trust her completely, I sense something more from her. I think that..."* His

thoughts were cut off as I felt him move a claw on my shoulder as if trying to reposition himself. At the same time, a gentle warmth built and flowed through me. I felt as if he was going to communicate more with me, but had paused when he heard Miriele speak.

"You know that I can offer you benefits that no one else can." Her hand traced up and down Mordric's upper arm and pinched his ear. "Will treasure and gems provide what I can offer you?"

Mordic stopped for a moment, as if he was actually considering Miriele's offer, before letting out a laugh from deep within his body. "Be gone, wench, before I decide to include you in their fate. I, and I alone, will claim the bounty. I will share it with no one—least of all you."

"What you mean you not share with us?" one of the two remaining ogres asked.

Miriele floated softly out of the way behind Mordic as he concentrated on the behemoths.

"Well, well, well, it looks as though you two finally got some courage. It's too bad that it is a little too late." Before either of them could react, Mordic snapped his wrists back and extended his arms at both of the ogres. From each of his arms two large snakes leapt on the creatures. They entwined themselves around each of the beast's necks, growing until they matched the ogres in size.

*"How are you doing?"* I asked Lumadian, still immobilized.

*"Patience, it is a difficult spell to break. I need a little more time."* I felt him moving his tail across the back of my shoulder. The heat he was generating felt good against the cold of the spell that held us. I managed to flex my index finger on my right hand and was hopeful he would soon be able to break the spell.

Mordic brought out a miniature hammer from one of his pouches. Moving his hand over it in slow circles, he murmured something under his breath. A large ghostly version of the weapon appeared. With a twist of the ogre's wrist, the hammer hit Jean-Luc sending him flying against the rocky wall, knocking him unconscious. His head snapped back against the hard surface, loosening some powdery rock from the ceiling. I was stunned, watching the ogres' life force drain away as the serpents squeezed their necks. The ogres tried stabbing the summoned reptiles, but their weapons had no effect. The behemoths fell, twisting back and forth until I heard sickly crunches from the necks of both ogres. In a puff of gray smoke, the snakes disappeared. The hammer hovered above me. Mordic spoke, "I will end your meddling once and for all. In doing so, I will escalate my position in the order, and for that, I thank you. Goodbye." He swung his arm behind his ear. The ghostly image followed, swinging back and poised to crush Lumadian and myself.

Suddenly, Mordic made a gurgling noise. Emerging from his neck, I saw a thin metal tip. He dropped the tiny hammer. The image disappeared the moment the miniature weapon left his hand. We saw Miriele floating in the air and grinning as she held the hilt of her sword still. Mordic captured the tip of the sword between his palms, and his hands burst into flame. The fire cascaded down the blade, penetrated his wound, and burst through the back of his neck, hitting Miriele in the face with an eruption of a fiery heat that knocked her into the ceiling.

*"That is what I needed!"* I felt Lumadian's claws tense on my shoulder. The fire from Mordic's spell leapt to the stalactites, breaking into five distinct columns. Wrapping like ribbons around the rocks, the flame spiraled down until it enveloped our bodies. The cold was instantly broken by the heat of the fire and, before any of us knew what had happened, we discovered we could move again.

Reaching behind himself, our foe ripped the sword from his neck, wincing from the pain of the sudden removal. He glared at Miriele and shook his head. "I'd expect better from you, dear. Not like you to have a heart. Or are you stringing them along like the rest? No matter. You will not be here to reproduce that, or any, mistake again." He aimed the weapon at Miriele and chuckled as a blue beam emerged from the tip. The beam broke into hundreds of strands surrounding her in something that resembled an iron maiden. The cage began to shrink.

Recovering faster than any of us, Lumadian flew with his tail extended in front of him plunging the tip into the gaping wound in the back of Mordic's neck. The creature yelled, snapping his head and neck back, and dropped the sword. Lumadian was launched back into the wall. Mordic clutched himself as he fell to one knee. A cloudy vapor surrounded him, obscuring him from view.

Diane rushed to Jean-Luc casting her healing spell, but he did not stir. She cast the spell a second time, and then a third before Jean-Luc finally opened his eyes. Helping him to his feet, she whispered something that I couldn't hear. Sweat dripped from the side of her face, and her expression was very tired. After checking him over one more time, she cast another spell on the both of them and collapsed. An orange radiance encased them in a protection spell I had not seen before.

At almost the same instant, a new spell came to me, its nature and purpose like a painting in my mind. I clenched my hands in front of my face and snarled in anger. Snapping my fists at the foe, I paused for a moment before raising my hands to the ceiling, open, palms upward. From out of the ground rose two large, spiked tentacles resembling octopus arms except for the fact they were stone. I rotated my palms at Mordic, pulled my arms back, and swung them down like pendulums, keeping my arms straight and rigid. The spiked arms copied my movements, swinging back and snapping forward, sending a volley of spikes at our enemy, before plunging into the ground with such force I nearly lost my footing trying to dodge the stalactites that were knocked loose.

Most of the thrown spikes hit the mist and disappeared. Some buried themselves deep in the bedrock around the vapor. Laughter echoed around the chamber as the mist faded. Mordic remained still, unaffected by my spell. The thorns surrounded him, but were stuck in some type of outer shell that protected him. The laughter deepened, reverberating against the rock walls of the cave then suddenly stopping, as if someone had deadened sound completely. Mordic puffed his cheeks out and blew, sending the thorns in every direction. The maelstrom of spikes knocked Cat, Lumadian, and Robert into unconsciousness. Even Miriele was hit and dropped along with the shrinking spell that trapped her. The spikes flung at Diane and Jean-Luc were incinerated by her protection spell. The ones that came at me simply altered their flight path and missed me entirely for some unknown reason.

Before we could react, Mordic reached down and picked up the shadows that surrounded him, leaving him devoid of darkness. After he rolled the shadows up into a ball, he hurled the mass at Diane and Jean-Luc. The ball splattered against the dome of protection like paint thrown against a round rock. The darkness grew until it completely snuffed out any sight of my friends.

Mordic chuckled and grinned, letting me see his green, crooked teeth. "So, it appears that your journey ends here. It was fun while it lasted." He laughed malevolently, each chuckle getting deeper and louder than the previous one. Something about the laugh left me powerless to do anything but stand and wait for the impending doom. He continued to chuckle, the vibrations ripping through my body as though he slashed me with a sword. His irises rolled up revealing the whites of his eyes. He bent his head back and bent his fingers on both hands, bending his palms toward the ceiling. His fingers glowed red, and he closed his mouth, summoning a spell. Suddenly a massive stalactite cracked from the ceiling and crashed down on him.

I heard the sounds of bones crushing and felt the effects of his spells wash away. I saw a pool of blood ooze from under the giant rock. Even the darkness around Diane and Jean-Luc disappeared.

Still stunned by the randomness of good fate, Diane sprang into action, taking a rose petal from one of her pouches and chanting something under her breath. The floor came to life with flowers, and the walls disappeared. For a moment, we were in the middle of a field on a warm summer's day. All my cares faded away, and I felt reenergized by her healing spell. I saw all my friends standing up, all the effects of battle instantly erased. We approached one another when her spell faded, and we snapped back into reality. Although we were still healed by her spell, the warmth dissipated. Diane immediately collapsed to the floor.

"That was… " Miriele paused for a moment to pick the right word. "…interesting," she finished, seemingly still a bit shocked.

I rushed to examine Diane. Jean-Luc reached her first and put his fingers under her nose. "She is still breathing."

Robert reacted in a flash, clasping Miriele by the neck with one hand and lifting her off the ground. "So, you think we are your pawns? I will not give you another chance to kill us."

Miriele flailed, trying to open Robert's iron grip. She could have easily reached her weapons, but instead tried to get him to stop. Jean-Luc threw a kick at Robert's arm, but it had no effect. Cat threw his weight against the pair, but simply bounced off. I was about to cast a spell but stopped myself when I sensed Lumadian flying in with his tail.

*"Stop!"* My mind called to my small friend. *"Lumadian, do not do it!"*

*"What?"* He veered away and up.

I was about to explain when Diane blinked her eyes, staggered to her feet, and stepped forward. "Put her down, Robert. Put her down now!"

For the first time, Robert acknowledged our presence and gazed down at Diane. He seemed puzzled, almost as if he did not recognize her. With the distant stare still on his face, he lowered Miriele and released his vice-like grip. Miriele coughed and tried to catch her breath, staggering into the wall.

"Robert," Diane said gruffly before calming herself, closing her eyes, and taking a deep breath. "Robert, can't you see what that creature was trying to do? Even in death he wanted us in strife." She smiled up at him and put both of her hands on his chest. "Remember who we are. I know there is good in here." She patted him on the chest with her right hand.

"But she..." he stammered. "Her actions could have..."

"No, Robert. Do not consider those types of possibilities. Her actions have spoken volumes. Even now, when you had her in your grasp she could have responded with her weapons, and yet she did not." Closing her eyes, Diane slid her arms around Robert and hugged him. A soft blue light bathed both of them for a moment. When it faded the rough, taut lines on Robert's face and neck had disappeared, replaced by a much calmer expression that I had not seen on him since before we arrived here.

"I am sorry," Robert apologized. "Everything about Elilith is getting to me. I fight the rage within me, and sometimes I lose." He offered a hand to Miriele who was getting to her feet and told her, "I am sorry. I guess I should be thanking you. We won because of the damage you did. You could have left, and you did not." He avoided her for a moment, and I almost thought that he wasn't going to look into her eyes, but he continued, staring directly into her face, "I will try to curb my anger so it won't happen again." With that said, he inspected his gear and grudgingly left.

We remained there in an awkward silence for a few moments before Cat broke it with a growl. I scanned the room for him until he growled a second time letting me see him in a hidden alcove that apparently extended deeper into the cave. We rushed to the opening, expecting the worst, but were pleasantly surprised when his growls were merely to draw our attention to the concealed passage. A cool breeze passed over us, and I enjoyed the sensation.

"Before we go further, we should search this mess," Jean-Luc stated calmly, already advancing on the monsters' makeshift camp.

We spread out to scout around, but only turned up a small satchel filled with a handful of burnished coins. Although I had never seen the image before, or seen the type of material the coin was crafted out of, I muttered, "Platinum. This should come in handy."

"How do you know that? What is platinum?" Diane asked me.

"I don't know," I replied. "I seem to know what they are, and that Kromar's crest is displayed here. Who knows? Maybe it's because of what the scientist did to us. Somehow we are becoming more and more comfortable..." I stopped and scratched Lumadian under the chin. "...with the mysteries that this world has to offer. I do not see how we can go back. I think that whoever sent us here, must have known something." I threw my head back, raised my arms, and shouted, "Why have you done this? What do you expect of us? Why? Are you even listening?" With each question, my voice got louder until I felt an impact on my side as Cat tackled me as a large piece of the ceiling came crashing down right where I was standing.

"Mrowl?" Cat stared into my face while he crushed my chest with his weight as if asking me if I was crazy.

"Fine, Cat, I will be fine. You can get off now," I managed to blurt out as his weight started to crush me. He licked my face with his rough tongue, then bounded off me. I sat up and shook off the effects of almost getting crushed twice, then got to my feet.

Diane came over to steady me. "We need to be going." She approached the hidden corridor next to Miriele. "What do you suppose is down this pathway?"

"Could be anything," Miriele replied. "I know that this cave had lots of minerals, both precious and valuable. If the ones in charge put this kind of guard in here, I'd think it would be something that is very much needed."

Robert grasped the pommel of his sword then marched to the tunnel. "In that case, we should capture it, or prevent it from falling into their hands." We gathered behind him, readied ourselves, and entered the passageway.

After taking a few steps into the downward slopping passage, our sense of smell was assaulted by the foul scent of rotten eggs. Although it was difficult to breathe, we decided to press on, determined now more than ever to discover what secrets this branch of the mine held. Before long, the passage opened to a large, domed chamber that could have held the entire ogre party four times over. The floor leveled off, and there were small pools of stagnant liquid everywhere. Along the back wall directly across from the entrance, about a dozen hideous creatures scratched the stone with their claws. The things were about my height. Although they appeared to be humans, that part of them must have died long ago. Their hair was long and greasy, their nails were longer than daggers, and their eyes were a dull white. Bits of flesh fell off of them periodically as they mindlessly performed their tasks. My nose told me they were the source of the smell. As we watched, the creatures gathered the stone bits and put them into a large box suspended by stilts. Moments later, a polished, glowing stone would fall out of the bottom into a catch basin that would be emptied by another creature and the stones put into a crate. Those crates were stacked neatly in the back of the cave. None of the things even acknowledged our entrance into the room.

"Oh my," Miriele gasped. "Jaspherine! I cannot believe that this was here and no one spoke about it. A handful of this stuff would dwarf any king's hoard in value."

"Well, who was going to talk about it?" Robert drew his sword from its sheath. "Dead things tell no stories." He approached the things. He progressed nearly halfway there before splashing in one of the pools and sinking up to his thigh. He yanked his leg out and placed it on solid footing.

The creatures stopped whatever they were doing and lumbered to Robert, as if he had become a beacon. Their stench increased greatly as they drew near, but we readied ourselves against their physical assault and ignored the smell for the moment.

Diane ran past me to Robert's side, casting her spell to deal with the non-living. As the spell came into existence, it appeared as though it was going to have its normal effects. But the spell's energy stopped short of the ceiling then seemed to gravitate down to the creature's claws, or more accurately, the bits of rocks stuck in their elongated nails.

Jean-Luc jumped into action, nimbly dodging the pools, and did a few somersaults to gain even more momentum before punching his opponent in the chest, hitting with such force that he collapsed the creature's chest. The sickly sound of crunching bones rang in our ears. The thing he hit merely bent back a little and groaned, not even breaking stride. It bent down and tried to grip Jean-Luc's arm, but my friend rolled out of the way and to his feet. In a series of fluid continuous motions, he tried a leg sweep, which did knock it off its feet. The thing simply tried standing up, ignoring the normal effect its injuries would have on a living being. Clenching one of its arms at the wrist, Jean-Luc pulled on the creature's arm as he jammed his foot under its chin, forcing the thing to its side and pinning its other arm. The pressure he put on the hold was too great for the decrepit being, and the entire arm came off in his hands. But instead of falling lifeless, the arm wrestled Jean-Luc's hold on it, eventually managing to loosen his hold on the appendage. Jean-Luc kept taking steps back to us, unsure of what to do, as the creature picked up its arm and re-attached it merely by holding it in place.

By the time Jean-Luc had rejoined us, some of the other creatures had managed to reach Robert. Robert sliced through his first opponent, cutting it cleanly through the chest, and continued his attack on another. As he was about to finish that particular creature off, it ripped into his arm with its claws, opening a huge gash on Robert's forearm. Another creature stepped in, biting Robert on his side above his left hip. Robert yelled in anger and anguish as he twisted his blade out of the creature it was currently buried in. Placing both hands on the pommel, he shoved his blade down into the neck of the creature that had a death grip on his side. He managed to sever the head from the body, causing the body to fall, but it stopped itself and held Robert's leg, imbedding its claws in his upper thigh. The creature's head still chewed on Robert's hip, seemingly unfazed by the sudden lack of a body.

I spun around, putting my back to the combat. Holding my hands in front of me, I bent my fingers to simulate holding a ball. Through our link, I could feel magical energy flowing from Lumadian, intensifying the spell as he helped me to concentrate on the sphere I was creating until the molten sphere of fire sprung to life. I felt flames attempting to leave the ball; tiny tendrils pulling at the rocks in the creatures' claws.

Tiny claws readjusted themselves on my shoulder and the ball pulled together into a solid mass of flames. "*Hurry,*" Lumadian thought to me. "*I cannot hold it together long!*"

Taking careful aim, I whipped the flaming mass at the floor near Robert's feet. The ball exploded the moment it contacted with the rocky surface, expanding to a wall of flame fifteen feet across. It rippled like a wave and headed to the back of the cave, washing over most of the creatures and igniting them. The moment the flame wall reached one of the containers half-filled with rocks, it was instantly snuffed out, although the creatures continued to burn.

Cat jumped into action, hitting the decapitated head with his full weight, sending it bouncing off the floor. Since its teeth still gripped Robert's hip, some flesh was still in its mouth as it landed in a puddle. Hitting the ground on his front paws, Cat back-kicked the nearest flaming mass, sending it flying into the back wall. But the blow seemingly had no effect on it. The thing hobbled toward us again.

A few of the burning creatures meandered to Cat, drawn to him as if he had a target painted on him. As they grasped his body, the fire migrated from them to him. The scent of burnt fur filled my nose, and Cat hissed. Through the fiery masses, I could see blood oozing from his wounds. He tried to escape their grasp, but they pinned him to the floor, pressing their claws deep into his body.

Something materialized between the creatures and the rocks. Worried that more trouble might be added to our already tense situation, we were relieved to see it was Miriele. She waved to us, took some powder from one of her many pouches, and poured it out. I watched as she took a tiny pinch of Jaspherine and set it in her palm. She examined the stone, nodded, and then slammed her palm into the powder. A bluish fire erupted from the union of rock and powder, obscuring Miriele from view as the fire engulfed her. The flames rotated counter-clockwise. The fiery funnel's speed intensified, whipping all the air in the room. Suddenly the creatures stopped attacking us, and were drawn toward the cyclone. I didn't feel the pull on my body, but I felt a tug on several of the objects I held: all of the magic items. The closer the beings got to the fire, the quicker they were pulled into the swirling flames. One by one, every single creature tumbled into the flames. Each additional one increased the size of the spell. When the last of the creatures hit the flames, it exploded in a brilliance that blinded everyone. After I could see again, there was no trace of the creatures left. In the center of where the magic began, Miriele lay unconscious, badly burned. The damage of the spell was not limited to her, however; bits of the roof also rained down.

"Get her!" I yelled to Robert, as I attempted a spell to hold the roof together. Magical tendrils crisscrossed like a net that pushed against the ceiling, but the strain cracked it further, bringing down larger chunks of rock. Robert and Jean-Luc joined Miriele, hoisted her up by both arms, and carried her out of the cavern as a massive rock crashed down where she had been. The rest of us ran out behind them as the chain reaction spread to the entire roof. I dove into the passage as the entire room collapsed on itself, sending clouds of dirt and rock into the corridor. Although we choked on the debris, none of us were hurt by the collapse.

Diane's hands illuminated with a pale blue light. She touched Miriele, and the soft energies cascading over her still body. At first nothing appeared to happen, but Diane concentrated harder. The light filled the corridor as she tried again. Lumadian hopped off my shoulder and landed next to Miriele, nudging her softly with his head. Diane gritted her teeth, but managed to complete the spell.

The spell softened Miriele's burns, melting them away to nothingness. We were not sure anything else was happening until Miriele reached up and scratched Lumadian under the chin softly and whispered, "You are such a cutie." Lumadian nudged her to sit up. The rest of her injuries disappeared, and Miriele breathed deeply, smiling at us as she extended her hand to me. I helped her to her feet then picked up Lumadian, setting him on my shoulder.

"What the heck was that?" I asked Miriele, choking a bit on the dust.

"Well, I figured the dust mixed with the magical rock would be the best way to attract the attention of the magically-created creatures." She paused to cough a few times before continuing. "I did not expect the interaction between the two to be so violent. I guess that happens when you try to be the hero."

Smiling, I told her, "I am glad you decided to try. It isn't often you meet a person willing to be a hero. Thank you for joining us."

"*I like her better than him*," Lumadian told me.

"Lumadian likes you, too, and he is hard to please."

"Of course," she said. "He is very smart."

I felt the pride swelling in my tiny friend again, and I tried to suppress a chuckle. "So, what exactly is a magically-created creature?"

Miriele tilted her head and raised an eyebrow. "You're a mage, and you don't know that?"

"What I meant to say was, I have never seen it used on those types of creatures to force them to work the way they were."

"Oh, that part is true. Usually ghouls are not meant as workers, but you should know by now that magic can do almost anything."

I nodded in agreement, even though I didn't know to what extent she truly was correct. "Well, let's get out of here and check the next corridor."

# CHAPTER TWENTY-THREE
## TRAINING

We arrived at the start of the next passageway, listening carefully. Hearing nothing, we cautiously entered the tunnel, which was the narrowest of the ones we had entered so far. We arranged ourselves so that Cat and Miriele were in front, Robert and Jean-Luc next, followed by Diane and myself.

I don't know how long we travelled before I spotted a soft orange light up ahead. I tapped Robert on the shoulder and showed him the light.

Robert touched Miriele on the shoulder and Cat on the tail to make them aware of it. "Rush in and take them by surprise," he whispered. He changed position to take lead, raised his fist into the air, then dropped it and dashed down the tunnel.

I followed last, trying to think of a proper spell, and ran into the backs of Robert and Jean-Luc who had stopped moving and were searching around the room.

"*Incredible*," I heard Lumadian think aloud—it was strange because, unlike anything before, I knew the comment wasn't directed at me—as his head swiveled back, forth.

I stepped back and gasped. The soft light came from a vast quantity of glowing butterflies that clung to the stalactites or perched on ledges near the ceiling. Their light warmed the veins of minerals in the rocks, making the entire room feel like it was bathed in sunlight. To the far left against the wall, I saw two pools. To the far right, was a crystal clear lake of water that reflected everything so perfectly, you couldn't tell where each part ended. Scattered about the cavern, large, spiral hourglass columns, going from floor to ceiling, were nearly covered in a leafy plant that resembled green cabbage.

"What is going on here?" Jean-Luc asked with shock in his voice.

Miriele shook her head. "I have no idea."

We cautiously explored around the perimeter of the round room, dragging our feet through the thick bed of moss-like plants at our feet. As we got closer to the two separate pools, we noticed two worn, wooden signs. One was marked "malez" and the other was marked "femalez". The male's pool had a scent of cinnamon and cedar, while the female's pool gave off an aroma of jasmine and lavender.

Diane reached down and ran her fingers through the female pool. "It's warm too. Do we have time to bathe?"

I nodded. "I don't see why not. We have to keep an eye out, but let's eat first." We pulled out our supplies and had a nice meal in silence. After we were done, we cleaned up the mess we had created. "Now that we are done, I think it is time to try out the water."

"Great!" Miriele joyfully proclaimed before stripping nude before us.

When we realized how far she was removing her clothes, Jean-Luc, Robert, and I all spun our backs to her. Cat, however, gawked at her with his eyes wide and his jaw open.

Robert coughed at Cat. "Cat, turn around!"

Cat hissed at Robert then huffed, spun around, and sat down on his haunches.

We heard the sound of someone getting into the water, and I was glancing at Miriele when I heard Diane. "Now boys, stay that way so I can get in." We waited until we heard the same sound and decided to strip down ourselves.

Robert, surprisingly, managed to get his gear off first. He faced the pool the women were in. "Miriele, check out a real man."

"Robert!" I yelled at him as I dropped my colorful garb. My vision diverted, and I saw both ladies submerged to the neck in the water.

Miriele chuckled and edged closer. "I am looking, Robert, but if you've seen one, you've seen them all."

I suppressed the urge to laugh as Jean-Luc jumped into the pool.

I inched to the edge and put my legs into the water. I held Lumadian so I could see his eyes as I thought to him, wondering if it reflected at all in his reactions. *"Does water harm you?"*

He responded by flying off my shoulder to midway between us and the ceiling, and nose-dived into the center of our pool. He stayed submerged for a while before bursting the surface of the pool and spraying all of us. *"I love to fish, too."*

I dove in and nearly melted. The water felt amazing. It tantalized my skin, and I could feel the dirt dissolving without the need for soap. I dunked my head a few times before leaning back and enjoying.

Miriele stared at Cat. "What about the kitty?"

Cat approached the water and touched one paw to it. He hissed, jerked his paw back, and shook the paw, but no water flew off.

Jean-Luc motioned to him. "Come on, Cat. Everyone needs to be clean, especially you in…" He stopped himself short as he glanced at Miriele.

Cat emitted a "humph," and did a belly-flop in. When he floundered around, we all burst out laughing as he figured out how to paddle.

We all enjoyed the warm water for a while as Lumadian circled above. When Lumadian flew over and landed next to me, I eyed him curiously. "How did you dry yourself off?"

*"My scales are water-tight, but there should be some trace—I don't know actually."*

I got out of the pool to examine Lumadian more closely, but the moment I was no longer in contact with the water, I was instantly dry too. All that remained was the light scent of cinnamon and cedar. I picked up my multi-colored shirt, dunked it under the water, and yanked it out. The garb was instantly clean and dry, as if I had spent all day scrubbing it.

Everyone got out and repeated my actions. When Cat managed to pulled himself from the water, he shook himself like a dog caught in a rainstorm, but his fur was dry.

Robert experimented with his metal objects, but like everything else, once he removed whatever was submerged, it came out dry and clean. Even his sword, which was a bit grimy, seemed brand new.

Diane dressed fully and stretched. "I wish there were more of these types of pools everywhere."

A shimmer of light ignited on the other side of the women's pool, and two creatures appeared, with arrows aimed directly at Diane's back. Time slowed to a crawl as I studied them. From the waist down, they had billy goat bodies. Their torsos and arms looked human, although with fiery-red skin. Their heads, though, were demonic, with long black curved horns. I watched in horror as they both released arrows, and I wasn't able to respond.

Robert, moving at a speed I would have thought impossible, scooped up his shield and cleared the distance to Diane before the arrows had even traveled half-way to their target. He shoved

Diane sideways into the pool and continued on, stopping at the satyr-like creatures before they could draw another arrow as time slipped back to its normal pace.

When Diane splashed into the pool, everyone else's attention was drawn to her. Jean-Luc went to the edge and helped her out. I tried to summon the balls of light, but instead a thick, black ooze flew from my fingertips and covered the creature's head. It dropped its bow and bleated loudly enough that the sound echoed off the walls.

Robert drew his sword and swung at the other, but it managed to block the strike with its bow.

The satyr spit phlegm at Robert, brought its head back, and head-butted him so hard, it dropped Robert to his ass.

I was about to cast another spell, and Lumadian flew off my shoulder when something else stunned both of us.

Jean-Luc, who had finished helping Diane, ran across the surface of the water and drove the satyr attacking Robert into the rocky wall. He jumped on the back of the other and choked him.

Miriele dashed to the thrown satyr and stabbed him in the chest before he could recover.

The rest of us hurried to aid Jean-Luc, but by the time we got there, he had already brought the creature down and twisted its neck with an audible crack.

From the back wall in the center of the room, a larger version of the ones we'd fought broke through some vines that were concealing a passage. It snapped its head in our direction and roared, the force of which threw everyone but Lumadian and me into the wall.

I had managed to throw my arms up in front of my face and summoned a magical force to protect us. After I felt the wave pass over us, I absorbed the energy from the shield, forced it into a ball, and hurled it at the demon goat.

I watched as the creature concentrated on my spell, and forced it to a standstill. It punched at us, and the ball reversed its direction.

*"Quick, concentrate together to force it back."*

I did as Lumadian instructed and tried to control my own spell again. I managed to slow its approach, but not stop it as I heard my friends getting to their feet and retrieving their items. My heart raced, and I sweated profusely as the ball not only drew closer, but grew bigger. I gritted my teeth as its shadow covered my body. The creature bellowed in pain, and I felt the spell fall back under my control. My eyes darted to it, and I noticed Miriele behind the creature. I propelled the ball at the beast, but felt a surge of uncontrollable power from within. The spell amplified with all my forced concentration, and when it hit, the impact exploded and shattered three of the support columns around it.

The ceiling crumbled down. "Run!" Robert commanded and darted for the entrance the thing had come from. When we got closer, we saw Miriele unconscious against the wall. Robert picked her up like she was a rag doll and continued to run. We all followed him into the tunnel as the rest of the ceiling collapsed and blocked off the entrance.

Diane came over with my items. "Here you go."

I splashed a little water on Miriele's face, and she came to. "How are you feeling?"

She hopped to her feet and brushed herself off. "Next time, let me get out of the way of your explosive spells." She peered down the tunnel. "At least there are no decisions now, so let's get out of here."

We hadn't progressed more than fifty paces when Cat crouched down and crept forward. His actions caused Robert to draw his weapon and shield and Jean-Luc to assume a defensive posture. Miriele followed closely as Cat continued for a few dozen steps. The passage crumbled under them. Robert dropped his shield and sword as he and Jean-Luc converged on Cat. The four of them disappeared under the falling rock and were out of sight in an instant.

When the dust settled, it was as if no hole had ever existed. It was completely smoothed over by the debris. We dropped and attempted to remove the rubble, but to no avail. They were lost to us.

"What should we do?" Diane sounded panicked.

We heard a noise from ahead of us, which we assumed had been the source of Cat's initial concern. We searched for anything additional that might hold up, but didn't see anything we could use. Robert's shield and sword had been consumed by the crevice.

Diane and I backed away, not knowing what to expect. From behind us, we heard growling. Confusion set in. We apprehensively stepped toward the first noise, unsure where to go.

"*Look out!*" I heard too late and a new hole gobbled up Diane, Lumadian, and myself.

# CHAPTER TWENTY-FOUR
## TRIALS

I awoke to a room completely devoid of light. It was cold and I could feel my breath around my face. I crawled blindly without finding anything. I sat and thought, "*Lumadian,*" but received no reply. A thought popped into my head, and I tried to shift my sight. It was difficult, but I managed to see a strange light coming from a roughly human-sized figure and one about my companion's size. Taking a flask from my belt, I knelt next to Diane and splashed a bit of the liquid in her face. She moaned and smacked her lips a few times before sitting up. I picked up Lumadian and did the same, but he didn't move. I handed him to Diane, who fumbled for a moment to find her symbol, then cast her healing spell. I watched her rub his belly until I felt a purring in my mind.

I chuckled. "He is fine. He likes the belly rub."

"*You are no fun.*" He jumped up and flew around us.

"I can't see an exit from here. Lumadian, can you?"

"*Sure, send the little one out, right?*"

"No, it's not like that," I said aloud.

"What's wrong?" Diane asked.

I looked in her direction. "He didn't like that we sent him out."

"But he is the bravest of us." Diane added.

With that added incentive, Lumadian flew off. It only took him a moment to reply, "*I found a tunnel my size. I will be back.*" With that, he left.

Time seemed to crawl, and the moments crept away. I do not know how long we sat there until I heard Diane say, "It is so cold." I heard a shiver in her voice.

Moving closer to her, I put my arm around her and pulled her close. "Is that any better? Once Lumadian finds a way out, we can go find the others."

I felt her put her arm around my back as she shifted closer to me. "That is much better. But what if there is no way out? The others might be hurt! What if Lumadian can't find an escape for us? I do not want to die in this land, in this cave—I had so many things I wanted…"

I stopped her mid-sentence. "We will be all right. Lumadian will find a way to get us out."

"He is a sweetie, but not as sweet as the one I am with now." She leaned even closer to me, resting her head on my chest. Her hand slid up and down my side. "You are quite warm."

"So are you," was my only reply. I rubbed her side as well, feeling her curves. I kissed the top of her head and inhaled, getting a full whiff of her soft perfume from the cleansing lake. She glided her hand over my stubble, stroking it until her finger tips reached my lips.

"Diane," I said, but was cut off by her finger.

The heat from her breathe burned my soul, causing me to exhale. I could see her face coming to mine, and our lips touched for a brief moment. We kissed again, this time a bit deeper. I wrapped my arms around her. Her touch jolted my body. All my worries seemed to disappear as I felt her perfect skin. I cupped the back of her neck and gently kissed her throat when she leaned her head back. My hands continued down to one of her breasts. I no longer felt the cold. One of her hands rubbed my back, coming around my side to my front. I touched my hand to her calf, and slowly worked my way up to the soft part of her inner thigh. I felt a purring and an immediate feeling of strong arousal that stopped me immediately. I broke the kiss.

"What…"

"Lumadian is here."

*"Don't stop on my account! This was just getting good."*

"What are you doing here?" I said aloud, as I tried to regain my composure.

*"Is that any way to speak to your savior? I found the others. They are attempting to open the door as we speak."*

"He found the others." I broke the embrace, but not before Diane managed a soft, teasing grope.

A crack of light entered the room and nearly blinded me. I blinked a few times as heat rushed into the room. I stopped my vision spell and shook my head to clear it. Jean-Luc pushed the stone aside. When my eyes adjusted I could see he was covered from head to foot in some type of ash.

"Well. Look who we found," Robert said, over Jean-Luc's shoulder.

Diane and I stood up, brushing off the soot. Gathering our supplies, we left the room. After leaving the cave, I could see rows and rows of stone slabs on both sides of the tunnel. It was a type of jail. The rocks were of various sizes and shapes, some not quite filling the gaps.

*"I was able to lead Cat to the outside, and he freed the rock in his holding cell, then the others freed you. I figured you wanted more time when I felt what you were doing."* He landed on my shoulder again.

"Where is Miriele?" I asked.

"She was separated from the rest of us. I figured we could take care of the beast first, then pick her up on the way out," Jean-Luc explained.

I was very curious at his sudden reaction to her. "Would you care to explain why you want to leave her behind?"

Jean-Luc tapped the end of the staff he had found—a nervous quirk that had begun upon our arrival in Ellilith. "The way I figure, the five of us have an emotional attachment to the necessity of freeing Cat. Miriele does not. If we only get one opportunity, I do not want to take a chance with someone without a stake in the game."

I thought about what he said for a moment. "But…"

Robert stepped up to me. "No 'buts.' She'll be fine. Let's get this done so she doesn't have to wait too long in her cell." Without waiting for a reply, he left with Jean-Luc and Cat at his side.

I exhaled sharply at Diane, sighed, and followed.

The passage was lit with braziers that seemed to burn without a need for fuel. Down one end, the corridor seemed to stretch as far as the eye could see, with an endless number of cells. On the other end, it opened into something. We followed the passage for several hundred feet until it ended at a large chamber.

At the back of the chamber an alcove was cut into the stone. It was semicircular in shape and reached twenty-five feet at its apex. At the left and right were two large metal disks about Robert's height across. Above the metal disk on the left was a plaque. In the middle of the room, near the back, four human-like monsters almost twice the height of Robert with purple skin marched at us. Each hand held some type of blacksmith hammer.

"I've got the one on the far left," Robert said before running off. He raised his shield in front of him and knocked the creature down. He spun around and smashed the end of the tear-shaped shield into the face of his foe, and laughed with glee.

Another beast lumbered to Robert's side and hit him over and over with the hammers, but Robert ignored the blows.

Jean-Luc swung his staff and poked at the monster on the far right. The thing side-stepped and brought down two of its weapons at his midsection. Jean-Luc had enough time to deflect the blows, but fell hard on the ground. The creature dropped its hammers, picked up Jean-Luc, and flung him into the wall with such force that he cracked the marble wall.

Lumadian shouted in my mind. *"Vish'Nar'Ru! Deadly protectors of dark places."*

I lifted my arms to the height of my chest and summoned eight prismatic orbs of light and launched them at our foes. Diane stepped in front of me. The balls streaked to the Vish, bounced off them, and flew directly back, hitting Diane.

She screamed in agony and her clothes smoldered. "Help!"

Cat slinked over to a Vish. When he got close, the thing breathed noxious yellow bile from its mouth and in a wailing voice said, "Motionless you are."

Cat froze. Even his tail stopped its hypnotic back and forth motion.

The Vish that threw Jean-Luc got behind Robert and pummeled him with the hammers, bringing my friend to his knee. The Vish that froze Cat added to the beating, causing Robert to lower his head.

I studied their attacks. "They must have orders to put prisoners back in their cells." I circled Diane as Lumadian poured magic into me. I held my arms out to my sides, palms to the ceiling. Smoke billowed from my fingertips. Then I saw something that chilled me to the bone and stopped my spell.

Robert gritted his teeth. His body shimmered with red light, and his eyes burned. He punched his fist through one of the Vish's chest. The thing fell face-first at Robert's feet. He raised his foot and crushed its head as though it were an egg.

The remaining two stepped back as if unsure what to do. They spun their hammers around to the opposite ends that had been sharpened, no longer trying to subdue.

Robert held his arm up to block the weapons. When the weapons hit his arm, they shattered like glass. The Vish was unable to halt its attack, thus destroying all its weapons. Robert kicked the creature in the chest, sending it flying into the wall, but instead of cracking the wall, the Vish sunk several feet into the solid marble wall.

The remaining monster crossed its hammers over its head and bowed its head to Robert. In an icy voice, it said, "I submit to you."

I watched as Robert planted his hands on the Vish's shoulders. In a quick jerking motion, he ripped its arms off its body. The monster fell on its backside. Robert clamped the side of its skull with his palms and dug his thumbs into its eye sockets.

The creature screamed in agony so loud that I felt the vibrations ripple through my body. Without thinking, I balled my hands so tightly that I pierced the flesh on my palms with my nails. I flung my fist in Robert's direction and shouted, "I steal your energy!"

Silvery bands of silk shot from me and streaked to Robert. When they touched him, they vibrated like lute strings. The yellow light that encased Robert seeped up into the bands and returned to encase me.

I yelled in anger, cracking the ground around me. Lumadian flew back and tried to speak to me, but it felt so distant and soft that I couldn't hear him. Staggering backward, grasping at air, my body shook for a few moments. I threw my head back and released a wall of energy in front of me.

As the wall passed over Cat, he instantly reverted to his human form. When it passed Robert, he blinked and spun around to me, any radiance snuffed out by the magic.

Before the spell hit the back wall, I felt something pierce my neck, and I blacked out.

*"You there? Come on, I didn't hit you that strong. Please wake up."*

I stayed motionless, trying to get the pounding in my head to cease. Lumadian bounced up and down on my chest. *"Wake up! Wake up! Wake up!"*

Robert grumbled. "Should we let it—Lumadian jump on him like that?"

Diane must have teasingly slapped him. "Quiet, Robert."

I felt Lumadian's claw on my chest and he scooted up to my neck to nuzzle me. *"I'm sorry."*

I reached around Lumadian and hugged him tight, eliciting a grumble. *"You have nothing to be sorry about."* Opening my eyes, I examined my friends. Cat had morphed back into his feline form and everyone's magical auroras that only I could see shone again. "How long have I been out?"

Robert extended his hand to me and yanked me off the floor. "About an hour." He sneered at Lumadian. "You are lucky he recovered when he did. I was getting antsy."

Lumadian glared at Robert. *"Yeah, and I would have stung you so hard, you would never have woken again."*

I rubbed my hands over my face and blinked my eyes a few more times, ignoring Lumadian's comments for the time being. Glancing at Cat, I said, "I saw you human again."

Before Cat could growl, I heard Lumadian. *"Your spell temporarily cancelled all magic. Normally, you can't do that with curses, but you did something I've never seen."*

"Is everyone else in good health?" "Can we check out that plaque now?"

Jean-Luc nodded. "We waited for you just in case."

I approached the plaque and read it out loud: "'If the prisoners run away, and all the guards start to sway, summon Almator who is no mere man, and watch all their faces pale.'"

"That sounds unusual." Diane came over and held my hand.

"We ready to do this?" I thought of a spell to ready, while waiting for everyone to respond.

Cat meow-purred at Diane.

"Cat wants to know if he should change back now," Diane said.

"Not yet," I stated. "If this is the beast with six arms, then jump away and change. Let's do this!"

Cat nodded, and we prepared. Robert blocked the front of the alcove, far enough away that nothing would appear on top of him. I got ready to step on one disk, while Jean-Luc got ready on the other. Diane was behind Robert, ready to heal him in the event it went bad. Cat hid behind Diane, waiting.

I yelled to Jean-Luc, "Now!" and we stepped on the disks. Moments slipped by, but nothing happened. We tried again with the same results.

I played the words over and over again in my mind and then stated them out loud, "Summon Almator who is no mere man, and watch all their faces pale." I repeated the phrase again. "'No mere man.' What do you think that means? No mere man—is the clue the word 'mere'?"

Diane joined us and took my hand in hers. "The plaque doesn't say 'man', it says 'male.'"

"It's the same thing."

"Perhaps," Diane said, "it means no 'male' can summon it."

"Great," Robert said. "What do we need? Chickens?"

"No, Rob, honey, no *male*," she said slowly. After seeing the blank expressions on all our faces Diane sighed. "Why do you think they have women in their ranks?"

"Are you trying to imply that women are somehow involved?" Robert asked.

I shrugged my shoulders. "I am as clueless as everyone else. Where are you going with this, Diane?"

"Perhaps, it takes a *fe-male*. You know no 'mere' male."

"Oh, that is great. So we cannot summon it," Robert said. "We only have one woman unless we go back and get Miriele."

"That is not entirely true," Diane said meekly, as she neared the black feline. "Cat," she said to him, "You must decide if you want to take that chance. As a cow you are a female and that might fulfill the plaque's requirements."

Cat paced back and forth for a moment before nodding at Diane and making a decisive sound.

Diane relayed his agreement and we arranged ourselves again. Robert set himself up in the same spot with Jean-Luc at his right. I was behind both of them and Cat stepped on the right disk.

I asked Lumadian, "*What do you feel would be a good type of starting spell?*"

"*Before we begin you should cast a protection. You never know what will happen when the thing is summoned.*"

Not knowing quite what to expect, I did as he suggested, concentrating on a protection spell. A dome-like barrier arose around the three of us. It distorted our vision slightly, like seeing a hot piece of earth in the distance on a warm summer's day. I yelled to Cat, "Go back to your normal form."

We watched as the shape of the cow replaced the jaguar. Diane jumped on the other disk.

At first nothing happened, and we all sighed with disappointment. Then a rumbling started, and a gigantic beast appeared in the alcove, nearly filling it. The beast was hideous, the stuff of purest nightmares. It looked like a massive human-like bull with six hideously deformed arms, each of which ended in a different type of claw. It had long sharpened horns on its demonic head that came out like a bull's. In its claws was a huge axe, nearly as tall as it was. It glanced to the right, then the left, smiling at Cat before locking its sight on Robert.

The beast swung its mighty axe at the three of us, hitting my barrier with such force that it shattered the spell like glass, scattering bits of light everywhere.

We were held transfixed by the blow. Jean-Luc recovered first, moving up to the creature and slammed it on the hoof with his staff. The blow did not have any effect.

Robert sliced the creature above its left hock and causing the beast to hop back. Again and again Robert sliced into the beast as blood gushed out the open wounds. The noise was deafening as the beast howled in agony.

Twirling the axe, the creature caught Robert squarely in the chest sending him flying across the room, down the hall, and out of sight.

Lumadian gripped my shoulder tighter. *"It is some type of minotaur, but I've never even heard of one like this, never mind seeing one."*

Jean-Luc stepped in front of the beast. The minotaur seemed perplexed by my unimposing friend, tilting its head to one side. Bringing its axe around, it swiftly cut down, but Jean-Luc deflected it as if it was a mere annoyance. The beast tried to kick Jean-Luc, but my friend's speed allowed him to avoid the kick with a counter-attack, hitting the creature squarely in his open wound. Unfortunately, it did not appear that he was doing any real damage. Yelling in pain and anger, the minotaur attempted to hit Jean-Luc time and time again, but failed to even come close.

Robert appeared at the entrance, blood painting his side wet. His eyes were wide open and fixated. His upper lip curled up, and he clenched his jaw tightly shut. He yelled at the beast in a death-curdling cry. He pulled his shield to his side and dove at the beast with his sword above his head.

At Robert's cry, the creature snapped its attention to the warrior again, eyeing his movements and waiting to see what Robert had in store for it.

Diane rushed over to Robert as she cast a spell at the creature. I watched the beast level its axe at Robert as he lifted his shield in defense. Diane finished her spell, casting pulsating, multicolored balls of light that darted around its head. The brightness seemed to confuse and enrage the beast. Its swing was off enough that Robert could deflect the blow. It was still so powerful that it sent the shield flying off of Robert's arm and across the stone floor. Both my friends dove out of the way as the beast swung wildly. Robert landed on his side, and moaned. Diane rushed to his side to heal him, but was caught under the hoof of the minotaur. She crashed down before she had time to heal Robert's injuries.

*It is funny how certain things tend to appear in your mind at the oddest moments,* I thought. *That jar I left in the room at the keep would come in handy right now.* Suddenly I could see it, sitting there all by itself. It was if I could reach out and pick it up. I reached out and was even more surprised when I actually did pick it up. Wasting no time, I opened the jar and gagged at the escaping odor. I'd thought it was bad when corked, but that was nothing compared to the overwhelming vileness that flooded around me. It also attracted the beast's attention. It stepped off of Diane and, snorting, lumbered to where I waited. Trying to remain calm, I summoned one more spell, extending a ghostly vision of my hands that carried the jar to its destination.

The creature stopped, curious as to why the scent was rising, until I lifted the jar to right about the creature's eye level, then dumped the entire contents directly on its nose. The creature cried out, dropping its axe. We all watched with curiosity, as the black liquid expanded and grew like a second skin. The creature fell on its stomach, trying to rub its face on the ground, but the liquid did not come off.

The commotion scared Cat, and the cow bolted into the corner mooing as if terrified.

Robert, stumbling about, retrieved his shield and tottered at the creature. Blood still gushed from the massive wound. The blackness covered its entire head and was moving down past the creature's chest. Removing the sword-length kris from his back, Robert hit the creature in the neck, pushing the blade in nearly to the hilt. The black ooze glided up the sword as well, causing him to release his grasp on the blade. Robert stumbled back and fell on his rear. He then slumped forward, eyes glazed over, and struggled to keep his eyes open, grunting in pain.

The creature stopped moving as the liquid covered its last remaining parts. I ran for Robert, and with some strength I did not know I possessed, pulled him out of the way before the beast rolled onto him. His face was white as a sheet and I could not tell if we had already lost him.

The stench was vile beyond my ability to put into words, and it was a miracle none of us were sick. We watched as the beast's breathing slowed and then stopped. The blood from its wounds dripped the same vile blackness that had consumed the beast.

Diane recovered from getting trampled and ran over to Robert, ready to heal his injuries. Her healing power began but refused to flow from her hand to Robert's body. She tried again and failed. She paused for a moment and summoned the spell one more time, putting every ounce of concentration into the spell. Suddenly, Robert jerked as the light flooded his body, covering him entirely in a golden light for several seconds. When it dimmed, we saw Robert breathing normally, but Diane slumped over.

Without stopping, I ran to Diane while Jean-Luc searched for Cat. I sat next to Diane and pulled her up to me. "Wake up!"

Diane's eyes fluttered open, and she groaned. "You guys have to take it easy in these battles."

Jean-Luc found Cat as his disheveled, human-self, huddled in a tight ball. He picked him up off the floor and hugged him. "Are you all right, Cat?"

Cat had a distant expression in his eyes and replied, "Moo."

We all cursed until Cat said in a soft voice, "Only kidding."

For a split second, we were all ready to pummel him… but instead we piled onto him, tickling the snot out of him.

"It is good to see you again," I said when I'd caught by breath.

"It is good to be me again." Cat stretched muscles that he had not been able to use for awhile.

"My aching body!" Robert sat up on the floor. Color was restored to his face, although I could still see the effects of the battle. "I see you are normal again, Cat. That is great." He attempted to stand, but fell down. He gritted his teeth, leapt to his feet, and recovered his items. "Let's get out of here."

Diane hugged Cat again. "Good to have you back," she said and kissed him on the cheek. "Now let's get Miriele and get out of here."

# CHAPTER TWENTY-FIVE
# MIDDLE AGE

Advancing down the hallway to the hall of doors, we were surprised to find that Miriele had already opened many of the doors and had a bulging backpack.

"There you are!" Miriele said with excitement. "I've been looking for you.—"

Robert scoffed and pointed at Miriele's pack. "You obviously were not looking *too* hard."

"—and in the process I found all kinds of goodies. Apparently, they never check on their prisoners. Where have you been? And who is that?" She asked, indicating Cat.

"Miriele, this is Charles Avery Thomlinson the Third. We call him. . ." I paused for a moment, taking in a breath.

"*Are you going to tell her who he actually is?*" Lumadian asked.

"Cat for short," I continued without answering my friend.

"Cat, eh? So this is the kitty who was rough with me. Very interesting talent there. It could be most useful against the druid."

"You mentioned a druid before. What does this druid have to do with anything?"

"Ah, so you don't know?" Miriele finished unlocking another door. "Rats!" she squealed as she opened it. Removing a short sword from her scabbard, she swiped at a dog-sized vermin as it attempted to run by her.

At the entrance, I saw the reflections of many red eyes. Without even thinking, I released half a dozen orbs of fire. The orbs lit the room for an instant before hitting the animals, searing them on the spot. We heard a snarl from the room as something shifted within it.

I shouted, "There is something big in there!"

We fanned out in a semicircle around the entrance, waiting for something to emerge. For a few agonizing minutes, nothing happened. Then the wall exploded, barely missing Jean-Luc. A horde of rats piled from the hole, forcing us back.

I lagged behind my friends and, when the last was out of the way, spun around and blanketed the floor with fire. "Back up! Back up!"

I watched in horror as the rats ran blindly into the fire and died. Wave after wave sacrificed themselves, and the sheer volume of rats filled half the height of the corridor. One leapt from the pile as I stumbled back, but Lumadian snatched it from the air and crushed it in his claws.

Cat transformed, and we lined up. We killed rats by the dozens, doing a good job at keeping them away from us until we heard a shriek from the dark room.

A grotesquely large rat shoved itself through the opening, scraping itself along the walls as it pushed a mound of dead rats ahead of it. Its ruby eyes radiated, and its fur was black with splotches of gray. It hissed, covering Diane, Lumadian, and me in mucus.

Robert wrinkled his nose and ran for the large rat, stepping on a few of the smaller ones in his path. He swung his sword at its head, but the rat batted the weapon out of his hand.

I summoned more fire when I heard Lumadian scream in my mind. *"No! What you are covered in is highly flammable."*

Jean-Luc leapt in, but the rat whipped its tail and lacerated his face.

Cat sprang on the rat's back, but his weight didn't even slow it down.

Robert punched the creature right between the eyes, and actually pushed it back.

The rat bared its teeth and lunged at Robert.

Miriele grappled with Robert in an attempt to toss him out of the way, but his bulk threw her off-balance. She managed to fling him to the floor, but left her back open to the rat. It crashed into her with a tremendous force, sending both of them sprawling. The creature used its weight to pin Miriele and locked its jaws on the back of her neck.

The rat crushed her neck in an instant. Miriele gurgled then went silent. We all tore into the beast, ignoring the bites from the smaller ones, trying to kill the leader by whatever means we could, but it simply clamped onto her throat again. Even Lumadian stung it several times, but it refused to die.

Robert retrieved his weapon and shoved it directly into the rat's eye, twisting the blade until the rodent moved no more. With the death of the large rat, all the others scattered.

We pushed the rat off of Miriele, but even in death it refused to release its prey. As Robert, Jean-Luc and I tried to pry the jaws open to release its grip on Miriele, Diane tried to heal her injuries. We heard Diane weeping as we cracked the jaws of the rat and slung it off Miriele.

The neck was barely attached to her body and we averted our eyes from the sight. In the briefest of moments, we had lost her. With everything that we had faced thus far, it suddenly snapped us back into reality. Death was as real here as it was in our old home.

"Is there anything you can do?" I asked Diane.

Closing her eyes, she knelt beside Miriele's still body. Touching her chest we watched as a purple-tinted cloud enveloped her hand. The cloud grew in size until it completely covered Miriele. The mist grew in opacity until we could no longer see Miriele or Diane. We all held our breath and waited to see what was going to happen. When the mist finally dissipated, Diane fell unconscious on the floor. Miriele was free from injuries, but remained still.

Cat changed back, carefully picked Diane partially up from the floor, and splashed water on her face. Her eyes flickered and she moaned.

"I am sorry," Diane began, "but she was too far gone."

Jean-Luc took out one of the torches from his pack, igniting it on a nearby brazier. Peering into the rat room, he and I saw trash strewn about. In the corner, a large nest twitched with small nestlings. Their beady eyes reflected the light from the torch. He tossed the fire directly into the center of the concave nest. Within moments, the fire engulfed the creature's young. We searched the room, but heard arguments from the hall and went to investigate.

"What do you mean we are going to leave her here?" Diane yelled at Robert.

"I am not going to carry her around until we can find somewhere to bury her. She's dead! It is unfortunate, but it is the fact. Say your blessings, and let's be done with it."

"You cad! You uncaring oaf! Her body is barely cold, and you'd toss her aside like yesterday's trash? She gave her life to save yours!"

I spoke up, trying to calm Diane. "Diane, be reasonable. We want to give her a proper burial, but we can't do that on these poisonous lands. For all we know, that is how some of the dead creatures come to life, and you wouldn't want that for her. Taking her body would bring unnecessary risk for us all. I for one, do not want to leave her here as a meal for any other vermin either. Would you be willing to allow a funeral pyre?"

Diane sighed, disheartened by the situation. She held my arm for a moment. "I know you are right. I wish circumstances did not dictate our actions. If we are to do this, I want to do it correctly. We should gather as much wood as possible."

None of us argued with her as we gathered wood from the debris in the empty rooms. We piled it to form a makeshift funeral pyre. When we were finished, we carefully picked Miriele up and placed her in the center.

"We should find the escape. The fire could trap us if we don't," Cat said timidly.

"Jean-Luc, Robert, could you find a way out while we finalize the preparations?" I asked them.

Both of them nodded without saying a word and began their search. Robert entered one of the rooms while Jean-Luc inspected the hall. After about five minutes, he returned. "Miriele must have found the exit before opening the door. A ways down the passage, there is a section of wall. The wall is actually a cleverly hidden door that appears to be like the rest of the stonework. It was open slightly, and a pike in the frame prevents it from closing."

"What of the items she found?" Cat held up Miriele's satchel.

"Let's put it with her," Diane replied. "I know that I would not be able to use any of them, knowing where they come from."

Robert looked as though he was about to say something but cut himself off and huffed.

Lumadian shifted his weight on my shoulder. *"You sure I can't do something to him?"*

I didn't reply to him but answered Diane. "I think that would be the right thing to do."

*"One moment please."* Lumadian swiftly and silently flew over to Miriele, landing on her chest as he gave her a gentle hug. He closed his eyes, and a soft sound came from him. He touched the top of his head, to the bottom of her chin. We all waited for him to finish as tears welled in Diane's eyes. After a few moments, he

circled around and hopped twice down to Miriele's hand. He picked up her hand and kissed it, placing it down then picked up the other and kissed it, too. Lumadian arranged one hand on top of the other then flew to my shoulder, nuzzling the side of my head. I scratched him softly. "*I am done.*"

Placing the bag on Miriele's legs, we stepped back and allowed Diane to say a few words, before lighting the wood on fire. We watched the flames grow until everything was ablaze before backing away and heading for the door. After everyone had safely passed through the door, I took the spike and closed the door. The stairs went up what seemed several hundred feet before ending in a ragged wall. Undaunted by its appearance, we fumbled with the door until we figured out how to open it.

Carefully peeking out, we saw what appeared to be someone's bedroom. We entered the room with caution, trying to ready ourselves for anything.

I nearly jumped out of my skin when Lumadian exclaimed, "*Look at that!*" My jumping caused everyone to jump before I heard what sounded like a timid, "*Sorry.*"

I ignored the puzzlement of my friends while trying to understand what Lumadian was telling me. Partially hidden under the pillow on the bed, was a slender piece of metal with strange carvings on it. I slipped it into my sleeve, and we left the room.

It took us very little time to figure out where we were. The corridor matched where we had been when Miriele led us to the food storage area. We hastened to leave the cave, our task completed.

# CHAPTER TWENTY-SIX
## TRADITIONS

A cold rain was falling as we broke from the darkness of the cave to the dreariness of the day. The wind was whipping the rain so that it came down sideways. We waited in the entrance of the cave for several minutes for any sign that the storm would break. We debated whether or not the weather should slow our progress.

Robert reached out and let the rain hit his bare hand. "It is only rain. Why are we stopped? If we linger here too long, someone will find us."

Diane arched her head to peek outside. "I was hoping it would let up a little."

I sighed and patted Robert on the back as I brushed by him into the rain. "Robert is correct. I don't want to stay *here* longer than necessary and be discovered. Cat, change into your jaguar, and keep smelling the air. That should give us warning if something is approaching."

Robert marched out without any more discussion. "Now that that is settled, let's complete our task. Whatever is to become of us, I want to guarantee we stay together." For the first time in a long time, I felt his words were genuine and that we had our old Robert back.

Once we left the cave and had taken a few steps, Lumadian nuzzled my ear. *"Wait a moment. Concentrate on the entrance with me."*

"Step back," I told the others and raised my hands in front of me with my fingers bent. I concentrated for what felt like a long time as the rain drenched my body. The cold seeped into my clothing and my arms ached while I waited for something to happen. I was about to give up when I felt my body start to shake, which I initially thought was due to the cold rain, but I realized that the feeling extended beyond me to the entrance of the cave. My fingertips felt as though they were touching rock, and I instinctually pulled down. I watched as part of the cave collapsed from the top down. Any dust was doused by the bad weather. I nudged Lumadian who finished helping me with the spell.

*"At least now they have to work on getting this back open and won't have time to follow us,"* he said to me.

I was about to say something to him, but I couldn't find the words to argue with his logic. I was about to say something to my friends, but they seemed unfazed, so I didn't feel any further comment on the situation was necessary.

After we had put the cave far behind us, we paused under a patch of low-hanging vegetation and pulled out the robes we had discovered in the keep. Even though they were all the same size before we put them on, the cloaks fit as though they were tailored to us. I was a bit surprised when I pulled the hood over my head and found that the cloak actually did a good job of keeping the cold rain away. Lumadian remained around my neck, so I covered him with the cloak as well. His warmth smothered the cold, and it quickly disappeared. It was more than feeling his warmth against my neck. I felt his warmth *as* my warmth. The wonderful feeling totally erased the cold, and I was very happy he was with me.

We traveled down the path of the forbidding forest for a while without incident. The weather never let up for a second, and it appeared that with every step we took, the forest grew darker and more sinister. The trees seemed bent at weird, impossible angles and their branches twisted around themselves. The trail flooded, slowing our movement further as we trudged through the mud. After traveling for hours without any changes, we saw a party in the distance. Without knowing who it was, we decided the best course of action would be to journey onward.

As we approached one another, we could see that the other party was comprised of a tall, gangly, bipedal creature with arms that reached down to its calves and nails that nearly dragged on the ground. Its skin was bright yellow-green with black splotches of hair growing from various parts of its body. Its face was a warped version of a tragedy mask with an overly-long nose. Around him, six creatures marched to a cadence grunted by the middle one. Their facial features were large, and almost comical with green-tinted skin and hair, but their appearance seemed more plant-like than human. It was apparent to us that they had seen us, and we prepared for the worst.

When we had come within striking distance of one another, I heard the leader barking orders to the other things, but could not understand a word until Lumadian translated for me. *"The leader, a troll, is telling them to prepare for battle and to be cautious."*

Having a gut feeling about how to handle the situation, I stepped in front of my friends and shouted out over the rain. "How dare you raise your weapons to us? Lower your arms, and stand aside before I have your hides for my new boots!"

The forest ogres—as Lumadian told me they were called—glowered at me, then back to the troll. One of them spotted my emblem and said something to their leader that sounded like gibberish to me. The troll grunted and was about to say something, but the rest of his companions lowered their clubs.

"What do you say?" I asked my companions, turning my back on the creatures. "Should we make an example of them?" I eyed their weapons, hoping they would pick up the visual clues. Without hesitation, Robert drew his weapons and stared at the troll.

Robert let out a small chuckle. "I say we punish him, since he is the dolt who leads them."

"We meant no harm, sir." I heard the troll's gruff tone.

"Interesting, it can speak our language," I said aloud. Marching over to the troll, I slapped him across the face with all my might. "Move on, and forget we met, understood?"

The troll gritted his teeth and said, "We never saw you, sir."

I nodded and motioned for my friends to follow as the creatures parted to let us pass. I kept stride, passing without so much as a glance back until I guessed we were sufficiently away from them. Glancing back, I waited until they disappeared before I spoke to my friends.

"I cannot explain why that worked, but for some reason I felt we needed to portray ourselves in that manner. With everything that we have encountered, it seemed reasonable to assume that enforcing a sense of fear is how things operate here. I guess I was lucky." We resumed our journey.

The sky darkened even more the deeper we went into the forest. Fallen dead branches littered our way. Deciding to seek shelter for the night, we saw the path branch in two directions. The two trails were very different, and I struggled to remember which path was the one we were told to take. The one on the left had virtually no debris on it and appeared as though the rain and wind were having less of an effect. On the right, the wind was howling even fiercer. The rain damaged everything it touched. The trees were a sickly gray which scared me more than the black we'd been seeing. On the path were several dead animals in various stages of decay.

"I suppose we must take the right, correct?"

Diane nodded. "Yes. You remembered?"

"No," I replied. "But I am resigned to it because that is how our luck is in this world."

Robert marched a bit down the path on the left. "No, J.D. We take this one. I don't care what scribbling you read. We *must* go down this path *because* it told us not to."

I was about to argue with him, but Robert didn't want for me to speak. He simply spun and marched on.

We ran after him, and Diane was the first to speak. "Since when do you alone decide for everyone else?"

Robert glanced around and retreated. "Since I am the one who seems to have the voice of reason."

I coughed, then laughed. "You? The voice of reason? Are you serious?"

Robert spun again and increased his pace. "Apparently. You see? Even the rain agrees with me. At least we are out of that accursed storm. And ano—"

Diane rushed up to the bend in the road where Robert hesitated and froze next to him. "Oh, my God!"

I reached Diane's side. "What's wrong?" I choked and stood still like Robert and Diane.

In the distance, on top of a rise, was a massive tree. Even at about a mile away, the tree blocked most the sky. It seemed as if the entire populations of Boston and New York could have easily lived in a quarter of its branches. But where I could envision the splendor of what it must have once looked like, currently the tree was ebony. Black was not the color, but its whole existence. I could feel evil coming from it, like heat radiating from sand.

I heard a gasp from Lumadian. "*The Tree of Conception!*"

I paused and asked him, "*What does that mean?*"

"*The Tree of Conception is where everything began. It is usually protected by guardians. That is why everything—including the elves—is dying. Someone must have taken the Gem of Life.*"

I cleared my voice. "Lumadian says the tree there normally gives life and energy to the forest. Someone defeated the guardians and stole a gem."

Diane crept ahead of us. "Why is the base of the tree white as new fallen snow?"

I stared. "We should take a closer look."

Robert drew his sword and marched to the tree. "Be cautious, everyone. I don't like this. Something doesn't feel right."

We followed Robert, and I watched constantly left and right. Cat roared as we reached the outer covering of the tree. He told Diane something.

"It is bones," Diane translated.

Robert spun the pommel of his sword then dashed for the trunk.

I was stunned only for a moment before I ran after him with the others close behind me.

When we got closer to the tree, I had to wade through thigh-high piles of bones. These were a varied assortment of bones: human-like creatures and large animals like elk and horse. I reached the trunk and leaned against it, trying to catch my breath. I glided my fingers into a recess which held something. When I touched the inner bark, feelings of pain and extreme anguish flooded into me. My body shook with violence, and I snarled at Robert. "Half-wit, next time drown yourself, and save us the trouble of saving your ass all the time."

Robert chuckled and leveled his weapon at me. "Really? You'd be dead if it wasn't for me."

I stomped up to him, clutched his shirt, and lifted him off the ground. "Are you serious, dumb, or both?"

Robert punched my arm, but I never flinched.

*"What are you doing?"*

I glanced at my friends. Cat panted at me strangely. Jean-Luc folded his arms over his chest and was indifferent as always. Lumadian licked my ear once.

I spoke aloud to Lumadian. "Mind your own business."

Diane came to my side. "J.D.?"

I stared into her eyes and tilted my head back and forth. Suddenly, I jerked the back of her head with my free hand and kissed her hard on the lips while still dangling Robert in the air.

At first Diane resisted, but then she leaned into the kiss. My body shook, and she held the back of my neck and kissed me with a fiery passion.

I dropped Robert and hugged her to me, feeling her warmth. I eased off the force with which I had been kissing her, but she continued until I broke it off and gasped for air. "What is going on?"

"*The tree is amplifying bad emotions. We have to get out of here!*"

"Run!" I yelled and bolted for the path.

We ran, almost making it to the edge of the tree when four blobs rose beyond the edge of bones.

"Yousss will sssstays with ussss," one hissed.

"Yessss, sssso nice for youss heresss," said another.

The biggest of the four chortled, "Yousss will ssstaysss with ussss foreversss and foreversss."

Robert rushed one and sliced it through the middle. His sword passed completely through the creature and emerged out the other side, but it didn't seem to do any harm.

"Yousss ticklessss ussss he doessss."

Cat ran up and swiped at the one that had remained silent. His claw made solid contact, but he couldn't pull it back. The ooze from the creature sucked at his forepaw.

"Youss joinsss ussss it willsss."

Diane tried summoning a spell, but nothing happened.

I created four balls of fire and tossed one at each. The balls immediately snuffed out upon contact with the creatures' skin.

"Ohsss thissss one issss powerful, he issss."

I asked Lumadian, *"Any suggestions?"*

He adjusted his perch on my shoulder. *"No. I've never encountered Shadants before. Just don't let them touch you."*

The one on Cat hissed in delight. "Oh, thisss onessss is tasssssty."

The rage I'd felt before returned, and I summoned four orbs, four *blue* orbs. The Shadants hissed and launched themselves at me. The one with Cat pulled him along as if he wasn't there. The orbs left my fingers and collided with the creatures, freezing them.

Cat yanked his paw free and shook off the excess ice. His paw was furless and red, but it didn't seem broken or bleeding. He reverted to human and I was pleased when the injury didn't carry over.

"We need to go. Now!" I yelled, running around the creatures and back to the path.

"Wonderful," Robert scoffed. "I can't wait to try out the right-hand fork. Are we excited?" Without waiting for an answer, he disappeared down the path.

Cautiously, we proceeded down the right fork, on guard for signs of danger, and were immediately assaulted with the full fury of the storm again. We tiptoed past the bodies of fallen animals and discovered an outcropping of rocks off the path. Vines hung over the entrance, almost concealing it from sight, but with the possibility of any reprieve from the storm and the heightened awareness of danger, the entrance nearly called out to us. It wasn't much—barely a den that would fit a bear and her cubs comfortably—but any respite from the harsh elements was welcome, and we staggered wearily into the cave. The cave also gave us the added comfort of a dry floor.

The vines covering the entrance not only blocked the rain, but also any chance of light entering the cave. I concentrated on a spell and produced the globes that I usually used offensively, but since I wasn't casting them at anyone, they merely floated around my body. The light wasn't much, but it was better than total blackness.

None of us wasted any time removing most of our soaked clothing. We left the innermost layers on for modesty's sake. I stumbled around the cave and nearly fell over a small pile of dry kindling that was neatly stacked in the corner.

"Cat, come here, and see if you can do something with this," I said, picking up the wood. He took the wood from me with a puzzled expression, but went to work creating a fire. With an amazing amount of skill, he had a roaring fire going and I thought Lumadian was going to jump right into it as he bolted off my shoulder to bask in its warmth.

In the firelight, I examined the cave. On the walls of the cavern were pictures of crudely drawn men throwing spears at some creature that was almost a woolly ox. Another picture has teepees and children wearing feathered headdresses and dancing.

"This is strange," I said to my friends who were more interested in drying off than anything on the walls.

"Not as strange as this fire," Cat said, trying to get my attention. "It produces no smoke."

Turning to the fire, I watched it with interest. Although it gave warmth, produced light, and crackled like a normal fire, it produced no smoke. "Perhaps it was the type of wood we used," I offered, although I did not believe it. I sat behind Lumadian. Picking him up gently, I settled him on my lap and rubbed my hands over him. "Are you hungry?"

"*I am sleepy,*" he replied. "*Just keep up what you are doing and you can feed me in the morning.*"

I kept stroking until I felt him drift off into slumber. I had been so intent on him, that I hadn't noticed everyone else had already settled down to sleep. Leaning back with Lumadian still in my lap, I drifted off to sleep myself.

# CHAPTER TWENTY-SEVEN
## LATER MATURITY

A chill in the air woke me, and I sat up to discover an empty cave. Even Lumadian was missing, which I thought was odd. Rubbing the sleep out of my eyes, I got up and looked around. The room was barren and none of our supplies were left. With suspicion and caution, I peeked out of the cave to see the storm had passed. The sky was clear and the sun very bright and high in the sky. The trees were full of vegetation, and I could smell the scent of wildflowers in the air. Sitting on a swing that I hadn't seen the night before was Diane in one of the finest dresses Paris could offer. She leered lustfully at me, and I walked over to her, feeling puzzled.

"What is going on, Diane?"

She slipped her arms around my neck. "Isn't this what you want, dear?"

My arms defied my mind. I found them slipped around her waist. I could feel her warmth against my body, smell her perfume, and taste her lips. I gave her a gentle kiss. I closed my eyes, struggling with the images, wanting to believe, fighting the voice yelling that it was not real.

I opened my eyes and was horrified with the sight before me. The trees and forest had reverted to the decayed state. The stench of decay and rot replaced those of the flowers. Instead of the beautiful Diane standing before me, there was a corpse whose skeletal arms were locked around my neck. The corpse had patches of moist earth on its face and a decaying dress. I could see worms crawling about in its skull. I attempted to pull away, but my feet were rooted to the spot, refusing any effort to pull them from the earth.

The thing before me spoke. "I control this realm. Your stay can be either very pleasant or a living embodiment of hell itself. Only you can choose. I will allow you some time to think about it." I watched, horrified, as it pulled me close to its skeletal teeth. The stench almost made me vomit. I closed my eyes, waited, and felt the bony claws touch my shoulders. Then, my face was licked by something warm. I opened my eyes and stared into Lumadian's face. His tiny claws held the sides of my neck.

*"It's morning. Time to eat."*

I looked at him in shock. My eyes darted left and right about the room. Everyone else was already up and getting ready to leave. I reached inside my pouch and produced a cherry red gem for Lumadian, still unsure if this was an extension of the dream. I sat up, and he scrambled to my shoulder to eat his treat. I rose and searched my supplies for anything edible. When my hands came in contact with a piece of dried meat, I gulped it down without even tasting it, then got ready to leave. By the time I was dressed, Lumadian was already napping.

We emerged from our sanctuary and discovered the rain had stopped. The smell of wet vegetation and moist earth was heavy in the air, producing the vivid images of my dream and making me sick to my stomach. A babbling brook flowed down the center of the path, taking some of the debris away to parts unknown.

Through the dismal gloom of the place, we carried on with Cat leading the way.

After we had traveled a short distance, Cat motioned for us to stop. "There is something very wrong here," he said, and leaned to whisper something more to us. "The animal bodies are gone."

"Perhaps the rain washed them away," I offered, trying to calm their nerves, although with the tension in my voice, I doubt it had the effect I'd hoped for.

Robert drew his weapons. "All of them, J.D.? Even you cannot think we are that gullible."

The sounds of the forest diminished to a whisper before disappearing completely. I felt the tension in my muscles building for whatever was about to happen. Even the noise of the water seemed to dim and wisp away to nothingness, as we waited for something to occur. Just as Cat decided to press onward, horrible animals emerged from both sides of the path.

Carcasses of various beasts approached. Their bodies had spotty remains of flesh from their former lives and only bare bone in other places.

Robert took the front, Jean-Luc fanned out to cover Diane's side, and Cat came to my side. One of the things—something that resembled a large dog or forest cat—leapt for Robert's throat, but Robert simply sliced it swiftly down the center, cutting it neatly into two pieces. We watched in horror, however, as the two halves came together and fused into the creature again.

Leaping across the path, Jean-Luc struck what appeared to be a large skeletal bear, but was too far decayed for me to be sure. Considering the creatures we had seen in Elilith thus far, it could have been anything. The force of the blow would have surely brought down any normal creature, but Jean-Luc didn't even move the skull. He fell hard. The bear wasted little time and pounced on his prone body. It picked him up in its maw and shook him violently like a rag doll before tossing him against a fallen tree pinning him with its bulk.

Robert charged at the bear with his shield in front of him. The force of the blow sent the creature sprawling on its back. Its state of decay added to its difficulties. He watched the bear with such an earnest zest that he failed to notice the cat-like creatures closing in on him from behind.

I yelled a warning to him, but was surprised to discover no words emerging from my mouth. In fact, it was then that I realized that there were no sounds at all. I watched, unable to do anything to assist my friend as the pack attacked Robert from behind, like lions taking down a zebra. He fell under their weight, into the undergrowth, and out of my sight.

I tried to reach Lumadian, who was finally stirring, and asked him what we could do. I felt the need to concentrate on a spell, so I focused on the bear that had managed to right itself. I saw a small red ball no larger than a clenched fist take shape in front of me. Curling my hands into my chest and thrusting out, I flung the ball at the bear. The ball hit the creature and consumed it in a fiery blaze. The fire continued to burn, taking a fallen tree with it. When the flames died down, all that remained were the charred bones of the bear still advancing on Jean-Luc. The decayed flesh had been incinerated in the hellish fire.

*"We need to concentrate together to eliminate this zone of silence,"* Lumadian told me. I slowed my breathing and tried to feel what he wanted me to do. Our breaths became one, and we tried to cancel the creatures' advantage.

I was concentrating so hard on the spell that I failed to notice Cat until he sailed over my head as a panther, hitting the bear head on, almost disrupting the union I had established with Lumadian. Cat managed to break the head off of the bear. The skull cracked into pieces, and the thing fell down. The victory was short-lived. The bear got to all fours again, the bones re-forming.

The bear, however, simply ignored Cat as it attempted to go around him to get at Jean-Luc.

Jean-Luc held his right arm limp at his side at a weird angle to his body, suggesting some type of grievous injury. His face was expressionless—not showing any hints of pain—and he held his staff in his left hand. Blood dribbled from a puncture wound in his neck, but he still advanced on the bear.

Diane was the next to react, calling forth the lights from above as she had done so many times in recent days. She seemed perplexed as nothing happened. I realized that the spell must have relied on sound, which was currently still nonexistent. She replaced the symbol Amilmadra had given her under her blouse, and pulled out her mace, readying herself against a large undead stag.

The deer lowered its head, aiming its impressive antlers at her as it charged. She sidestepped and swung her mace, but didn't move far enough. Diane managed to smash the entire side of the beast's rack to bits, but the sheer momentum of the creature's shattered bones cut her badly on the arm. Unlike our attempts, the bones did not re-form and remained lifeless.

I closed my eyes and concentrated harder on the spell. At first, nothing happened, but I could feel the rhythm of even our hearts matching. Lumadian and I acted as one. Warmth spread throughout my body. I welcomed the change. The cold dampness around me melted away. I felt a surging sensation course through every part of my body. At first, it was a mild feeling like going outside on a summer's night in a lightning storm. It built until it was hard for me to stand still. Opening my eyes, I could see the vibrations were not limited to me. Everything, from the dancing of little pebbles to the ripples in the puddles, was in motion. Its magic spread outward in a ring from me, creeping along. Without warning from Lumadian, my body suddenly felt as if it was on fire. The feeling shot through my body from my head, through my feet, and into the earth. All the action that had been raging around me slowed to stillness. Everything from the leaves to the chaos of combat was affected. It covered my friends, our enemies, the trees and even the air itself, leaving nothing untouched.

"I am going to destroy you all!" Robert screamed, shocking me with the sudden burst of sound. He struggled, but managed to stand in the brush. I could barely see him. His back and extremities were covered with the cat creatures. Their bones were stained crimson from his blood. He reached behind himself, literally tore one of the cats off his back, and threw it into a large stone. The rock cracked from the force of the impact, fracturing the bones of the cat. Robert picked up the sword from where he had dropped it and, in a blur of actions, slashed the other four monstrosities from his body.

The remains of the bones jittered slightly at his feet, and I could not determine if it was a residual effect from my spell or if the creatures were still trying to re-form. At least they were much slower than before.

Jean-Luc swung at the bear with his staff, but his injuries and the wet vegetation proved too much for him, and he slipped down. The bear reared up on its hind legs, ready to swing, when it was suddenly hit on the side by Cat. The two of them tumbled around, neither one gaining an advantage over the other.

Diane swung her mace again as the buck tried to gore her a second time. This time, her blow landed true and sounded like thunder when it crashed into the bone. The entire frame of the animal froze. The bones glowed with a golden light, starting from the point of impact, but swiftly traversing the bony structure right down to the tail. The light grew to a blinding luminosity before dissipating into mere water, adding to the already muddy field. The whole process took mere seconds, but it seemed much longer.

Robert crushed the cats' bones and kicked them into the forest, scattering the tiny fragments everywhere. He noticed the bear struggling with Cat. He went by Jean-Luc and swung his sword hard over the two, completely severing the bear's back, but the power of the blow continued, and the blade cut deeply into Cat's back. Cat growled in agony. Robert simply pulled the blade out of Cat, kicked him to the ground, and then wiped the blood from his sword onto Cat. The bright red appeared as a prominent swathe against the black of his fur. Robert eyed me standing alone in the path. "I am tired of you doing nothing!" He screamed and ran at me with his weapon raised.

Reflex took over, and I tried to stop him with a spell. Robert quickly closed the gap, but stopped when a vine latched around his leg. He sliced at the vine cutting it off his foot, but two more wrapped around his thighs. He cut those free, but more replaced them. His face was red with anger as he came closer to me. He attempted to cut more of the vegetation away, but the vines eventually wrapped around his arms, confining them to his sides. The forest wrapped him like a mummy, leaving only his neck and face exposed. He had a crazed demeanor and struggled against the confinement.

Diane clutched her symbol and attempted to cast her spell again. She searched the sky. Her chant was answered as the forest opened, and the clouds in the sky parted to let the sun shine down. The rays touched everything and felt warm. We watched as the light wrapped itself around the skeletal remains, much as the forest had done to Robert. The light broke the bones of the creatures into fine dust, scattering them in the wind. When the light faded, there was no trace of their existence anywhere.

I rushed over to Cat and Jean-Luc. I could tell their injuries were worse than I'd feared. Cat bled badly, staining the moss crimson. The cut on his back caused his legs to twitch uncontrollably. I wrestled my cloak off and pressed it against the wound in an attempt to stop the blood. As I pressed down on the cut, causing Cat to whimper, I glanced at Jean-Luc. His arm was separated at the elbow, and the two bones had broken through the skin. I shuddered at the injury, wondering how he endured the pain with no expression on his face.

"Diane!" I called. "Get over here now! I can't stop Cat's bleeding."

Diane dashed over and fell almost on top of us. She gently touched Cat's muzzle, summoning the lights she used for healing. I watched the lights more closely than I had in the past. Like ribbons of light they entwined as they reached out over my friend's body. They went under the cloak I was attempting to use as a tourniquet, emerging on the other side and sliding down Cat's tail. The light continued moving in one continuous stream, reaching out to touch Jean-Luc's arm. The energy widened, and the lights swiftly encased his arm in their healing touch. From there, they leapt out toward Robert, but tapered off to nothingness before reaching him. On the other end, the lights from her hands had crept up Diane's arm and wrapped around her shoulder where the buck had injured her.

I held my cloak to Cat's injury and felt the pulsating from the blood fade away. I peered under the cloth to see that the light had intensified, blinding me for a moment. Blinking in an attempt to get my sight back, I was relieved to see that Diane had managed to heal the wound. I was pleasantly surprised that Jean-Luc's arm was normal again, with no trace of injury remaining. Even the blood that had spattered both of them had been cleansed.

Diane fell to her knees, as she had on that fateful night when we fled Salem. "I did not know I could heal more than one person—at least, not more than one with these types of injuries." She got up and tentatively went over to Robert, who had fallen to his back, and was still held tight by the vines. Bending down, she summoned the healing again. Although the lights did not have the same intensity as before, it was the same healing that she had performed in the past. I was confident that Robert had been healed.

"*He is still poisoned.*" I heard Lumadian in my mind.

"What do you mean?" I asked aloud, so everyone knew I was talking to him.

"*Those ocelots poisoned him somehow. Diane needs to cure that as well.*"

"Diane," I said. "Lumadian says Robert was poisoned, and that is the reason for his actions. Could you heal that as well?"

"I don't know how, but I will try." She closed her eyes and concentrated on Robert again. Instead of a soft light, a bluish fog formed. The fog grew until it covered Robert like a large blanket. The vapor passed through the vines and his body into the ground. Seconds later, Robert blinked his eyes.

Robert struggled to break the bonds. "What happened? Why did you tie me up?"

# CHAPTER TWENTY-EIGHT

*Why did I ignore the signs?* J.D. thought, stopping the story to reflect on everything he had written. Slowly, he rose and staggered to the now clear ice wall. Dawn had broken, and the rain had stopped. He felt his strength returning and stretched the kinks out of his system. When he touched the wall, he felt a rush of depression, thinking about his story. His body twitched, and he fought the rage that wanted to escape, but rational thought prevailed, and he remained silent.

*"No!"* he thought, as tears streamed down his face. *"I must finish!"*

He saw the image of Robert with a demonic grin, knowing full well what he had done to J.D. "At dusk of the tenth day of Sorrows, we shall end this once and for all, my friend. I give you time to *grieve* your losses."

J.D. shuffled back to the desk, but paused before he reached it. "So, this is where it ends," he said aloud. "In nine nights, we shall see what Fate has in store for me. Before that occurs, I must finish my tale." He took a few deep, calming breaths of the crisp, morning air, carefully sat back down, and continued writing.

# CHAPTER TWENTY-NNE
## UNDERSTANDING

I concentrated on the vines that held Robert to release him from their grip. They receded, leaving him free to move.

"We were ambushed. You were poisoned," Jean-Luc said blandly.

"You tried to attack us?" I asked him, hoping he could fill in what he could.

Robert looked around as if trying to recall what had transpired. "I don't remember anything after the animals jumped on my back."

I tried to read anything I could from him, but he seemed sincere, and I accepted his explanation. "The hut should be close now. Diane, could you find the passage in the diary about what we should do once we get there? I don't remember the phrase we are supposed to say."

"Sure," she replied. She pulled out the diary and read the passage to us:

*"Go to the door and speak these words, 'The stranger gives me strength.' That will give you access to their base of operations. You need to defeat*

*Grazalian. Doing so will shatter their will and will cause strife as others attempt to take his power."*

"Her?" Cat asked, having transformed back to his normal self. "Miriele said a man was in charge here."

"I do not remember," I said. "Let's keep an open mind as to whom or what this person might be. Remember this land is very different, and it could be anything."

"In that case," Cat said, "I better take cat-form." I watched my friend meld into the form we had been so accustomed to already. It felt weird to me that I was thinking of him as a fifty-fifty mix of cat and man—as if this cat shape was one I had known all my life.

We proceeded down the path, looking into the woods for any signs of life. Like before, all was silent. Constantly on guard for an attack, we slowed our pace to a crawl. After about an hour at the agonizingly slow pace, Cat growled a warning and bounced toward a concealed building.

The wooden shack was barely bigger than a double outhouse. Moss and the forest had grown over it and, if it weren't for Cat's keen eyesight, I would have missed it. The wood was very weathered, but it was a solid structure. When we approached, the wood smelled fresh with decay and rot, but none of us could find so much as a knothole to see what was contained within. I crept up to the door, but there was no handle, no keyhole, not even one of those magical mouths we had discovered on the vampire's door.

Clearing my throat first, I spoke. "The stranger gives me strength."

At first nothing happened. After about a minute, I was about to ask my friends what they thought we should do when the door faded from sight, leaving a portal of pure blackness. The void was darker than any we had experienced. We watched as shadowy tendrils emerged from the entrance. Robert and Jean-Luc held their positions, but the rest of us took a step back. The appendages were transparent as they touched all of us at almost the same time. Instantly, we lost some color, like clothes that fade from too many washings. Even Lumadian's skin had changed to a dull red.

"*We have been marked as allowable to pass through the portal,*" he informed me.

"Robert, you take lead. Jean-Luc, follow him up. Diane, you will be in the center, with me after you, then Cat to cover the rear. Be ready, my friends."

One by one, we proceeded through the portal, fading completely from view. When my turn arrived, I examined the doorway closely. No matter how hard I peered into the room, I could not see anything. Taking a breath and holding it, I walked through.

# CHAPTER THIRTY
## OLD AGE

Have you ever woken up after a night's sleep and stayed there with your eyes closed? You drift between a dreamy state and reality, wondering where you happen to be at any given moment. That is how I felt as I passed through the portal. I had closed my eyes as I continued, but the surroundings filled me with a sense of peace. After several feet, I felt a warm sensation on my face, and the darkness in front of my closed eyes lightened. I waited a few more seconds, before I decided it was safe and opened my eyes.

The death of the forest had been replaced by rolling hilltops, alive with fresh flowers and green grass—not quite the spectacle of brilliant flowers the elves' lands presented, but impressive, nonetheless. The sun was high in the sky on a clear day. Each of us was about ten feet apart from one another, in the order we had entered the shack. In front of Robert were two figures. The first was dressed in brown and green leathers. He carried a large quarterstaff in one hand and on the opposite shoulder perched a large crow. The other person was dressed in a suit of polished silver metal. He wore a pure white cloak. Its hood was drawn over his head and obscured his face. Both of them stood with their backs to us. In front of them, about two hundred feet away on a rising hill, I could see some kind of construction going on.

Humans the heights of the tallest giraffes moved stone slabs in a clearing. Their skins were pale purple, as if they had never been in sunlight, and they only wore tattered, black pants. Each of them had complex tribal tattoos of animal heads emblazed in blood-red on their chests: an eagle, a bear, a wolf. In the center of activity, a single one slammed a rectangular, bluish stone into the ground horizontally. The dirt and mud from its actions splattered everything. It grunted and pulled out a large skin of some kind, then cleaned the rock. Around him, white stone slabs as tall as the creatures were being erected vertically in pairs, capped with a stone that covered the two, and arranged in a horseshoe shape with a central stone at the opening. Around that, vertical gray stones were arranged in a circle with stones on top touching end to end. Bustling throughout were normal-sized figures dressed in leathers similar to one of the men standing before us.

"What is this for again?" The man with the crow asked.

"That is not your concern, Grazalian. Make sure this is completed. My calculations tell me that should materialize roughly four thousand of my years ago in the Salisbury Plain west of a town called Amesbury. There will be *consequences* for you if it is not completed." I could see him twirling a smoky, blue glass sphere in his hand as he spoke to Grazalian.

"Should I have any of my acolytes there?"

"Only those acolytes who show the most promise. They will not…"

The cawing of the crow interrupted his voice. I had been so attentive in listening to their conversation that I failed to notice Robert who was within striking distance. The man in armor barely shifted out of the way of Robert's swing, twisting his body violently to escape being cut into two by the blow. As he twisted, we could see he was the individual from the moving tapestry, the one who caused the accident. The blade of Robert's sword nipped the man's outstretched arm, causing him to lose his grip on the glass bauble. I watched as it bounced on the ground, rolled down the hill, and smashed on some rocks, hissing as the smoke escaped.

The man pushed Robert in the chest so hard, he sent Robert flying into Jean-Luc. "You fool!" He glared at Grazalian. "Deal with them any way you want. Prove your worth to me." He gestured, and a shimmering, oval portal appeared beside Grazalian, and the man entered it.

Robert screamed, "Noooooo!" He leapt to his feet and, with a tremendous burst of speed, Robert dove through the portal as it disappeared.

The smoke from the orb grew in size and intensity, and a sickening odor wafted on the wind. Grazalian slammed one end of his staff down, which produced a thunderous sound. Purple light shot from the top of the staff up to the sky as far up as I could see.

The large men building the monument dropped whatever stones they had and charged us. The quicker, smaller figures dove out of the way of the falling debris, but not all of them were fortunate enough to escape. As the titans ran in our direction, they ripped up trees, roots and all, for weapons, and I got a better view. At about twenty feet tall, the creatures were like oversized humans, but their upper bodies were so deformed—like the entire torso and arms were one solid muscle—that it was hard to think of them as such.

Instead of focusing on the approaching mass of trampling giants, I was terrified of the mist that was rapidly expanding. It had already grown to a sphere taller than me. My eyes confirmed what my nose picked up first: the stench of rotten and dead vegetation. The ball of mist killed anything it touched. The smell from the cloud raised bile in my throat, and I nearly choked. I could hear chanting from Grazalian, and the sphere pulsated slower than a heartbeat. Unknown instincts kicked in, and I wrapped my arms around myself. A circle of blue light clung at our feet, rooting us, as the sphere exploded to hundreds of times its original size.

I knew the effect was instantaneous, but for me it appeared drawn-out. The sphere expanded, I could see blackish trees taking the place of the green ones, as if someone was painting a new landscape around us. It washed over my friends and me with no ill effect. When it passed over Grazalian, he looked meaner, more menacing. Even the crow on his shoulder changed. Its talons grew, and its eyes erupted in a flaming red.

The mist continued its growth, passing over the giants, but most of them were painted out of the picture, dissolving them as it passed over them. As the mist reached the circle of stones, a strong, green light pulsated from the ring. For an instant, the blackened mist stopped, and it looked like the light from the stones was going to defeat the power of the mist. Any chance of that happening was wiped from existence as the mist continued, painting its version of the forest over the stone ring, removing it from this world. As it passed beyond my range of vision, the forest resembled the forest we were in before entering the shack.

Time returned to its normal pace, and I was assaulted by the terrible smells of the dead forest that completely surrounded all of us. The smell of wet, moist earth, the rotten stench of death and decay, and a sickly acidic gas filled my nostrils. If I'd thought the smell from the mist was bad, this was much worse. The odors were so powerful that I had to fight with myself not to be sick.

Grazalian cackled and inched slightly toward us as my spell faded. "Well, well, well. It appears that I am going to have the honor of a few permanent additions to my forest." Staring icily at Cat he said, "And when you die, you will forever remain a panther

268

under my control. You will always remember your friends, even in your deathly state."

Cat's anger had reached its boiling point as he lunged at the druid, but Grazalian simply laughed again as the forest bent to his will, ensnaring my friend in thick vines. Cat struggled under the grip of the vegetation, biting some of the tendrils in two, but every time it seemed that he would free himself from their grip, more would join.

Jean-Luc dashed off to the side, dodging the moving verdure as he confronted the two lumbering at us. Every time something tried to grab him, he easily jumped out of its grasp. It appeared to me that the further Jean-Luc retreated from us, the less influence Grazalian had on the forest. In no time, my friend confronted the giants. Both of them stopped to watch what their new adversary was going to do.

I watched Jean-Luc artfully dodge their blows until something out of the corner of my eyes caused me to dive into the moist, rotten leaves in time to avoid getting hit by a black sphere of energy that was tossed in my direction. Its impact against the trees behind me decayed the trunks to dust. When I looked up, I realized that the effect didn't come from the druid, but rather from his familiar which had darted to a branch.

"*I will deal with the crow,*" I heard in my thoughts as Lumadian flew off to fight Grazalian's pet.

Getting to my feet, I concentrated on the druid. My eyes were momentarily distracted by Diane trying to free Cat, but I focused and watched Grazalian. He lifted his arms, smirked at me, and snapped his fingers. In front of him, the vegetation gathered in a clump of moving leaves. The debris broke into two smaller balls. The balls mirrored each other as they grew in length and taking on a familiar shape. A maw ripped in front of the leafy vegetation, with spiked thorns for teeth. An eerie yellowish radiance burned out where eyes would be, and they were like copies of Cat. One of them jumped at Diane, knocking her down as the other crouched low on its haunches, waiting for me to react.

# CHAPTER THIRTY-ONE
## JEAN-LUC'S BATTLE

Jean-Luc watched the behemoths, eyeing the both of them as they circled around to flank him. The giant with the tattoo of a large bear head on his chest also had blood-red runes tattooed all along his bald head.

Jean-Luc glared up and down at the giant. "You must be the leader."

The giant held his stomach and chuckled. "Yes, little man. You will find out soon enough."

Jean-Luc bolted for the other giant, one with a wolf's head on his chest, with his quarterstaff tightly clutched in both hands. That giant simply bounced the tree trunk in his hand. The staff's end glowed white, and my friend slammed it into the giant's foot.

The giant yelled in pain and held his foot, hopping in place.

Jean-Luc yelled, "One less scum to deal with!" He raised his staff over his head, this time the entire staff glowed ember white.

From behind him, the leader's somatic movements pulled the very shadows and darkness from the trees and surrounding forest as though it had substance. It chanted in an unknown language and pressed everything into a sphere. He skipped it across the ground, engulfing Jean-Luc like a snowball rolling downhill before my friend could complete his attack.

Jean-Luc tried to break the shadow-ball's grasp on his body, but was unable to even move as the sphere rolled to the other giant. That giant stopped it with its sore foot. Taking careful aim, the giant hit the ball with his tree trunk using all his might to launch Jean-Luc into the air. The ball prison broke through branches until it crashed against the trunk of one of the old trees, popping the bubble. Jean-Luc fell from nearly the top of the tree, bouncing off some of the bare branches, as the sound of his crunching bones echoed throughout, until he sank into the mulch and disappeared.

# CHAPTER THIRTY-ONE
## LUMADIAN'S BATTLE

Lumadian flew at the crow with his claws extended, ready to rip it apart, but when he got close, multiple images of the crow appeared, and Lumadian's attack hit air, dissipating one of the illusions. He scrutinized the number of crows, trying to pick out the real one, but the delay allowed the bird to unleash an attack of its own. All the remaining illusions mimicked the same actions, as balls of lights that struck him from all sides. I cringed from the pain, feeling the spells' effects.

My tiny friend contorted and released a spell of his own, making the hairs on my head stand on end when he released a lightning bolt through the crows and into the heavens. The thing hissed, and the rest of its illusions vanished. Lumadian followed up his spell by diving at the crow, but it recovered faster than he anticipated. It called forth a shield of snow and ice, plunging the temperature downward. Lumadian plowed into the icy defender head first, cracking the ice somewhat, but the spell held.

Lumadian shrieked, but shook off the effects of the impact and used his claws to shred the ice. The delay, however, allowed the crow to escape into the shadows that surrounded us.

I scanned the canopy for the black terror, trying to help my companion.

Lumadian felt my eyes on him. *"Pay attention to your own battle!"* he screamed in my head, diverting his attention to me for a second.

The delay was long enough, however, to allow the crow to appear from its hiding spot, send a volley of shadowy arrows at Lumadian, and then disappear back into the shadows.

Lumadian dove to avoid the arrows, but two managed to find their mark, hitting him in his wing and in his lower thigh. Lumadian twisted as he fell, his limbs wildly flailing with his tiny claws extended. The entire tree canopy lit up like a thousand fireflies on a field of black. Bouncing off the mulch on his back, Lumadian flipped over on all fours and scanned upward, locating his foe's outline against his fiery spell. He muttered something under his breath and clenched his teeth. The crow was encased in a light of its own. The backdrop flickered out, making it impossible for the crow to hide again. Lumadian launched himself into the air and clutched the crow. The two tiny creatures locked themselves together in a death grip as they spun in the air.

# CHAPTER THIRTY-THREE
## DIANE'S AND CAT'S FIGHT

Diane swung her mace from her prone position, catching the vegetation-cat by surprise. She jumped to her feet and squared off against the deadly foe. When she swung the mace again, the creature dodged to one side and took a swipe at her extended arms, opening a wound. She lost her grip on the weapon and dropped it into the muck and mire. She held her arm for a second before bending down to get the weapon, but that action proved to be too slow. She was stopped by the abomination which had jumped on top of the mace. Diane froze, staring into the creature's hypnotic, yellow eyes. The cat crouched and snarled before leaping at Diane, but was broadsided by Cat, who had freed himself enough to help her. He wasted no time leaping on the creature's back, biting hard on its neck until he had completely bitten off the thing's head. The monstrous beast collapsed back into a heap of lifeless vegetation.

The second cat jumped on Cat's back. It locked its maw onto Cat's neck, sinking its teeth deep enough to draw blood. Diane recovered her weapon and swung at the creature. The mace gleamed with a golden radiance as it stuck the beast. The light fused itself with creature, rippling down its back like cracking ice.

The creature on Cat's back lost solidity  and fell down into piles around his paws.

Grazalian simply snapped his fingers. The heap of weeds animated to his will, growing up Cat's limbs amazingly fast and covering every inch of him in a matter of seconds. Even his tail was assaulted by the weeds. Diane took a step back as a cold set of yellow eyes stared back at her. Cat growled at her and advanced. The pink of Cat's mouth was still visible against the dark green of the forest that encased his body.

When the forest lit up from Lumadian's spell, it distracted Cat for a moment, and his eyes returned to normal.

"Fight it!" Diane yelled to him, as she held her weapon before her.

Cat strained against the leaves, looking back at Grazalian and taking a step toward him. So powerful was the action that the druid's spell fizzled and died as he stared at the new foe. He took a step away from Cat.

Cat leapt at Grazalian, hitting him square in the chest as Diane rushed over to me, trying to see if I was injured. Cat growled at the helpless man while standing on his chest, stomping a few times. He clamped his maw on Grazalian's neck, wanting to prolong his suffering. The fire from the canopy died out. The new darkness blinded Diane for a moment as we tried to adjust our eyes. Cat simply stopped moving, not dealing the death blow. I watched as Cat slid off Grazalian's body and spun to her. The yellow light in his eyes returned to full intensity.

# CHAPTER THIRTY-FOUR
## TRANSFERENCES

Facing the leafy-cat my friend had become, I waited for his attack. I glanced at Jean-Luc, and when my eyes left Cat's, he swiped at my leg. I managed to roll out of the way. *"Jal'Ra Tuz!"* I yelled shoving my hands straight out, palms at Grazalian. The air in front of me rippled, and an invisible wall appeared between me and the druid allowing me to deflect his spell. The dark sphere he had thrown bounced harmlessly, absorbed by the shadows.

I rolled away to avoid Cat's attack, drawing my dagger as I got to my feet. I faced him, getting ready for his next attack. Grazalian called forth massive tentacle-like vines that attached themselves to the wall I had crafted and ripped it down. At the same time Cat jumped at me. I fell straight back and felt a sharp pain from phantom wings and my right thigh. Then Cat sailed clean over me.

A large talon covered my torso and pinned me down. I fought against the confinement, trying to push it off me, but the claw pressed into my chest, forcing the air out of me. I saw Cat snarl, and then something else caught his attention, and he leapt over me and out of my range of vision. I glared down, past my feet to Grazalian. He had one arm extended at me. His hand had changed to resemble the claw that had me pinned, and he clenched it.

Just then, the trees lit up with a powerful light spell, distracting the druid so much that he retreated. When he did, the claw returned to normal size, allowing me to stand.

Cat snarled and pinned Grazalian to the ground again, which allowed me to try to help my scaly friend. I felt scraping over my body and noticed Lumadian in a pitched battle with the crow, twisting in the air as he tried to sting it with his tail.

I went to aid Lumadian and happened to see, in the periphery of my vision, the druid standing with Cat at his side. He reached down and said, "Now now, pet, you will eat soon enough." He murmured something under his breath, and the temperature dropped. I watched a huge ball of ice appear from nowhere and hurtle at me. Instinct kicked in, and I crossed my arms in front of me. The ball rolled over, dropping me to my back and knocked Diane out.

I shook off the effects and moved to Diane. Her body was ice cold, and her lips had become blue. I held her to me, forgetting about what was going on around me. My only concern was her well-being. I glanced at the druid, scowling as I felt hatred building in me. Carefully placing Diane on the vegetation, I stepped over her body. The druid cast a few spells at me, but they simply hit my body and vanished. Cat leapt at me, sent by his new master, and I simply slapped him away with my hand as if he was a rag doll, sending him flying some fifteen feet. The druid called the vegetation to his will, which wrapped around my lower half.

I stared at Grazalian. My fists filled with power, and I held them up in front of me to show the druid. The magic became a fire. I snickered, held my fists over my head, and slammed them on the ground producing an earth-shattering explosion. A fiery inferno wall appeared over me and moved in a wave. It destroyed all the growth on me. It destroyed the growth on Cat, leaving his body smoky, but not on fire. It passed over Lumadian without effect, but burned some of the feathers off the crow, leaving it stunned. It passed over the druid. He crunched into a tight ball and hit the earth face-first. When it was done, the wall of flames had destroyed the entire forest in front of me, leaving a huge fifty foot cube of nothingness.

"It's over, Grazalian," I said, watching his form as it pulsated. Although part of the sky was now visible, it was still dreary and gray.

Some magical effect washed over me from behind, and I heard Diane get up.

"Did I miss much?" She went over to Cat's body and touched him with her own magical power.

"No," I answered, "I got a bit angry." I went to Lumadian and stopped when I saw him sting his foe.

Lumadian returned to my shoulder. *"I am alright. Pay attention to Grazalian!"*

I focused my attention on the druid, and he raised his head to me. Instead of a human, a creature stared back at us. His red eyes seemed like fire against his black body. He was about ten feet long, had four sets of limbs, and long tusks like a boar. The druid's new shape was short-legged, and each of the paws had long, sharp claws. The skin was pulled paper thin. Bones were easily visible on the gaunt body.

Grazalian sniffed his fallen familiar and nudged it with his muzzle. The creature the druid had become shrieked like a wounded animal. Cat joined us, and we all watched as the skin fell of the crow's body, leaving the bones and a strong yellow light gleaming from its eyes. It flew over to Grazalian and landed on his back. When it landed, the fire-scorched earth cracked and pushed aside from underneath. Bony skeletons clawed their way to the surface and came to his side: an army of the forest's dead.

# CHAPTER THIRTY-FIVE
## JEAN-LUC

Rising from the brush, Jean-Luc held his arm for a second. He picked up his simple staff and rushed at the wolf's-head giant, yelling at the top of his lungs. Jean-Luc used his staff against the giant, hitting it squarely in the shin, but the behemoth merely laughed at my friend as his staff vibrated against the blow. Jean-Luc studied the situation for a moment. A look of slyness slowly replaced his look of despair. He laughed so loudly that it drowned out the confused giant who stopped and stared. Jean-Luc took a small object from his pocket. He rolled it back and forth in his fingers before placing it on his finger and calling, "*Elorath*."

The air around the three came to a standstill and all remaining life in the trees around the trio stopped moving. The bald giant's face flushed with anger and confusion as he rubbed the bear tattoo on his chest a few times. The giant's muscles bulged as the tattoo pulsated red. An evil snarl crept over his face, before he used the tree as a club. The swing was deliberate, but his motions slowed to a stop until the tree was mere inches from where my friend had been standing. Jean-Luc had already rolled out of the way.

A foul wind blew violently around them, carrying in snow on the North Wind. Both giants froze and their skin became as blue as a clear day back home. As if they were part of a nightmarish dream, the giants began to shrink. The giant who had attacked Jean-Luc lost its grip on the tree, as it shrunk, and the trunk slowly fell. They shrank in size until the two of them were in front of Jean-Luc, eye to eye. The color of the leader's skin returned to normal, while the other one remained blue. The spell slowing everything disappeared, returning the scene to a normal pace. The bulk of the tree slammed on top of the blue giant, shattering him into a thousand shards and sending pieces into every direction. The sound of the trunk slamming the earth echoed.

The remaining giant seemed shocked as bits of his former ally covered parts of his body. Jean-Luc took advantage of the situation, slamming the end of his staff into his adversary's neck. The giant clutched his throat and stumbled back. My friend immediately followed up by kicking him in the chest with both his feet, sending the giant flying back.

Jean-Luc didn't stop his assault and attempted to strike his foe, but the giant tossed a handful of some powdery substance in his face. The giant lumbered to his feet, and his neck thickened. Long claws grew from his hands as Jean-Luc stumbled back. The giant still clung to his throat as his muscles thickened even more. His stomach bloated, and fur erupted from his skin, everywhere, all at once. He lurched to Jean-Luc. After picking up one of the shards, the giant drove it into Jean-Luc's damaged arm, causing him to scream in agony. Jean-Luc returned a punch of his own with his good arm and at the same time planted his leg behind the giant to trip him. Jean-Luc frantically snatched some wet mulch and attempted to wipe his eyes.

Jean-Luc picked up the giant and punched him in his enlarged stomach a few times, ignoring the pain in his arm. He stopped and glared into the giant's blackened eyes before he punched it one last time. He planted his feet into the giant and fell on his back, sending the leader over and behind him.

The giant went flying, crashing through the brush and into a tree. As it rushed back, the wall of fire overcame it, barely missing Jean-Luc in its destructive path.

Jean-Luc blocked his eyes from the fire and the light. The body of the giant fell smoldering to the barren ground. Jean-Luc readied his staff and waited a minute for the giant to rise, but it didn't. As he was about to join us, the flesh melted off the giant, leaving behind a skeleton, which rapidly gained height until it was back to the size it had been while it was alive. Jean-Luc paused for a moment before the earth broke open with more shapes. With such a force confronting him, he ran for his friends.

# CHAPTER THIRTY-SIX
# DEATH

Jean-Luc, Cat, Lumadian, Diane, and I faced the army of bones going back to the edge of the wasteland I'd created. Fog rolled in at their feet, obscuring some of the smaller dead, but their creepy yellow eyes shone through the gloom.

I stepped toward Diane, who was already preparing a spell. "Cast the spell that destroys these things!"

She called forth her magic, but nothing happened. The only thing coming down from the sky was more darkness. The creature that Grazalian had become only hissed an evil laugh that was repeated over and over by his dead army.

Jean-Luc and Cat jumped first, trying to attack the druid, but were cut off by his protectors. I tried one of my spells, but it bounced harmlessly off my target. I felt a burning in the pouch at my side. Fumbling for the source of the heat, I pulled out an acorn—the gift from the elves. The amount of heat coming from it was beyond anything that words could properly describe. I drew my arm back and heaved it over their heads, into the center of the undead.

A massive oak grew from the acorn, shooting up and up and up, breaking anything that still remained above it, and piercing the sky as the girth of the trunk tossed bones aside. A light shone down from the sky as the life from the tree expanded, and the ground around the base sprang to life. When the light pierced the gloom, popping could be heard as the bones broke apart in miniature fiery explosions.

Diane seized the opportunity and cast her spell, pulling the light down and obliterating Grazalian's left flank. Before anyone could react, she cast her spell again, destroying the other side with the same effects, until only the giant, eight or nine animal skeletons, and Grazalian remained.

We stared at each other, not moving, waiting for someone or something to make the first move. It was not long. Lumadian hissed in my ear, and I stumbled back feeling a bit dizzy. Grazalian and his forces took advantage of the situation, and he led the attack. I felt the back of my neck, my fingers met the warmth of fresh blood. A cold stare gazed back at me when I wondered about Lumadian. I attempted to contact him mentally, but he blocked me. I fell, ready to be trampled by Grazalian when Cat jumped in the way, moving the creature the druid had become enough to deflect him from me. Diane rushed to my side as I started to get lightheaded.

Her hands flowed with magical energies as she called, *"By the power of the Ancestors, I purge the filth from this body!"* I felt the gentle touch of her hands caressing the back of my neck and a slight tingle of cold ebbing from my wound.

The giant grasped the huge rack of a moose skeleton that was still moving and twisted its head off. It grunted, "I kill you now." He stepped forward and swung the antlers at Diane and me.

"Not today," Jean-Luc called as he jumped on the antlers, bringing the would-be weapon down. Rolling to a standing position as the bony prongs lodged into the rocky soil, Jean-Luc shoved his staff in front of him horizontally and shouted, *"May those I face slow to a breathless halt."* The creatures were bathed in a purplish light, and their skin went from a bone-white color to a dull gray as they stopped moving.

Lumadian wrapped his tail around my neck, squeezing like a boa around its prey. He hissed at Diane as she finished her spell. He watched her as she pulled something from a pouch. I desperately tried contacting him, but could not hear anything. I had become accustomed to his voice in my mind, and without it, I felt empty, as if he simply did not exist anymore.

"Here Lumadian, I kept this for you," Diane said, holding out a dark green gem, with flecks of gold reflecting in the sunlight.

Lumadian twisted his head to the side, and stared into her smiling face. He shook his head taking the gem from her. He uncoiled his tail from my neck as I heard him say, "*Sorry, he was in my head!*" He gulped down the treasure, and we focused on Grazalian and Cat.

Grazalian snarled at Cat, then attacked with all his fury. The druid bit at Cat's shoulder, opening a wound. Scraping Cat's side with multiple arms, he opened gashes in Cat's body before kicking him, coloring the soil red as my friend's body rolled. Cat went to get up and stopped when he discovered the razor claws had done more damage to him than even he had realized. Blood poured from the wounds as his intestines spilled from the wounds. He tried holding them in, but mess oozed around his attempts.

Jean-Luc ran to the druid and slammed the end of his staff into the druid's ribs. Grazalian's expression turned demonic, and with the weird shadows, I swear I saw horns. I watched as the staff Jean-Luc wielded blackened at the tip where it contacted Grazalian's body. The spot corroded with a dark sable light that ate the wood, disintegrating it into ash. The decay spread to Jean-Luc's hands, then engulfed his body. When it faded, all that was left on Jean-Luc were tattered remains of his clothing—barely enough to keep his pride intact. He tried to run, but his feet were embedded, covered over by foliage and dead topsoil. He fell face-first, breaking both ankles.

Grazalian moved fast and swift, pouncing on Jean-Luc's prone back. His claws embedded themselves in Jean-Luc, and the druid's great weight pushed him down. He gnawed on one of Jean-Luc's ankles as he lay on top of him, tearing bits of flesh from it. He waited for Diane and me to notice, then shredded Jean-Luc's back like a cat trying to create a comfortable bed.

Diane tried to go over to Cat in order to heal him, but a vine around her leg pulled her off-balance. A large purple and white flower opened, like one a trap-door spider would use, and pulled her underground. I blinked, dumbfounded by what had happened in the span of seconds.

I stared at the druid, filled with a burning hatred. I slammed my wrists together, and then let my hands fall to my sides, my palms hitting my thighs as they continued their path behind me. A surge of water erupted and took the shape of a hand that engulfed Grazalian, enveloping the beast's entire body.

I backed up, keeping my main focus on the druid as the watery hand drowned him. I laughed out loud when I heard the druid gagging on the water. With my spell still active, I glanced down, trying the find the door to free Diane.

"*There it is!*" Lumadian brought my attention to the correct spot—as if I saw it through his eyes.

I spied the enormous flower, pulsating like a heartbeat, getting a bit smaller with each beat. Lumadian flew into the crevice, latching his claws on one of the enormous petals. As he attempted to peel the petal like the husk on a stalk of corn, I was hit in the chest by a dark bird. It dissipated as it passed through me. I was hit again and stumbled back. I was hit a third time, knocking me on my backside, and lost concentration. My spell collapsed.

Grazalian jumped into the air. I thought I was going to be pounced next. But instead of trying to land on me before I could stand, the druid simply jumped straight up, inhaled a deep breath of air, and landed with all his weight on top of Jean-Luc, producing a sickening crunch that echoed in my head and still haunts me to this day.

*"It's too strong, and I can't take the chance of stinging Diane,"* I heard in my mind.

*"Get up here! Now!"* I shouted.

Lumadian abandoned Diane and flew to my shoulder as Grazalian stalked me. I tried to duplicate the same fire effect as before, but something prevented my efforts. I glanced at my friends. Cat had stopped moving. Jean-Luc's body was partially crushed, shredded, and his lower leg's bones were exposed. Diane's body was visible like a hand in a glove as the flower continued to contract around her.

Four balls appeared before the druid, hovering in front of and above him. The balls were at four corners, marking a square. Each one was a different element: a ball of water, earth, fire, and air. They began spinning in a circle, faster and faster until they bled into one another, becoming a solid ring. The speed kicked up the wind, then created a funnel effect as debris was caught up in the cyclone. I was hypnotized by the effect as it washed over Lumadian and me.

Something clicked in my head. I snatched my friend, and like Grazalian had done before, formed a tight ball with Lumadian in the center. I hit the ground as the maelstrom overwhelmed me, obscuring us from the druid's field of vision. I closed my eyes when I heard Grazalian howling laughter as the spell ripped at my body. I felt my clothes easily shredded. The debris dug into my skin, and my body ached from getting buffeted. I pulled Lumadian to my chest, feeling his warmth. He helped slow my breathing.

*"Hold on!"* he told me.

New strength coursed through my veins, and I no longer cared about anything, not even the maelstrom which I could no longer feel. When I opened my eyes, I easily spied Grazalian through the whipping turmoil. I snarled, shambling around on all fours as I glared at him. Everything was painted in red hues by my hatred. I took a step toward him out of the cyclone. I noticed something was not right. I examined myself and discovered that a transformation had occurred. I had become a much larger version of Lumadian, right down to the nick in the wing that he had acquired in his recent fight.

I scanned for him until I heard from his thoughts. *"I am here, don't worry about me. Finish this!"*

I stumbled clumsily to the druid as his spell dropped. I chuckled and glared down on Grazalian. I towered over this creature, nearly twice his height. I tail-slapped him hard, flinging him against an oak, which cracked and fell on him.

The tree lifted off of him, and hurled at me like a javelin, hitting me in the crown of the head. Squinting, I shook off the effects and scanned the forest for him again. Instead of the creature, Grazalian confronted me in his human guise.

I leapt into the air, far above the tree line, and I hovered there momentarily distracted by the view. In the distance, I saw the mountains that would later become my home. My focus was brought back when something bounced harmlessly off my armor. I dove, leaving an impression of my massive rear claws into the dirt, crushing Grazalian. I hopped back, my rear resting against the trees, and I looked for the fallen druid, but all I found were the impressions I had left.

I heard clapping from Grazalian as he stepped out from behind one of the dead trees. "You are both easily fooled by illusions. Good. You will be a nice addition in that form. So, it has come to this?" Grazalian asked me, lifting his hands above his head. I felt a tree branch entwine around my left rear foot. I easily broke free. Another branch grabbed hold, and then another. More and more of them wrapped around my leg until I could no longer break their hold on me. I concentrated, trying to burn loose with a flame, but the spell would not burn any of the wood or vegetation.

Without answering Grazalian, I summoned ghostly hands that reached for his neck. With an air of arrogance, he simply deflected the spell, backhanding them into the top of the trees. The apparitions snatched the top of one of the trees and bent it all the way down and tied it to my right forearm. The tree attempted to snap back into place, lifting me up, stopped only by the fact my other limb was held firm by the vines.

"My, you are in an unusual predicament, are you not?" Grazalian circled around to face me. "Here, let me help you." He snapped his fingers with a smug look on his face. Erupting from the earth, more vines wrapped around my free hind leg. One of the trees at the burn line bent to his will, wrapping around my only remaining free limb. It lifted me up, pulling me taut, and making me feel like I was going to be drawn and quartered. I struggled against the restraints, but they held like iron.

"I was intrigued by your audacity, but now you and your friends will join me. Forever. My master will be pleased with my victory and by your foolish friend who jumped through the portal. What a delicious bonus he will be. Goodbye." He held his arms to the heavens with his fingers stretched apart. He crossed his arms in front of his chest, bowing his head and closing his eyes. I felt the vines and trees vibrate, ready to rip me asunder.

Suddenly, I spied a warm light growing behind Grazalian. Diane pulled down the light. Flowers grew over the statues the dead creatures had become. Using the vines as a sort of slingshot, I thrust my body forward and snapped my tail, hitting Grazalian square in the chest. The force of the blow sent him back into the sunlight, breaking his concentration. He screamed.

Warming winds kicked up and I was free. I jumped to all fours and glared at the druid.

Grazalian shrank away from the clear sky, and his face contorted. He tried to lunge back into the darkness, but it seemed the field itself held him in motionless. The drab colors of his clothing were being replaced by the splendor of nature. His face cracked and hissed as he lost mass.

I bowed my head, exhausted.

"*Look!*" Lumadian's scream jolted my attention to where Grazalian had been. From beneath the clothes emerged a small creature. I was no expert on the wildlife of the strange realm we were in, but it appeared to me as if the druid had become a wolverine.

I scrambled at the wolverine when he tried to escape into darkness. Chasing him, I hesitated for a moment, not sure what would happen when I entered the field. I knew I could not allow Grazalian to claw back to where his power was greater. I snapped my jaws at him. He dodged, trying to get around me. I snapped at him a second time, this time trapping him completely in my mouth. Without thinking about it, I snapped my neck back and swallowed the vicious creature, feeling it fight as it descended down my gullet and into my stomach. The sun enveloped my body, and the light expanded. The heat from the sun made me drowsy. I felt a strange need to find a warm rock. I lumbered over to Grazalian's clothes and sniffed them. When I pushed them aside, I saw a large green emerald pulsating like a heartbeat. I picked it up in my claws.

"*The Gem of Life! We've found it!*"

I sniffed the gem a few times, licking it.

"*Don't you dare!*" Lumadian warned.

A strong sense of serenity surrounded me, and I felt myself shrinking. I closed my eyes letting the euphoria take hold of me. I feel Lumadian adjusting his claws on my shoulder, and I opened my eyes. The emerald was still in my hands. I twirled it a few times.

I asked Lumadian, *"When we return this to the Tree of Conception, will it repair the forest?"*

Before my friend could respond, the gem answered my question.

The blackened forest dissolved around me and gave way to a new forest teeming with life and vivid colors. As the effect passed over each of my friends, they mended. Cat's body was first. His innards were eased back where they belonged, and his wounds closed. The light, when it touched Jean-Luc, wrapped his body in a golden energy. He sat and inhaled deeply through his nose, exhaling through his mouth. His eyes remained closed. The light continued, passing over the hole that held Diane, changing the man-eating plant into a blanket of daisies. I could smell her scent and knew she was safe. All my friends came to my side.

"Is that it?" Cat asked, having assumed human guise. "What happened?"

"I managed to defeat Grazalian. When he stepped into the sunlight, it weakened him."

*"Are you going to tell them what you actually did to him?"* Lumadian asked me.

I rubbed my full stomach. *"Not at this time."* I felt unsettled thinking about what happened.

"Is there anything wrong?" Diane touched my shoulder.

"I will be fine." I stared into her starry eyes. "It's good to have you all back."

Holding my hands in front of my chest, I spoke. "Hold on, hold on. We should go and return the gem back into the tree."

We rushed for the portal and stopped. The magic from the gem had restored the portal to what I assumed was its real appearance. A golden archway, nestled in front of a trio of birch trees, greeted us. On both sides of the portal, blue water flowed and orange and green birds splashed.

"Let me go first." I held the gem up in front of me like a torch. I strode through the gate.

With every step we took, the gem restored the forest to its former glory. I could hear life breathing back into the trees, like the entire forest was a living creature. We ran faster, around the bend, and down the path until the tree came into view.

Dark shadows rose, but I dashed past them and slammed the gem into the empty socket in the tree trunk.

Colors exploded, knocking us all off our feet. We felt the effects of an earthquake. But instead of destruction, waves of life spread from the epicenter. The rumbling ceased and colors shot out in every direction. The dark beings behind us liquefied. Songs from all types of creatures sang out in triumphant euphony. Brilliant colors restored the darkest of places to their former glories.

I managed to stand. "We need to get back to Su'nard and see what has happened in the lands of the elves. We cannot help Robert, but maybe Amilmadra can."

# CHAPTER THIRTY-SEVEN
## REBIRTH

We retraced our steps out of the forest. The trees along the path were bright green and so alive that we could actually feel the energy radiating from them. The sky was bright blue with fluffy white clouds.

We traveled down the path, seeing all kinds of wildlife. I spotted families of animals with their young—some of which seemed weeks old. Advancing down the road made me feel good, washing my cares away. It was a profound feeling of being at peace with the forest.

As we passed the cave, we saw that the rubble had been cleared away, replaced by flowering trees. The wooden door and the feeling of foreboding were completely gone.

With every step, we beheld visions of beauty: serene waterfalls and trees full of flowers in bloom. Our actions slowed, because we wanted to take in the splendor. We stopped at the fort, amazed that the healing effect wasn't limited to living things.

Brilliant white stone gleamed in the sunlight, and any flaws had been erased. At the top of both parapets flew green banners on tall poles. Perched at the apex of each pole was a falcon, keeping watch over the land. The drawbridge was bigger and stronger. The moat was crystal clear, and we could see all the way to the bottom. Small fish, dazzling in their bright yellows and oranges, swam around each other in circles.

I shielded my eyes and pointed to the banners. "Should we go in to investigate who flew the flags, or should we continue on to find Su'nard?"

Diane answered, "I think we should…"

A man with shredded clothing barely clinging to his body staggered out the door and over to us. "What is the date?"

We shrugged, not knowing what to say until Lumadian informed me, *"It is the third Cloud day in the month of Rains, in the year forty-two twenty."*

I put my hand on the man's shoulder to try to calm him. "Easy now. Everything will be fine. It is the third Cloud day in the month of Rains, four thousand, two hundred, twenty…"

It had no sooner rolled off my tongue than the expression on his face changed from dread to shock. He stepped away from us. "What did you say? It cannot be!" He fled, but Jean-Luc blocked his way.

"Easy Jean-Luc," I said. "Now, take it easy. Tell us, friend, what is wrong?"

"I know I was imprisoned in the mansion for a time, but I can't believe…" His voice trailed off, and he swallowed. "I was captured some time ago and forced to work for the Drakoto. They, in turn, worked with Grazalian to poison the land. When the mysterious powder took hold of my mind, Zalikan decided I was a test subject, locking me in that room after I killed many of his men. Once the plague lifted, I found myself normal again. The door that sealed my prison melted away. Are you the saviors of the land? You have saved me, too."

"Whoa, hold on there for a moment," I said. "I don't know about being called 'saviors of the land.' Yes, we defeated Grazalian, but we only did what was needed, nothing more, nothing less. And we lost one of our own. My name is John, and this is Diane. Jean-Luc is behind you and over there," I nodded to Cat, who was at the drawbridge peering into the water at the fish, "is Cat. And you are?"

Making a fist with his right hand, he slapped the back of it with his open left hand, and he held his hands in front of him at chest height. "I am Hastidor DeGuirre, first son of the House of DeGuirre. I am eternally grateful for what you have done." He bowed before us.

"It was our pleasure to save you and the land. Please, you do not need to bow." Diane stepped forward.

Looking up at her, he took her hand in his and gently kissed the back of her hand. "The pleasure is all mine, lovely lady." He glanced at us. "Shall we leave Von Breinenhouser's home together?"

"Just a moment, please." I motioned for everyone to gather. We stepped aside. I whispered, "What do you think?"

"I think that the land of evil might have cleansed him as well," Jean-Luc said.

"Can we trust him that easily?" Cat chimed in.

"*Have Diane examine him with one of her spells,*" Lumadian said.

"How can Diane examine him with one her spells?" I asked aloud, so my friends knew what was going on, but not quite loud enough for Hastidor to hear me.

"*Have her study his aura, and watch that he is not resisting the spell.*"

"Diane, concentrate on his aura and determine his true merit." I left the group to address Hastidor directly. "I need you to allow Diane to examine you with her spell."

"Of course," he replied.

Diane stepped forward and closed her eyes. She held out her symbol and opened her eyes. They pulsated with yellow light. So did her outstretched hand. A ball of bright white appeared at her elbow and spiraled down her arm, over her hand, and zoomed over to Hastidor's feet. The ball circled him, moving up his body until it reached his head. It took the shape of a halo for several seconds before dissipating. Diane smiled. "He is fine. I sense good intentions in him." She winked at him. "We should get out of here."

We decided to hasten our pace, stopping only briefly when we reached the river. It, too, had been transformed. We could see some kind of fish swimming in the clear water, and it was so inviting that I dove in. The small wooden bridge that spanned the creek was very sturdy. As we crossed, I had to test the bridge's degree of ruggedness. I jumped up and down when I reached the middle of it.

"What are you doing?" Cat asked me.

"I cannot believe the stability of something that was not here when we passed by the first time," I said, and Cat grinned.

We continued until we reached the spot where we had entered this land. The trees were still densely packed, and the only passage was through the archway, but the scene had changed.

The trees were a deep shade of red—like rosewood—and smooth, as if they had been worked by a lathe. On the surface of the trees, the agonized faces had been replaced by smiling, inviting faces, and I chuckled. The trees were still bent to form an arch, but instead of decay, a white and indigo flowering vine connected the two trees. From the vine, hung bright yellow orchids with a cinnamon and sandalwood scent. Even the grass at our feet was bright green redolent of freshness. Perched on the pinnacle, a single white owl hooted at us.

A voice rang out with power and authority. "I bid you greetings, saviors of the elven race. We will sing of your deeds for generations to come." From behind one of the oaks emerged Su'nard, smiling at us with his arms outstretched. "We should travel back now. The queen will be happy to see you."

We met more elven folk on the way back to Nesh'tirai. When we were within viewing distance of the hamlet, we saw Amilmadra standing at the edge of town waving at us.

There was a whirlwind of activity as elves of every age came to see us. As night fell upon the village, a feast to end all feasts was presented, and I felt like our ancestors must have at their first feast in 1621. Their food melted in the mouth, delighted the eyes, and filled our stomachs. We partied into the night and I was feeling the effects of the elven wine when Amilmadra called me to the gathering tree. Sitting on the table was Lumadian and around it in comfortable chairs were Diane, Cat, and Jean-Luc.

I bowed to their leader, and she gestured me to an empty chair.

"I am pleased that you are enjoying yourselves." Amilmadra chuckled. "I wanted to tell you more good news. We dispatched riders to all the edges of our land, but I am confident that the plague is completely gone." Raising her hand, she snapped her fingers and a beautiful elf woman entered the room. She wore leathers and she looked as though she was ready for traveling. Slung over her shoulder was a mandolin. She pulled out some scrolls and a feather that danced with energy of its own and sat in one of the empty chairs. Amilmadra continued. "Please relate the tale while it is fresh in your mind so that our bards can sing it for ages to come."

I held my head for a moment and blinked. "Your majesty, perhaps in the morning when the effects of the celebration on our bodies have eased somewhat?"

"Nonsense," she answered. "I realize that you may not be accustomed to our celebrations, but your story is more important than you know. I would have it now."

"Very well." I took a deep breath, trying to clear my mind. As I was about to start, Hastidor came and blocked the door.

"Please join us, Hastidor." The queen motioned for him to take the chair next to her. He nodded and sat. All eyes focused on me.

After pausing for a moment, I told our story. I chuckled a few times when Lumadian chimed in to emphasize his actions and to add things so I didn't leave anything out. I even related how I defeated Grazalian, much to the chagrin of my friends. When I was done, the bard nodded at me, bowed to the queen, and left the room.

Lumadian flew to my shoulder and Amilmadra closed her eyes and concentrated for a moment. We remained silent, waiting for her to finish.

"I am sorry, my friends. Robert is hidden from my view. But, after hearing your tale, I think I could assist you in trying to find your friend. It is my belief that if you assist the people of the land, you will eventually come to the attention of the cause of the misery that has befallen everyone. The Drakoto are an evil race of part lizard and part human creatures. They capture humans for slaves, and they are more dangerous now than they have even been. Normally they are a xenophobic race. They would not have expanded beyond their swamps without aid. When we have completed our celebrations, you will journey south to their lands. Hastidor can show you the way. The gifts I have given are yours to keep. Use them well." She stood and started for the door. "And I think you should also take your friend, once she has finished resting." She opened the door to reveal Miriele sitting comfortably on one of the beds. Shock spread to our faces. "Lumadian managed to hold on to a piece of her essence, which was revitalized by the field. We were able to bring her back when we celebrated the start of the next four hundred year cycle."

Anticipating my question, Lumadian explained. *"When I flew over to her body, I removed one of her fingers. The elves were able to use that to bring her back. I knew it was very unlikely that it could be done, but I figured even a slim chance was better than none.*"

"That reminds me, what exactly did we do?"

"*That is a tale for another day,*" was his reply.

"Once Miriele has recovered, we need to journey to Hastidor's lands, but for now we should enjoy the hospitality of the elves. Tomorrow we set out for new tales."

# EPILOGUE

John sluggishly rose and rubbed his weary eyes. He picked up the stack and, after opening a drawer and removing some twine, he tied the stack together and set the bundle in the left bottom drawer. Moving away from the desk, he stretched his legs a few times to work out the kinks. He slowly shuffled to the entrance. The ice wall had almost completely melted. He stared into sky. The gloom of the clouds hanging low in the sky blocked out the sun. A blustery wind howled, causing him not only to shiver, but to remember the fateful day he'd left Salem. He crossed to the hutch and opened the doors. "Cinnamon and honey milk, warm." Instantly a cup appeared and filled with the frothing mixture. With shaky hands, he picked up his drink and lumbered to his bed, slouching down on it. He sipped the mixture that always lulled him to sleep.

"So much to tell. Will I have the time? Should I be doing something else?" He gulped the rest down and tossed the cup on the dusty, rock floor. He stretched out on the divan.

"Lumadian, come here, I need comf—" his lips quivered, and his red eyes filled with tears. He snatched his friend's small pillow and clutched it to his face, inhaling the scent. He faced the wall with the pillow clutched to his chest.

"Tomorrow is definitely a day for new tales," he murmured before falling asleep.

# About the Author

Greetings again.

I hope you've enjoyed my novel. When I started it back in 2002, I never dreamed it would grow as it has. From small origins, it grew to a five volume tale.

I have so much of the universe that I have created, that I wanted you to experience it also in my short stories series: Dragon's Bond, which is available in e-book format.

I have many things planned for the future, so I ask for your patience as I attempt to get it all in print.

Thank you,


John DeJordy